Part One:
Meeting

OPEN WIDE

OPEN WIDE

JESSICA GROSS

HARVILL

1 3 5 7 9 10 8 6 4 2

Harvill, an imprint of Vintage, is part of the
Penguin Random House group of companies

Vintage, Penguin Random House UK, One Embassy Gardens,
8 Viaduct Gardens, London SW11 7BW

penguin.co.uk/vintage
global.penguinrandomhouse.com

First published in Great Britain by Harvill in 2025
First published in the United States of America by Abrams Press in 2025

Copyright © Jessica Gross 2025

The moral right of the author has been asserted

This is a work of fiction. Names, characters, places and incidents are products of the author's imagination or are used fictitiously. Any resemblance to actual events or locales or persons, living or dead, is entirely coincidental.

Penguin Random House values and supports copyright. Copyright fuels creativity, encourages diverse voices, promotes freedom of expression and supports a vibrant culture. Thank you for purchasing an authorised edition of this book and for respecting intellectual property laws by not reproducing, scanning or distributing any part of it by any means without permission. You are supporting authors and enabling Penguin Random House to continue to publish books for everyone. No part of this book may be used or reproduced in any manner for the purpose of training artificial intelligence technologies or systems. In accordance with Article 4(3) of the DSM Directive 2019/790, Penguin Random House expressly reserves this work from the text and data mining exception.

Printed and bound in Great Britain by Clays Ltd, Elcograf S.p.A.

The authorised representative in the EEA is Penguin Random House Ireland,
Morrison Chambers, 32 Nassau Street, Dublin D02 YH68

A CIP catalogue record for this book is available from the British Library

ISBN 9781787305021

Penguin Random House is committed to a sustainable future
for our business, our readers and our planet. This book is made
from Forest Stewardship Council® certified paper.

For Matt

1.

It was on one of those unreal early-summer days, the window boxes violently in bloom, that our merger began. As I walked, I ran my digital recorder as I did constantly, collecting sounds the way other people collect stamps. A bus hissed and screeched. Someone yelled, "Yo! Shithead!" Playground swings creaked on their hinges. A dog retched and a child cried out, "Tata bawfed!"

A woman approached, icy blond, with a face cut into impossible angles and shrouded in a pair of oversized hexagonal sunglasses. Her shapeless shift dress still revealed her tininess. As she passed, and I pointed the recorder toward the ground to pick up the clack of her derbies on the concrete, I watched her chew a wad of gum as though it had affronted her. It was too bad I couldn't hold the recorder up to her mouth. You can tell a lot about a person from the way they chew their gum. Her jaw worked in circles, her lips parted—every so often she'd crack it against her teeth, just the way the popular girls in high school used to do it. She was probably loved. Her footsteps receded. She hadn't even looked at me.

The route to the food pantry where I volunteered took me past a restaurant with sidewalk dining, where couples and girlfriends brunched with grating merriment. People squealed greetings over the clanking din of forks and knives, and one blessed diner said, "I want to eat her face." A hacking cough wafted from an open window. A teenage couple strolling hand in hand tried to kiss while walking, then laughed when they missed each other's mouths.

As I watched the two of them, I regretted having made myself look as crappy as possible. I had, I admit, begun volunteering in hopes of meeting a man. Throughout my twenties I'd tried various gambits: I'd gone to open houses for expensive apartments across downtown Manhattan (I only met one man who was single, who also repeatedly used the phrase "right on"); reserved a seat in the movie theater next to an open spot on the aisle, hoping it would be claimed by a solo moviegoer; brought a book to my neighborhood bar. Failing to strategize, I brought the novel I actually happened to be reading—Tessa Hadley's *Late in the Day*, a tender exploration of marriage—which, at the bar, two different women interrupted to tell me they'd loved. On my next attempt, I instead brought a book on the history of geometry that I'd received from a coworker; an excitable older man approached me to explain that the ancient Greeks had written the first-ever mathematical proofs. (I knew this, as I had just read it.)

While these forays were unsuccessful, they made for entertaining stories at my expense. "Why don't you try crashing a funeral?" my oldest sister, Romi, asked. "I hear tons of people meet at those." I laughed along. She'd been with her husband since college.

By my thirties I had figured out that volunteering gave me the best chance yet of meeting someone kind who liked other people, qualities I'd recently decided to prioritize in a mate. And unlike fake apartment hunting, which left me feeling desolate, ladling out food at a soup kitchen or reading bedtime stories to children at a recreation center was a really nice way to spend time. For a few years I'd hopped from one New York Cares opportunity to another, but early in the summer, I'd lucked into a gig at a food pantry not too far from where I lived. Unloading cans and packets onto the shelves had a lulling rhythm, the mostly consistent group of volunteers had a casual intimacy that I slipped into without too much difficulty, and the guests who came once we'd fully restocked the shelves became familiar to me over the weeks, lending my Sundays the pleasurable comfort of returning home.

Today I'd dressed ugly, in some hometown youth choir T-shirt that someone had left in one of my college dorm rooms and cutoff shorts I'd made from a pair of baggy jeans, as if to prove to myself that I was really volunteering because I was *so* selfless, or perhaps to forestall disappointment. My singlehood had been a nearly lifelong era, punctuated by rare, swift romances. Mostly I'd lusted from a distance. At middle school sleepovers, I'd begged my friends to tell me everything about what kissing felt like, how the two sets of lips moved against one another, how each person knew which way to turn, what another tongue felt like in your mouth. As we got older, even before I'd kissed anyone, I'd had friends giving blow jobs, and I needed to know all about that too: what penises looked like, how they tasted, how hard "hard" was, what to do with your lips and teeth and tongue. Was it true that boys' pupils got huge when they were horny? Was it true that when boys jiggled their legs, it meant they were trying to conceal a boner? I dreamed of pressing my whole body along the length of a boy's. Yet whenever one was interested, I found myself running away.

My adulthood, too, had unfurled in long dry spells of yearning. It seemed to me I could never really access men, but perhaps it was that I found it hard to let them access me. It was still that childhood compulsion to flee. I worried at times that I was incapable of being in a relationship that lasted longer than a month or two, or that there was some secret part of me, deep inside, that wished to be single forever. Was my discomfort with dating possibly a discomfort with any sort of exposure at all?

Maybe this is why I was drawn to radio—because it offered intimacy with parameters, and at a distance. Not only that, but at work, I was in control: the intimate revelations came from my subjects; my only role was to elicit their confessions. Even recording people on the sidewalk or in casual conversation, then listening later to the tapes I'd made, was a way of marshaling chaos into order, and winning for myself after-the-fact dominion.

Usually I listened to my recordings all the way through, playing them while I was washing the dishes or folding laundry or cooking, as though they were podcasts. My intent was, at least in part, to amass a library of sounds: If I came across tape I could thread into a radio piece as background noise, I would jot the timestamp down in my phone or in my little red notebook, if it happened to be near, and bounce the clip later on. With these kinds of recordings—street noise or restaurant din or laughter in a park—I had no problem excusing my habit, given that it was for work, and besides, it wasn't hurting anybody. It seemed far more innocuous than taking photos of strangers with a smartphone and posting them all over the internet. The be-derbied woman I'd taped on the street would be none the wiser.

Secretly recording my everyday conversations, though, was another matter. I tried to convince myself that this practice, too, was a necessary or at least helpful part of my job. Years earlier, my voice—more nasal on tape than it sounded to me in life—had made me wince, but I'd used the recordings to work on my speech, to deepen and round it, to make it more professional.

But I didn't just use the tapes for work. I also scrutinized my social performance, noting missed opportunities for bon mots and practicing retorts, and studied details my friends had shared that I could refer back to in later conversations. As a result of this strategy, I'd been told on multiple occasions that I had a "very impressive memory." I stored up successful conversations to listen to as company later, fights as potential future ammunition. (I'd never played back a tape of a conflict to prove anything, and promised myself I never would, but I didn't delete them, either. They were my rainy day fund, and having them around gave me solace.)

Ultimately, I couldn't stop myself. It was something I'd been doing since I was a child, and I felt no more capable of quitting it than a binge eater does ice cream. I reasoned that, unlike with my tapes of street noise, I never used my recordings of conversations for anything; they were entirely private. Even if I'd wanted to use them for a radio piece, the sound quality of voices recorded from my pocket wasn't anywhere near good enough. I'd need to place the recorder in plain sight, as close to whomever I was talking to as possible, to mitigate the interference of background noise. So what could be wrong?

Yet I kept the practice to myself. At least, then, I did.

The food pantry was in Brooklyn Heights, at a beautiful church at the end of the street: brownstones layered like expensive cake, trees bursting out of their fenced-in pockets of dirt. Even the air conditioners hanging out of the windows hummed more quietly than they did in Clinton Hill, where I lived. From down the block, I spotted Martine, who'd been the shift leader for years, holding a box in one arm and pulling a ring of keys out of her back pocket. Today she wore high-waisted shorts, a crop top, and chunky white sneakers: now *that* was how you were supposed to dress on a Sunday. No wonder she had a husband. She'd gotten a new haircut since last week—buzzed on one side—and though I'd seen it in the photos she'd posted, it looked even better in real life.

I slipped my recorder into my back pocket as I neared, making sure the microphone was still exposed, and called out a greeting, to avoid the awkward scenario in which I startled Martine from behind and dissolved into too-high laughter. She waved back.

"Wow, great haircut!" I said, as if I hadn't seen it online. Though it was pathological to *not* e-stalk people these days, with acquaintances it was embarrassing to bring up, in person, details of their life you'd ferreted out, even though they'd consciously made them available for your consumption. I'd relearned this my last time in New Orleans, when I'd run into someone I'd gone to elementary school with and asked how her baby's birthday party—the preparations for which she'd posted in a string of Instagram stories—had gone the week before. The conversation had concluded quickly thereafter, leaving me ashamed. It was as if your online avatar alone was supposed to know these things, and you-in-the-flesh was not.

Martine gave her new hair a sassy shake, asked how my week had been.

I said I couldn't complain—"Or I can, but I won't."

"Girl, same." What she had to complain about I couldn't fathom. She and her husband lived in downtown Manhattan; they had met at some bar or other while Martine was in law school and he was working as a hedge fund analyst. (I knew a few of these but somehow still had absolutely no idea what the job entailed, and amused myself by imagining them commanding pens full of hapless hedgehogs.) They'd fallen immediately in love and gotten married within the year. I'd found all this out at my first shift, throughout which I queried, maybe interrogated, Martine and her husband, who were volunteering together, frequently touching each other on the arm or back or waist, sometimes murmuring to each other and laughing at their private joke. They looked a bit like siblings, I'd thought, and wondered if they ever mused about it or if they'd even noticed. I wanted to scrutinize their seemingly perfect life in the hopes it would infuse me, through osmosis, with similar fortune.

But as I'd listened to my recording of the conversation the night of that first shift, my optimism had curdled into an angry lust. The contrast between Martine's life and mine was too extreme: I shared my two-bedroom with a twenty-four-year-old woman named Ava I mostly hated but felt compelled, for some reason, to pretend I adored. I invited her everywhere, even though she rarely came and had never invited me (which only made me more ragefully determined to win her over). Ava had an overabundant social life: a Saturday might hold day drinking in someone's Bushwick backyard, a museum date with a friend, dinner with other friends in Williamsburg, and then some party or other. In bitter moments I wondered why it was that she needed quite so many friends, something that made me suspicious she was intent on not becoming intimate with a single one.

Mostly, though, I was jealous. Friends my age had increasingly coupled up, leaving me stranded. Unsure what else to do, I continued inviting people to do things with me as I had in my twenties: I'd email a few dozen people asking if they'd like to join for any of the events I'd planned for the summer (Green-Wood Cemetery tour one weekend; karaoke the next; paint-your-pet's-portrait, anyone?). I started something called the Moon Club, where I set out watercolor paints and we all, literally, painted the moon in whatever phase we found it in—really an excuse to drink several bottles of wine and talk about whatever was happening with our bodies lately. (On one visit, my mother found a pile of terrible moon paintings I'd stuffed under my coffee table and demanded I hand them over to her; a couple months later, a package of framed moon paintings arrived in the mail.) For my thirty-third birthday, I picked three Saturday evenings a few weeks apart and invited thirty-three friends to choose which evening to come to: "Feel free to bring a guest!" My goal was to introduce people I loved to each other, which did happen, but also to "meet someone," aka someone to date, aka a boyfriend, aka my soulmate, which I did not. (I did, however, pawn moon paintings off on my guests as joke party favors.) Increasingly fewer people came to my events—their partners needed them, their babies needed them, of course I understood, next time!—but I forged on like a deranged mountaineer. When coupled friends couldn't make it to the plans I proposed, they'd often reply, "sorry ☹." The insertion of the emoji gave the apology a pitying flavor—not *I wish I could*, but rather, *I can't, and how it's going to hurt you!*

I took the box from Martine so she could unlock the door and trailed after her into the building. Our footfalls echoed through the old church. The box—full of records of inventory, X-Acto knives, paper and markers for signage, guest check-in sheets—went on a table in the way back. Martine idled there with me while we waited for the other volunteers and a truck full of the nonperishables a local business had donated. I asked Martine whether her husband was coming, wondering if they'd fought and he'd bailed, but he was just stopping by the hardware store for a few extra X-Actos on the way over.

"Quick, show me photos of Felix before everyone gets here," Martine said—I'd mentioned my dog the first time we'd met and every shift thereafter. Gratefully, I obliged: Felix curled up on the bed, curled up on the couch, curled up on the rug, and then, in the park, beaming with a stick in his mouth.

Martine's husband arrived, and they kissed: showy, I thought, after such a brief time apart.

The others trickled in: Kam and Noah, mid-fifties, who'd been on this shift for years; Binita, newish, whom I was in the process of befriending; Dahlia, who kept her headphones in throughout the shift and was, by my account, our only aloof member. Binita and I exchanged tentative new-friend back-and-forths—I told her she smelled like flowers; she showed me her perfume and I held out my wrist to request a spritz. Martine called to us that the truck had arrived, and we went out to meet it.

I waited until the others had cleared out with their first load of boxes before climbing inside. Transferring heavy boxes to the back of the hall was my least favorite part of volunteering here. I lingered alone in the truck, scanning the remaining boxes' neat labels, looking for a light one. Not canned soup, not canned fish, not peanut butter or loose dried beans. Jam: heavy *and* fragile. Tea: bearable. I started gingerly shimmying the package off its pile.

"Hey, let me—"

The voice from the street surprised me so much that I yelped and dropped the tea.

"Fuck!" I said, but then started laughing, and he did too. I turned to look at him.

When our eyes met, we stopped laughing.

Thick eyebrows, dark unruly hair, a delicate and beautiful face. His eyes were soft and boyish, giving the sense he was not quite an adult, not yet capable of navigating the world on his own.

"I was going to say, 'Let me help you with that,'" he said. He had his hands braced against the truck bed, and I could see the bluish tint of veins threading through his forearms. The skin there looked soft and hot.

I noticed that my toe was throbbing; the box of tea had fallen on it.

"Ow," I said, belatedly, as though speaking to him through a dream.

He hoisted himself into the truck, swinging one foot up between his hands like he was getting out of a swimming pool. His shorts hiked up his leg, and as I watched him come up and over the edge, my eyes caught on the tendon that hitched onto the back of his left knee and ran along his thigh. Above was a soft, shadowy hollow. My heart started to pound. I felt crazy.

It reminded me of watching my skinny friend do the monkey bars in elementary school: she had those sharp tendons also, running down her forearms. I would watch for them as she grabbed one rung after another: those two lines, one fainter than the next, stretching down from her wrist toward her elbow. I had wanted to touch them, too; the thought of running my fingertip lightly up and down her forearm had made me want to cry, it was so tender.

"I'm Theo," he said, and reached out to shake my hand.

"Olive."

He had a firm handshake. His hand was warm.

"It's great to meet you," he said, and we let go.

"Same." It seemed I could only produce one syllable at a time.

He smiled, and I saw he had a space between his two bottom teeth. It felt to me like a shared secret.

The rest of the shift is suspended, in my memory, in a sepia haze. There was the way he smiled at me—more with the left side of his mouth than the right—as we passed each other walking into and out of the building; the shock of his hand on my back as he squeezed by me; the snippets of conversation as we bagged and weighed almonds side by side.

"Do you like them?" he asked. "Olives, I mean."

"Wouldn't it be horrible if I didn't?" My heart was pounding, but my voice came out smooth. A radio trick.

"I knew someone named Cookie who hated cookies."

"Well, *Cookie*—that's just mean."

"She changed it, I think—"

"To something like Jane, I bet."

"I think it was made-up; I'd never heard it before."

"Like Florg?"

"Just like that."

I liked his voice, which had a quirk I'd always loved: "L" sounds came not from his teeth but from deep in his throat. A speech impediment of some kind, but—like his tendon, or the gap between his teeth—it betrayed a certain delicacy, like when a man can't help but shiver. It felt private, meant for only me.

I miss his tooth gap. (His voice, I don't need to miss; I can access my recordings of it at any time. Of course, this isn't the same as talking to him.) I liked the way that, when he spoke with Martine's husband outside the truck, he put one hand on his shoulder and leaned in, a gesture that conjured both the vulnerability of not being able to hear and the gentle offering of proximity.

We'd talk when the other volunteers were busy elsewhere, then stop when anyone joined our circle. There was something pleasurably illicit about making conversation behind the others' backs, as though their presence contained us. From the soup aisle, as I stood nearby, chatting with Binita while we bagged loose tea—I asked about her plans for the week, making clear that I had free evenings and movies I was dying to see—Theo caught my eye and let his mouth form that lopsided smile. I raised my fingers, so subtly it might have been nothing.

He turned back to his task, bending down to grab a few cans from a box on the floor, then straightening to slide them onto a high shelf. He was facing away from me, so I couldn't see what was revealed when he lifted the hem of his shirt to his face to wipe the sweat, but I imagined his wiry torso. Did a line of hair cut a line down the middle? Above, I knew what I would find: like a door flanked by sentries, the gap between his two front teeth.

An hour before the end of the shift, I found Theo in the back alley, breaking down cardboard boxes. The other volunteers were still unpacking and helping guests indoors. Theo and I were alone.

"Need help?" I asked.

"No," he said, and my stomach lurched. "But I want it."

We manipulated the boxes in silence. I observed, covertly, the muscles flexing in his arms as he tore the tape from a box and collapsed it, his hair swishing against his forehead as he flung the cardboard to the side. As he focused, I let myself stare openly at his face: beautiful more than handsome, its angles elegant and precise, but with those boyish eyebrows and hair. He grabbed another from the pile and began again. Glanced up at me. I looked quickly away. He asked what I did for work.

"Radio producer," I said. "And you?"

"Tell me more about it."

"I asked first."

He raised his eyebrows.

So I told him I was a radio host at WNYC. My show, *The Process*, interviewed writers in the middle of working on a project, rather than after it was completed—in the gunky period, rather than the shiny one. The show was a counterargument to timeliness; I explained to Theo that in most cases journalists, even cultural ones, need a timely "peg" for each show or article. The window in which any work is considered timely is laughably narrow; in the few weeks surrounding a book's publication, the author gives a dozen different interviews, says the same thing each time, and then disappears. I knew a critic who'd held on to an essay about a novel she'd loved, which had come out five years prior, until the author died and it was again relevant enough to publish.

"Seriously?" Theo had paused his work as I'd spoken; focused on me, he probed between his bottom teeth with his tongue. I wondered—already, in that moment—what that gap would feel like against my finger, my lips, my own tongue.

"All hail the peg," I said.

My show was the rare exception. I'd interviewed Nora Lee, who hadn't published a book of poetry in a decade; Tory Ann Waters, who was undertaking the epic project of translating all of Tolstoy; Adelyte Müller, an unsubtle but impressively prolific novelist; and Tatum Bly, a science journalist who'd taken a hiatus after a book of his was widely panned. As I spoke, I continued peeling tape off of boxes, folding them flat, and throwing them to the side. I had started sweating again as soon as I'd come outside and hoped that Theo hadn't noticed, or that if he had, he didn't care. The sheen along his arms only made me want to lick them.

Even if writers weren't ready to describe in granular detail what they were working on, I said—it sometimes happened—they'd usually tell me how it was going, the phase of the process they were in, if they wrote at a desk or in bed, with a pen or a laptop.

Theo told me he hardly ever listened to the radio for lack of time, but if he had, he was sure he would've heard of my show. "Is it okay if I listen?" he asked. He crushed a box between his hands and flung it onto the pile, his shirt fluttering up for a moment. Yes: there was a slash of dark hair.

"Of course," I said, as a mixture of glee and terror rose in me. Part of me desperately wanted him to listen to every episode I'd ever made; the other part felt already embarrassed. "Now your turn," I said.

"I'm a surgeon." He flattened another box, threw it onto the mounting pile. Muscles flexing in turn, hair swishing. An image solidified in my mind of him bent over a body, flashing metal tool in hand, hair screening his face. No; he probably wore a surgical cap. I revised the image. Did he probe his teeth with his tongue as he made the incision?

"What kind of surgeon?" I asked.

"Colorectal." I revised the image again, moving Theo down from the patient's head, where I'd placed him initially, to his gut. Digging the blade into the soft flesh, eyes squinted at the bloody slice.

"Do you like it?" I asked. "Cutting people open." I wondered what sound it made, slicing into someone's skin.

"You really want to know?"

"I'm not squeamish."

"I love it," he said, then looked at me, smiling. He tossed another box onto the pile. "Is that gross?"

"Not unless it's in a murdery way."

He laughed, ran his hand through his swoosh of hair. "No, not like that."

"Is it that you like seeing what people look like, inside?" I found myself squinting at him, the way I did when I asked an interviewee a question I really wanted the answer to. Quickly I rearranged my face, softening it as though meditating, but Theo hadn't flinched or looked away under my scrutiny.

"In the beginning, it was," he said, a little smile curling the corners of his lips as he remembered. "Before I got used to it. When I was an intern, an attending asked if I wanted to reach inside a patient's belly, and I felt like a kid who gets to stick his hands into a bucket of worms." He tossed a box and grabbed another. "I think that's the difference between me and all the doctors who don't want to be surgeons."

"What does it feel like?"

"Warm," he said. "Squishy, and slippery. There's fluid in there, and a layer of fat that covers all the organs. Which are mostly bowel: slippery, shiny, very soft coil, over fifteen feet long." His guttural voice had sharpened, as though thinking of the body cut any excess from his speech.

I realized I'd been standing still, listening to him, with a box in my hands. I ripped the tape off and squeezed the cardboard flat.

"It sounds like pasta," I said.

"That's just what it looks like. Really thick, pink pasta. Above are the liver and the stomach. The more you dig, the more you'll find."

"What's on your hand when you take it out of a body?"

"Some slime; maybe a little oily stuff. Like if you'd stuck your hand in a pot of stew."

"Cool," I said dumbly. I threw a box to the side, causing my hair to fall in front of my face; I tucked it back behind my ears, which I knew made me look prettier. Covertly, I dabbed at my upper lip, where beads of sweat had accumulated. I wanted to ask what he thought my insides looked like.

"It's *so* cool," he said. "But it feels different now than it used to—more routine and relaxing, like how people describe knitting. When you're knee-deep in an operation you really do need to keep your eyes on it at all times. So on TV, when people say, 'Hand me the scalpel'? That's real. That's what I love now: focusing so hard the rest of the room falls away."

The door to the building creaked open, startling us both. Martine called me back indoors to help with a guest who'd asked for me. Theo stayed outside; there were still plenty of boxes to break down. I kept my eye on the back door throughout the rest of the shift—as I restocked shelves, helped guests find items and carry their baskets, took inventory—silently pleading with Theo to come back inside. I'd have to run home to walk Felix as soon as the shift ended, so I wasn't sure I'd be able to say goodbye. The shift sign-in book was right by the door and, after a moment's hesitation, I copied down Theo's number.

At noon, I found Martine chatting with Binita by the door and told them I had to dash, as usual.

"Who else walks their dog four times a day?" Martine joked. "The 'lunchtime walk'?"

"How *is* Felix?" Binita asked.

From Theo, who'd approached from behind: "Who's Felix?"

I waited a beat, as if testing him: *Would you mind if I had a boyfriend?* His expression was unreadable. I watched him swallow, which could have meant nothing or everything.

"My dog," I said.

Did he breathe out then and smile a little?

Let's say he did.

2.

Felix was waiting by the door, his whole butt wagging. He's a shaggy mutt, fur sprouting from the ridge of his nose, with one pointy ear and a floppy one that used to wave in the air like a little flag as he ran. He pressed his head between my calves. I scratched the crown of his head, his favorite part, and behind his ears, his other favorite part. He made a noise of assent deep in his throat that seemed an incarnation of my own desire.

We walked. I thought about Theo. I'd been imagining him nonstop since I left the food pantry for the subway: as I looked briefly back over my shoulder, though I knew Theo had gone back inside for his things; as I swiped my MetroCard, missing it four times before it hit; as I walked through the turnstile, the grimy metal pressing sensuously against me; as I waited on the platform, as I sat on the train, as I walked home and ascended the stairs and unlocked the door. The sweat stains beneath his armpits. His hand, briefly, on my back. His tendon, and the shadowy dip above it. I had fixated on men in this way before, and still fed on the details when I closed my eyes—the thick parentheses of this one's eyebrows, the smoker-hoarse quality of that one's voice—but rarely had I felt that maybe, just maybe, the fixation was also going the other way.

Back home from the walk, I went straight to my room with Felix and closed the door—Ava wasn't in the apartment, but she could return at any moment. I plugged my recorder into my computer and downloaded the file from the shift. Three hours and forty-seven minutes. I did this every time I recorded anything, but downloading the Theo file felt intrusive in a particularly sickening-thrilling way. I sank to the floor as the file transferred, pulling Felix into my lap, his dog-limbs askew. He indulged me, nudging his head into the crook of my neck.

I was painfully aroused. I wondered if I should masturbate with Felix on my lap—he was usually in the room with me, anyhow, so was this really different? Sometimes, he'd look up at me from the floor as I touched myself in bed, and we'd lock eyes. I'd read on the internet about a woman who'd put peanut butter between her legs for her dog to lick off. That felt like a step too far, but when it had got to be a long time since I'd had sex, the knowledge that I could gave me a sense of calm. I wondered if men put peanut butter on their penises, or if they worried about being bit; but when Felix licked peanut butter off a knife, he never bared his teeth, so it was probably not an issue. I had noticed, when I'd remove my vibrator from my vagina after coming, that Felix's nose would twitch interestedly in its direction. By this point it had become a ritual: as soon as I'd come, I'd offer him my vibrator to lick. So, in a way, he *had* been between my legs, by proxy—like kissing a tallit to touch the Torah.

The computer dinged: the file was ready. I lifted Felix from my lap onto the floor beside me and reached toward my laptop. I fast-forwarded through the walk to the pantry (bus, swings, barfing dog), through my conversation with Martine, through my chitchat with Binita, until I could hear Theo's voice. It had more air in it than I remembered, closer to a clarinet than a trumpet. *I was going to say, "Let me help you with that"* . . . *Is it okay if I listen?* . . . *The more you dig, the more you'll find.* . . .

It was hard to touch myself over my shorts, but I didn't want to take them off and *commit* to coming. Instead I lazily stroked myself over the fabric, watching as Felix sniffed around the floor for crumbs, tail twitching back and forth with each step. I closed my eyes: Theo's T-shirt, the pitchy circles of sweat. His guttural voice. His thick hair, almost as dark as mine. His eyes, a rich brown with tiny slivers of green. The gap between his teeth.

I managed to wait three days before I texted him. It was night, and I figured he would be home from work at the hospital. I also, strategically, would have getting-ready-for-bed tasks to busy myself with if he failed to respond.

> **Me:** Hi Theo—it's Olive from the shift
> **Me:** At the food pantry!
> **Me:** I took your number from the sign-in book, I hope you don't mind

I tossed the phone onto my bed so I couldn't keep looking at it, then laid Felix on the covers beside it. Slowly I got ready, changing into a cute pajama-shorts set I had gifted myself as a "summer treat." Ava was at her boyfriend's, so the bathroom was all mine as I washed my face, patted it dry, methodically smoothed cream around my eyes. Felix let out a yip and I returned to him, curling myself around him, scratching his chest, willing myself not to pick up the phone. My usual replying-to-a-man strategy was to wait at least an hour, and I figured men did the same, so I shouldn't read much into his lack of reply, it really didn't mean anything at all.

The phone buzzed. I grabbed for it.

> **Theo:** So glad you wrote
> **Theo:** I do not mind

My cheeks went hot. I clutched the phone to my chest, a gesture I would have been mortified for anyone to witness.

Me: :)
Me: So glad you wrote back
Me: Touch any "pasta" today?
Theo: I ate some
Me: I meant pasta as in guts
Theo: Me too

"It's happening," I whispered to Felix. I crawled under the covers, tenting them over my head, the phone beaming into the sheeted dark.

Me: What did it taste like?
Theo: Like spam
Me: I've never had spam
Theo: Are you vegetarian
Me: Nope
Theo: You gotta try spam
Me: Do I really?
Theo: Definitely not.

We texted for three hours. I asked the best gift he'd ever gotten, which was a chemistry set when he was young—prompting us to wonder whether it was possible to get a "best gift" as an adult, when your propensity toward elation had been (necessarily, if unfortunately) tempered. He asked which I preferred, opera or pop. (I said pop; he said opera. We converged on classical.) We traded favorite words (quixotic and cubby), things we found most disgusting (spiders and gagging noises), favorite dreams from childhood (flying and eating extremely chocolatey chocolate-chip pancakes). We slept for five hours, then resumed texting the next morning.

Me: Good morning
Theo: [sun emoji]
Theo: Sleep well?
Me: I did
Me: You?
Theo: Mm-hmm
Me: Any dreams?
Theo: I think one had a bison
Me: Doing what?
Theo: Charging?
Theo: I think
Theo: Or eating? I can't remember
Theo: You?
Theo: Dreams I mean
Me: Something involving a giant hand

The hand's giant pointer finger had pressed upon my clitoris to explosive effect.

Theo: Comforting? Scary?
Me: Comforting, I think
Me: I can't remember

I asked what he was going to eat for breakfast: two hard-boiled eggs, the same as every day. (Actually, he'd already eaten and was on his way to the hospital, a revelation that prompted me to exit my bed.) He asked what I was looking forward to once I got home from work: vanilla ice cream with whipped cream. (Also, of course, texting him.) By the time, several days later, we'd made plans to go on a run that weekend—we'd figured out that we both loved running, and it was the first slot of time he wasn't working or on call—I'd also learned he'd grown up in Poughkeepsie, was thirty-five, had no siblings, was a dog person (thank God), collected notes he found on the subway, and had one plant (a cactus). I, meanwhile, had shared that I'd grown up in New Orleans, was thirty-three, had two sisters, took Felix on four walks a day and was obsessed with him, was Jewish but loved cheap Easter candy from the pharmacy, and kept my handwriting small so that it could be misperceived as neat. I started typing out a text about my recording habit, wanting to share everything with him all at once, but it took me too long to figure out how to put it, and Theo pressed send faster.

Theo: Should we put a moratorium on texting til we see each other?
Theo: So we can learn some things by voice

I felt, absurdly, the flush of tears. How could I bear to wait the fifty-seven hours until we'd see each other? But I was also relieved: it was too soon to tell him about my recordings. I'd tell him once he knew me better and could really understand.

Me: Great idea
Theo: Just two days
Me: We can do this!

We'd planned to meet in Grand Army Plaza on Sunday afternoon. The hours until our meeting dripped by. I wrote and deleted dozens of texts, refraining from sending them by bribing myself: if

I didn't text for the next thirty minutes, I could have three squares of chocolate. After another hour, I could masturbate. After another hour, three more squares. By the day of our run, I had eaten enough chocolate that I thought I might be sick of it for some time. But it had worked: I hadn't texted. Unfortunately, neither had he.

Theo had to go to the hospital that morning, while I went to the food pantry, where his absence left a cavity. I still hadn't heard from him and wondered if he was going to bail. When Binita asked if anything was up between the two of us, I admitted we were going running later that afternoon, if I didn't shit my pants first.

"If you do, just go home and change!" she said. "This is amazing!"

I didn't tell the others, especially not Martine, whom I could not imagine comprehending the concept of pre-date jitters. My meetup with Theo felt freighted, important, and I couldn't stand the thought of anyone shrugging it off as no big deal.

I put my phone away for the last hour of the shift. When I finally checked it, he had messaged.

Theo: See you soon?

At home after the shift and my mid-morning walk with Felix, I stood in front of my closet, deliberating. Most of my running clothes were ragged things I'd been washing and rewashing since high school or college. Would such an outfit look nonchalant? Like I was so confident I didn't even think about what I wore?

No. It would look bad.

I decided on my Hot Workout Outfit™: spandex with a cropped black tank top that left a sliver of abdominal skin visible when I raised my arms. This one outfit, which I'd gotten from my mother as a birthday present, usually embarrassed me to wear; it read too fit-Upper-East-Side-mom. But I was not about to meet Theo in a shirt with frayed seams and a hole in the armpit. I applied a light layer of makeup I thought would read as "natural" and rolled on a healthy dose of powder-scented deodorant.

I arrived a few minutes early and paced around the plaza, unsure where to wait. Sit on one of the benches? Stand with a hip jutting out to be "casual," to counteract my try-hard outfit? I didn't want to *look* like I was waiting—eager, awkward—but I didn't want to become immersed in checking my phone, either, so I'd be startled by his arrival. I split the difference and did some stretching. Quads, so I could keep a lookout.

I was nervous. Usually my first dates were shrouded in both alcohol and night. Even then, I tended to slip into the role of interviewer, relentlessly craning the spotlight away whenever it pointed in my direction. Something about Theo had made this midday date seem possible: he was open, which made me trust him. Open and, even better, weird. And: he seemed to like me. Yet as I waited for him to arrive my impending exposure revealed itself as fraught. What if I stumbled awkwardly during our run, obliterating his attraction to me? What if he'd revised my appearance in memory so that, seeing me in person again, he wasn't into me anymore? Or what if he'd never been attracted to me at all, and this wasn't even a date? Was that why it'd been easy for him not to text for two whole days?

A few minutes after our proposed meeting time, I caught him loping toward me from the north. He was a light runner, really good, seeming to hover in the air a second extra between each step. It was a beautiful thing. *Is*, I should say, though it's possible I'll never watch him run again. He was wearing a T-shirt and shorts that came a few inches above his knee, so I could see the muscles working in his thigh as he ran. My heart thunked in my throat and I looked to the side, pretending I hadn't seen him.

I waited until he spoke to turn toward him with a start. It was horrible acting. He apologized for being late. He was breathing only a bit more heavily than usual, like running was that easy for him.

"Hardly late," I said, looking at my wrist as though there were a watch on it. "Did you run here?"

He nodded, wiping the sweat from his forehead, then making a gesture of embarrassment that he was sweaty. So he was nervous, too. I wanted to touch him.

"It's good to see you," I said, and he smiled, the gap between his bottom teeth beckoning me like a black hole.

"The loop?" he said, gesturing to the park's main path, just over three miles long.

"Let's do it."

The first few minutes passed in silence. I was conscious of how heavily I was breathing, my heart beating far more quickly than our pace justified. Perhaps we should have chosen a more standard first date after all. It was one thing to talk "privately" in the spare moments of the food pantry shift or over text, but meeting up, just the two of us, in person, for a pre-planned date in the sunshine, was so intense I thought I might cry.

"It's a nice route from your place to here," I said, trying to get all the words out between breaths. He lived in Brooklyn Heights, he'd told me over text. "All the brownstones."

"It really is." He still wasn't out of breath, or at least much less than I was. I thought he might not notice, until he said: "How's the pace? Do you want to slow down?"

"It's great," I said, but I was rasping, which mortified me almost as much as catching myself in the lie. I might have been a good runner, but he was marvelous. "I mean, it's challenging, but I like a challenge." I asked how long he'd lived in Brooklyn Heights.

"I lived in Manhattan until a few months ago," he said. "My first time living in Brooklyn."

"And?"

"It's better," he said, glancing at me and grinning.

I smiled back, rehomed my gaze on the ground. I wondered if, until a few months ago, he'd been living with a partner. Unlike the radio producers and journalists I knew, Theo's social media offerings were minimal; his Twitter account was strictly about medicine and his Instagram account was private. Somehow, I'd stopped myself from requesting to follow him, self-restraint of which I was proud. I'd found just a few photos in my Google Image search: one from his LinkedIn, another from an old local newspaper article about his high school soccer team (he was mid-kick, hair swishing in front of his face—he still had the same haircut), a headshot from an essay he'd written for a medical journal. I kept each open in a separate tab to peek at before bedtime, my new nightly ritual. He talked about where he'd lived in Manhattan—the East Village when he was younger, then the West.

"Do you live alone now?" I asked.

"I do."

"How is it?"

A pedicab passed by, blaring a jingle. Birds conversed with one another. A maintenance cart backed up, beeping. Our breath came out in huffs.

"It's strange," he said.

"Why?" I asked.

"If something moved, it's always because *I* moved it. Plus, no one to talk to."

"What would you talk about?" I thought: *If you lived with me?*

"The most bizarre thing I'd seen that day."

"What was yesterday's?"

"A woman who brought her bird with her to the hospital."

"You made that up."

"Swear to God. A blue and yellow parrot named Cheese."

I laughed, which, because I was out of breath, made me start coughing.

"I'm fine," I said in between coughs, before he could ask if I was okay, which would only have mortified me further.

When I'd recovered, he asked, "How about you? Live alone?"

"No. I never have."

"Who do you live with?"

"Her name is Ava. I hardly know her. She's young—and loud."

He laughed. "Loud, like . . ."

"Like her voice," I said. "And when she cooks. You know, she bangs around the kitchen. . . ." He was laughing again, and now I laughed along, glancing at him so quickly his beautiful face was a blur. "And, yeah, that too," I said. A few months into our roommate-ship, Ava had started dating Brody, whom I'd privately nicknamed Blob. He came over multiple times a week, played games on his phone without using headphones, and jiggled his shoulders up and down as he laughed, like a cartoonish impersonation of a laughing person. He boiled time flat. When they had sex, Ava's headboard banging against our shared wall, she came as though auditioning for a porn film. But Ava and Blob might not be such a problem for me soon.

I looked at Theo, then back at the path. Trees arced up on either side of us. Every so often, when the road curved, he got a pace or two in front of me and I could admire the apostrophes of his calves. His feet punched the pavement. I wanted to lie underneath them and be pummeled.

"What you told me when we met, about reaching into a belly for the first time?" I said, panting every few words. "I couldn't get the image out of my head—"

"Oh God, sorry—"

"No, in a good way." I didn't tell him that I'd listened to the recording of this conversational snippet dozens of times, but I did share that his description reminded me of the Mütter Museum, a medical museum I'd visited in Philadelphia years before. He hadn't heard of it.

"It's incredible," I said. "Very gross. It has a book bound in human skin, and slices of Albert Einstein's brain, and a fucked-up skeleton of a woman who wore a corset." The sentence had a lot of words and left me gasping for breath. Again he asked if I wanted to slow down; this time I conceded.

"Is there a wall of eyeballs?" he asked. "At the Mütter?"

"Is that your thing?"

"What if it is?"

I waited a few beats, our sneakers drumming beneath us. "I'm into it."

"I knew it."

The path rounded a lake rimmed with trees that beamed back to us, blue and green. The place was packed: kids throwing bread to the ducks, a few old men sitting in the gazebo smoking cigars, a stream of other runners. I tried to tune out everything but Theo's steady footfalls, steady breaths. It was another steamy day, and as I looked out across the lake, the trees on the other side seemed to shimmer.

I told Theo how when I'd visited the Mütter Museum, I'd come across stillborn conjoined twin fetuses floating in a jar. It was one of the more gruesome sights on display, but as my disgust mounted, I'd continued staring at it, because it was also magnetic. As I'd stared, I had conjured the image of Little Red Riding Hood's wolf, who ate Grandmother whole: sealed her inside himself, completely subsumed. "More like a baby than a murder victim," I said to Theo. I wondered aloud if the wolf ate the grandmother as an inversion of his own wish—to crawl inside someone, to be protected—and as a tantrum that it couldn't be fulfilled. I imagined him feeling the grandmother heavy inside him, pushing against his gut and wiggling furiously at the sound of her granddaughter's voice. I imagined the wolf picking one of her hairs out of his teeth. Why, he might have wondered, would she want to escape?

"You make it sound good, getting eaten by a wolf," Theo said.

"Wouldn't you want to try it?"

"I'd rather do the eating."

"Why?"

"I feel like a grandmother would taste good—like cloves and rum."

"I want to meet your grandmother."

I asked Theo to tell me more about his work. He was nearing the end of his fellowship, he said: "a much better schedule than residency." Then, he'd been at the hospital whenever he wasn't sleeping; now, he ostensibly had nights and weekends off. Fellowship was less predictable, though. More often than not, he'd sit down to dinner only to be paged a moment later. "In residency, I knew I would have no life; now, I can have one, but it can be interrupted whenever."

"More time, less predictability," I said in a breezy tone that I hoped masked my sudden anxiety. He could be whisked away from me by surprise, at any moment; he was needed by others, elsewhere, whom I'd never know.

"The great compromise," he said.

"At least you love it," I said. "Doctoring." I told him that what he liked about surgery was what I liked about interviewing people: getting inside them. "But," I added, "I'm sure there's nothing like *really* doing it." I was envious, I realized. I'd never contemplated becoming a doctor, but he made surgery sound appealing in its intimacy—its intrusion.

I glanced at Theo. He glanced at me. My heart started to hammer. As if by instinct, we both slowed our pace to a walk and strolled off the main path onto a slim, secluded one. We crossed a bridge over a narrow span of water; Theo stopped and leaned his elbows on the railing. I echoed his posture, staring at the water. My heart was pounding so loudly I could hardly hear the children shrieking in the Nethermead nearby. Our bodies were almost touching; there was a film of sweat along his forearms. I shifted closer and brushed my thigh against his shorts. Slowly, I turned my head. His lips were parted just slightly, his breathing shallow and quick. He made as if to say something, then closed his mouth and swallowed, his Adam's apple moving up and down. I reached a hand toward his hair and ran my fingers through it—thick, brown, a horse's mane. His mouth on mine was like a cave.

Theo came home with me to walk Felix. As I unlocked the door, I prayed Ava was out, but as I cracked it open her typical "Hi-i-i" drifted from the living room.

"Hey," I called. I held up a hand in greeting.

"Oh *hello*," she said to Theo.

"Theo," he said, giving a wave.

She came over and stuck out her hand. "Ava."

"And this is Felix," I told Theo, as Felix—having roused himself from slumber, his face-fur flattened on one side—sidled over to us and pressed himself against my calf.

"*Buddy,*" Theo said. He knew how to pet a dog, scratching Felix right behind the ears. His surgeon's fingers were nimble and long.

"We came by to walk him," I told Ava.

"Oh, I just took him out."

I blinked in surprise. This was the first time in the history of our co-dwelling that she'd walked Felix unprompted. I wondered if she even knew how to properly clip him into his harness.

"He seemed like he really needed to go," she added. She had a backpack in one hand, and as she spoke she walked briskly around the apartment, collecting items and dropping them inside: water bottle, old-school camera, apple, comb.

I thanked her for walking him, privately cursing her for making me look neglectful. "Are you heading out?" I asked. I was aware of Theo's every movement: his subtle shift from foot to foot, his fingers running through his hair. I knew I couldn't really feel heat streaming from his body a foot away, but couldn't I? Couldn't I taste his sweat?

Ava nodded. "Tanya's having a birthday party in Red Hook," she said. "Sunny's?" I knew the bar and resented her assumption that, aged or uncool as I was, I did not. I also resented the way she dropped the names of her friends without context, as though she were famous and I kept abreast of the minute details of her social world.

But she was leaving. I shivered with relief.

"Have fun!" Theo and I said in unison, and Ava said, "You two are so cute."

And then we were alone.

"Do you want a tour?" I asked. The memory of his mouth on mine throbbed silently around us.

He did.

I led him around the living room first: mostly my furniture, including a few bookcases beyond filled; a shag rug, for Felix's enjoyment; and a bar cart I'd found on a solo day trip to the Hudson Valley, stocked with a handful of bottles of wine from me, hard liquor from Ava.

Theo gestured toward a book splayed open, face-down, on the coffee table. He asked if I was reading it, what it was. It was Eleanor Aldine's *Urbania*—a group biography of writers whose work captures urban isolation—which I was rereading, as I'd soon have Aldine on my show. This book had come out a year earlier; Aldine had also written three collections of essays, two biographies, and a travelogue. I'd figured her next project could be anything at all, and my producer's pre-interview with Aldine had proved me right: she was working on her first novel. Reading *Urbania*, I'd been struck by her image of loneliness—people floating through time and space, totally removed from each other even as they resembled one another—which I found tragic.

"When I'm done reading, I'll lend it to you," I said.

"A loan." He raised his eyebrows. "That's serious."

"Too serious?"

It felt like minutes before he answered: "Just the right amount."

The art in the apartment was almost all Ava's, a combination of things she'd collected from jobs—she worked in a gallery—and pieces she'd been given by a grandmother who had moved to a nursing home. Ava's irksome qualities notwithstanding, she (and her grandmother) had great taste. She'd hung about twenty framed pieces behind our sofa. Theo and I stood looking at them together.

"Are these yours?" he asked.

"Only this one." I pointed to a framed page from an old magazine, which featured an illustration of a young girl lying splayed out on the floor like a starfish. "My mom had this hanging in our house growing up; she said it reminded her of me."

Theo examined the image, then looked at me.

"I think I can see it," he said. "But can you lie on the floor, to be sure?"

I lowered myself to the shag rug. My head felt light.

"Like this?" I asked.

"Do what she's doing in the picture."

I stretched my arms over my head, spread my legs into a vee.

"That's good," Theo said. "Can I come down there?"

I nodded. He lowered himself to the ground and lay beside me. I could feel my heart hammering away, and tried to enjoy it. I concentrated on the image of the contracting muscle flooding my whole body with blood. It was nice to know it was working hard to take care of me, pounding so forcefully I could feel it in my back, beating against the floor. Light streamed into the apartment. I was conscious of my sweat-sticky hair, the sheen of my forehead, the likely pungent scent between my legs. Theo fingered the hem of my shirt. "Okay?" he asked, and I nodded and sat up so he could pull it over my head. I stripped his, too, and there was his body: lithe and rangy, curls of hair spreading across his chest and down into his shorts. I pressed my hand against his stomach as if to absorb him through my palm. Felix whimpered and yelped as Theo leaned toward me; I ran my tongue along Theo's teeth, trying to find the gap, to make it mine. He wrenched my sports bra over my head and said, "Fuck," before closing his mouth around my nipple.

Felix nosed his way between us and Theo laughed. "I'm sorry," I said, "he's really possessive," and Theo said if he were Felix he would be too. "We'll share," Theo said, and I straddled him to block out Felix and yanked down his shorts. His penis snapped against his stomach; I pulled his shorts below his knees and off one foot and then the other. I traced my fingers along his tendon—how much I wanted to lick it—then all the way up his thigh. His breath rasped in his throat as I took him into my mouth, but before he could come he rolled me onto my back and pulled down my spandex, then wedged his head between my thighs like I was giving birth to him. As I came, Felix peed on the floor for the first time in years. Theo asked if I had a condom and I did but I shook my head, and then he was inside me, skin on skin. He touched his lips to my ear. "Olive," he said.

3.

By the time I interviewed Eleanor Aldine two weeks later, I'd revealed to Theo things I hadn't told anyone else I'd dated: that I had snooped through the bedroom of every roommate I'd ever had (Ava, unfortunately, did not keep a diary). That I had long wondered if Felix was my soulmate. That with women friends, I'd fall into easy, rapid, maybe excessive intimacy; with men, not so much. Not before him, anyway.

Daniel: whenever I thought of him, I pictured the mattress on the floor of his bedroom, in an Alphabet City apartment he shared with a couple other guys and a girl I felt threatened by. His small window had been covered by a pale green curtain that, as I'd sink into the underwater of sleep, looked like a bit of algae floating by.

A few years later: a guy I'd met working at the Food Coop. He, like I, worked in radio; we both lived in Park Slope at the time; we had pets (though his was a cat). We were similar, but only in ways that didn't matter. Half the time I put my hand on his shoulder, he shrugged me off. His primary mode of interacting with his friends was mutual mockery. As soon as we finished having sex, he'd pull his boxers right back on. I'd try to pull my clothes back on even faster.

I'd learned that, contra my imaginings, Theo hadn't had a serious relationship since college. He'd dated only a few women, and none for very long, but—once I'd followed him on social media—I scoured for photos of them anyway. His most recent ex looked as though she'd just returned home from summer camp, with clear pink skin and lips like fruit. But the fact that they had only two months' worth of photos together comforted me. His work had absorbed him, he said—but now, for the first time in years, he had some freedom in his schedule. I got the sense that this was a cover; plenty of doctors had relationships, after all. The more I learned about his parents, the more I felt it must be insecurity or fear that had kept him alone: they apparently bickered as though it was their love language, and had chastised Theo for minor errors since he could remember. "Lovingly assholish" was how he described them, but to me they sounded like plain assholes. At work, at least, he could live up to their expectations: he could be perfect and in control. But now he was with me, and I would love him so hard it would obliterate what they'd done.

Though he was passionate about his career, he seemed to feel distant from his surgeon friends, whom he'd told me cared more for procedure than for people. The flavor of curiosity demanded by the profession was specific, of course—what caused a woman's skin to turn a putrid yellow; what caused the pain she felt just below her ribcage. But her surgeon did not need to know why she'd kept all her stuffed animals from grade school for her future children, except for the orange cat from her aunt, which she'd tossed in her early twenties in a black garbage bag that she knotted twice.

Theo was different: he wondered about people. (Surely, now, he's wondering about me, though I'd like to think on some level he knows everything, and understands.) This was why he collected found scraps of paper that people had scrawled notes on by hand: they were portals to other minds. Early in our relationship, he unearthed them from somewhere in his closet and we riffled through them together:

one Post-it displayed a grocery list on which someone had crossed out "apples" and, in different handwriting, written "ooples." On a piece of printer paper was scrawled, in purple marker, "STOP PLAYING THE GUITAR!!!" There was a letter addressed to someone named Hal from one Geronimo Strange, who claimed to have spotted Hal having a private dance party and said it was the most beautiful thing he'd ever seen.

Theo was drawn, or so he told me, to my own rabid need to figure out everybody's *why*. There was a rigor to my inquisitiveness, he said—not that this was news to me. I'd often felt self-conscious of what I saw as my nosiness, which I was largely unable to control, even outside of my tape recordings. I worried that my digging, relentless as it was, could push people away. At times, it had. During our first week living together, Ava had rolled her eyes while describing a friend who'd never figured out how to drink without blacking out. "She vomits literally every time." I asked why Ava thought that was. What was her friend escaping? I remember resting my chin on my hand, squinting at Ava in concentration. But a dismissive look crossed her face: "She's not escaping anything," she said. "It's just fun."

Work was where I was allowed to give this quality free rein. It was an asset, if not a prerequisite of the job. I thought it might be the only place I could express my intense curiosity without embarrassment, aside from with my sister Talia, who mirrored it. That is, until I met Theo, who told me that he'd been unknowingly seeking such inquisitiveness—meaning *interest*—for his entire life. He'd never known anyone who asked the kinds of questions I did, and he liked it. On dates, we would make up stories about the people we saw at nearby tables: the elderly woman was, after long refusing to do so, passing her family business on to her two daughters, who sat tensely on either side of her.

"But which of them will be CEO?" Theo asked me.

"They have to compete. Their mother has two months left to live, and that's her final wish."

"And the competition is, they each have to paint her," he added.

"She'll choose which best represents her."

"But not her likeness: her soul."

"It's a company that has nothing to do with art, though."

"Of course not. They sell life insurance."

I laughed.

"What would your soul look like?" I asked.

Theo pushed his tongue between his teeth.

"You tell me," he said finally.

"A knot, waiting to be unraveled." I winced inwardly at my cheesiness. But Theo chewed the inside of his cheek, trying not to smile.

"What about mine?"

"A long conversation."

"Which looks like what?"

"An infinite strand of DNA."

So I'd found "it." But Theo's work was an issue. Though we would usually sleep together for two nights in a row—one night at my apartment, one night at his (Felix loved it there)—we would then separate for a night while he was on call. The on-and-off nature of the arrangement brought me sharply back to childhood: after my parents' divorce, I became a boomerang between their homes. My mom's lacked my special quilt. My dad's lacked my favorite tree. Both of them, of course, lacked one parent, and the complete family I had loved.

But even before their divorce, I'd slept with my mom anytime my father was out of town for work. We would lie face-to-face with our knees curled up and talk about the events of my life: the book I was reading for school; the friend who had mocked my purple lunchbox; my nervousness about an approaching birthday party. Before we went to sleep, she would touch her fingertip to my nose and give it a little kiss. "Night, pumpikin." Never pumpkin; always pump-ee-kin. "Too wet," I'd moan, wiping my nose with my hand, but I didn't want her to stop. When my father returned from traveling—he was a consultant before he became a teacher—back out of their bed I'd go, into my own, to spend the nights alone.

My antipathy toward sleeping by myself hadn't abated in the decades since—but sharing a bed with Theo often made me so hyper with lust that I could still barely sleep. Sometimes I'd lie for hours staring at the ceiling, willing myself not to turn my head to look at him, since it would only make me more aroused. I would often notice with relief that I was finally drifting off, which would wake me up again. Other times, I'd linger in the liminal pre-sleep state, half embedded in a dream. I'd imagine Theo was saying something to me: "Do you like deviled eggs?" I once thought I heard. (The next morning, he asked why I'd mumbled "scrambled.") Or I'd imagine we were doing something odd in bed, like baking a cake, and I'd start searching through the sheets for the flour. Or I'd have the sensation, as I had several times in childhood when I'd slept in my mother's bed, of her hovering over me. I'd feel her warm breath bathing my face, her finger on the tip of my nose. When, back then, I awakened with a start, my mother—strange and beautiful above me, her sharp chin outlined in the moonlight—would swiftly retreat, saying she'd been admiring me, I was so beautiful.

I'd still loved sleeping with my mother—loved feeling her stomach against my back, her head against my neck, the cocoon of her body. The bed was warmer with my mother in it. My strange memories of her likewise had no bearing on my desire to sleep with Theo as often as possible. In fact, when my eyes snapped open from a vision of my mother to find only Theo sleeping beside me, the contrast between hallucination and reality only made me more grateful. (And, unfortunately, horny again.) I did wonder why I thought about my mother so much when I was with him; but didn't everyone's relationships make them think of their parents?

My nights apart from Theo were more of a problem. I didn't make plans, in case he became available for a phone call. If he wasn't, I listened to the recordings I'd made, which I was trying to limit. Beyond that first food pantry shift, I'd recorded only two meals (a dinner we'd cooked together in his apartment and another at a restaurant, the background noise overwhelming); one evening of innocent sleep; one almost-fucking session (he was tired from work and we ended up cuddling); and one actual fucking session (from the following night, when I had seduced him with a determination bordering on vindictiveness). I would fall asleep listening and wake up the next morning to my computer still open on Theo's pillow, and always, too, to an early-morning text from him, telling me he missed me.

Except for the day of the Aldine interview. Theo and I had spent the previous evening apart, but when I'd awoken, my phone lay messageless, as it had remained. As I prepped for the interview, leafing again through the dossier my producers had prepared, which I'd marked up by hand, I repeatedly checked my phone. If I made it a full minute before glancing at it I was proud. While there was no reason to suspect Theo had neglected the routine on purpose—he was probably stressed, or merely forgetful—I felt sick. We had met only three weeks ago and been dating for two. I knew I was cute but not beautiful, and an acquired taste; I had stupidly told him that I had wondered if my dog was my soulmate. It would make too much sense if Theo had changed his mind. But he would be decent enough to at least *tell* me it was over, wouldn't he? Which would mean I'd have the chance to convince him to stay.

Aldine was on UK time, so our conversation was early: a necessary distraction. I left my phone at my desk and relocated to the studio, where I reread the list of questions—three pages, single-spaced—over again, aloud. Though Aldine would be in a separate studio, as my guests often were, I wanted to get my questions in my head as well as I could so that I could listen and respond, not read my notes out loud like I was auditioning for a school play. Interviews usually went at least twice as long as airtime, so a lot would land on the cutting room floor, which meant I didn't need to worry about sounding stupid on air or leading us into a dead end—though, for fear of embarrassment, I worried anyway. There was a part of me—not my most professional-journalist part—that hoped Eleanor Aldine and I would connect so well during our conversation that it would blossom into a friendship. I fantasized about going to her beautiful home in Cambridge, England; we'd eat bread with cheese and fig jam in her garden, which, per Instagram, rivaled New Orleans's best.

When I'd finished rereading the questions, I put the sheet to the side and did my vocal warm-ups ("Eddie edits," "tittle tattle," "Betty Botter bought some butter, but she said this butter's bitter"), letting my eyes roam around the booth, its corrugated sound-insulating walls, its microphones with their pop filters, its little window with the control room just beyond it. I could see my producer Jenny there, her head tilted down toward the mixer, hair falling in curtains around her face. While I sat in this dark, cushioned room, Theo stood in a sharp, fluorescent one. Was he bent over a patient right now, squinting into the red recesses of her body? I imagined that when he was operating, he was focused solely on the task at hand, had no room for any other thoughts. Maybe that was why he hadn't texted me yet. Hopefully that was all. What about when he was talking to a patient—was it the same then? Did his mind ever wander, or was his attention total? Where did I go for him when his mind severed its tie with the concept of me?

Aldine was on the line. I put on my headphones, gave my standard preamble about the show. I asked her to describe what she'd had for breakfast that day so that Jenny could adjust the levels: "A strong cup of coffee, and then two more. I don't eat breakfast; it makes me sluggish." Her voice was crisp like fizzy cider, her sounds clipped and high.

I started by asking about her extant work. I always began this way, warming guests up with material they were practiced at speaking about before moving on to the less comfortable terrain of their work in progress. I could feel myself laughing a bit too loudly at Aldine's minor jokes, and thought again about my desire to please or befriend her, a fantasy that elided the power dynamic inherent to interviewing. I was always the one asking questions and also the one who, along with my producers, would edit our conversation before the show aired. I couldn't dictate what Aldine's responses would be, but I had a lot of power to shape which parts made it to the public. Although I was awed by her, and felt small in her shadow, in reality I held the dominant role in our duet.

Unlike with Theo. He was clearly the dominant one in *our* duet. He was the one who texted, or didn't; I was the one who waited, possibly forever. Yes, surgery was absorbing, but he'd remembered to text me every other morning, before he'd even gotten to the hospital. So what had changed? Perhaps he had grown so comfortable in our relationship that he didn't feel the need to announce himself all the time. Or he'd become ambivalent, and was taking the day to think about whether he wanted to break up with me. Would he do it over text, à la "I've been thinking..."? Would he come over tonight as planned, and do it then? Or would he just ghost me? If he didn't message all day, and didn't come over tonight, maybe I could go over to his apartment tomorrow evening anyway, as if nothing had changed—by then, he could have reconsidered, or on seeing me again might remember something good about me. I was above begging, I thought; then again, maybe I wasn't.

Jenny gave me a thumbs-up: Aldine's levels were good to go. I scrambled for my list of questions—I'd gotten myself so addled that, despite my preparations, they'd flown from my mind. In their place swam visions of Theo climbing into the truck bed, running his hand through his hair, pressing his forehead to mine, sleeping next to me. I stared at the page until the first question came into focus.

> **ME:** Tell me about the physicality of writing for you: computer? By hand? Pen, pencil?
>
> **ALDINE:** I go back and forth: I'll write by hand until there's so much on the page I feel the anxious pressure to type it up, lest I get lost or overwhelmed. Typing it up also lets me get a handle on what I've written, so when I've reached the end and go back to drafting by hand, I can do so with a better global understanding of the work. But that's for the first draft only. Once I'm revising, it's a whole other thing: I print out portions of the manuscript and cut the pages up with scissors, glue the bits onto new pages, handwrite new matter in between.
>
> **ME:** Does that help you see the work anew, as if someone else wrote it?
>
> **ALDINE:** It does, yes, and it helps me to literally see more of it at once—easier when it's printed out than when I'm scrolling on the computer. And then there's the matter of tricking myself—always necessary when I'm doing the scary business of writing. In this case, I trick myself into believing I'm doing arts and crafts, and it's all fun and games.
>
> **ME:** How else do you trick yourself?

ALDINE: I often write in bed rather than at a desk; then, I'm not *really* working, am I? It's horrible for my back but excellent for my momentum. Or I'll journal *about* the work instead of diving straight in, pretending to myself I'm not hoping that the journaling will bleed into writing, though of course I am.

ME: You mentioned feeling an "anxious pressure" to type up your work at a certain point. What would you say is the relationship between anxiety and writing for you, in general?

ALDINE: They're intimately linked. With a new project, especially, the anxiety about beginning mounts until I can't stand it anymore, and then it's time to turn to the page. After the first few minutes, I'm in a groove and the anxiety releases. But that phase cannot be helped.

ME: So many writers describe this torturous feeling. Why endure that at all—why not do something that produces less dread?

ALDINE: Everything produces dread. Getting out of bed in the morning is dreadful. So why do we do it?

ME: We have to, I guess.

ALDINE: And there is something on the other side.

ME: So where are you in your current project? Anxiously dreading beginning? Or have you made it to the other side?

ALDINE: To clarify, every day is a matter of making it to the other side, where writing a first draft is concerned. Revision is another matter; there is more security there, more control. But with drafting, every single day.

ME: Is that where you are now—drafting?

ALDINE: Unfortunately, it is.

ME: And what can you say about what this new work concerns?

ALDINE: It's a novel, the first I've written.

I paused, long enough that if she'd wanted to delve into what it was about, she would have. In the pre-interview, she'd said only that her new project dealt with the limits of what we can know of another person's mind.

I waited another beat. She stayed silent. But she knew the premise of the show and had agreed to participate, which meant that at some point, unless she'd changed her mind, she would go into it. I didn't press further right then: that kind of pushiness, that level of unresponsiveness to an interviewee's cues, could make them withdraw like a prodded turtle. It could shut down a whole interview. Instead, I saved my intrusion for the end, when it didn't matter if I perturbed her, because I'd got everything else I needed, minus her friendship.

This entire transcript, I should say, is an approximation; I don't have access to my work recordings anymore. But I listened to it so many times in the course of editing that it's imprinted on my brain.

ME: Earlier, you mentioned working on your first-ever novel. How has it felt wading into this new and differently defined terrain? Freeing? Overwhelming?

ALDINE: Both, definitely. It's also opened up new channels of curiosity for me. I'd gotten into something of a rhythm with essays: each is an answer to a question, so curiosity is baked into the narrative performance, but still, it had begun to feel a bit routine. Ditto biographical works, of which I've now written two. Writing a novel lets you deal with questions in a more indirect, exploratory way, like a thought experiment.

ME: What are the questions you're dealing with in this new work?

ALDINE: The main one is, how well can we know each other? What is the perimeter of our access to another person's mind? I'm curious, too, how our knowledge of others relates to their capacity to introspect: can we comprehend in others what they cannot in themselves, and vice versa? To what extent? And, as a corollary:

how do we deal with those limits emotionally? *[Laughter]* It's a lot of questions, actually.

ME: No wonder you need a whole novel.

ALDINE: Right.

ME: Through what relationships, what premise, are you exploring these questions on the page?

ALDINE: Mainly through a couple that's been married for ten years. They have a young daughter, and the bonds between the two of them have begun to fracture. Parenting has brought out things in each member of the couple that the other finds alarming. They wonder how they could've missed it—which begs the opposite question: how could they have seen it?

ME: I assume their daughter is another mystery? Inaccessible to them, to a certain degree?

ALDINE: She is, though whether they accept her inaccessibility is another matter. One sees her as a person with a private mind; the other sees her as an extension of themselves, or a possession. But, by the way, this all may change. It may be that by the time this book comes out, it's about a twenty-something single person mystified by a pet. Or a divorced woman with no kids, trying to understand where she and her ex went wrong.

Just like me, I thought—though Theo and I hadn't even been together long enough to warrant a divorce. My insides squeezed unpleasantly and I refocused on Aldine. The conversation was going better than her earlier silence had suggested it would; she was surprisingly open. Perhaps she'd just needed to get comfortable, and my approach had done the trick.

ME: What about the prompt for this inquiry—is there a relationship in your personal life in which you've experienced this kind of mystification about the other person? And the resulting frustration, or panic, that you can't know everything inside them?

ALDINE: Oh, I'd rather keep my personal life out of it. There are reasons I'm writing this as a novel, beyond how big the questions are.

ME: Can you tell us, then, if this is something that generally comes up for you in familial relationships, romantic relationships, friend relationships? All three?

ALDINE: I would rather not.

At once, my pleasure at our dynamic dissolved into mortification. If I sometimes overstepped socially, when I was interviewing, the boundaries of acceptability were wider, and so I was usually better at staying within them. I had wanted to be the interviewer who incited Aldine to say, "I haven't told anyone this before, but . . ." I had wanted to wear our intimacy as proof of my skill. Instead, she'd shut me out.

With my final few questions, I fumblingly brought the conversation back around to comfortable, if dull, terrain. Once the tape stopped rolling, I blurted—even as I thought, *Olive, don't*—that we should get coffee when she was next in New York. Aldine offered a polite "How lovely" that made clear that we would not meet.

Back at my desk, my shame about my gaffe was pierced by the sight of my phone, which sent an icy prickle across the back of my neck. Had Theo messaged? I stared at the black screen for a few moments before pressing it on. Nothing. Miserable, I threw the phone with a clang into the bottom drawer of my desk, dumped a packet of index cards over it, and slammed the drawer shut.

Using a program that rendered my voice and Aldine's as separate visual tracks, one above the other, I went back over our conversation, excising the disastrous questions about her personal life in advance of sharing the tape with my producers in the afternoon. I sewed together the sentences she'd said before and after the blunder so seamlessly that the listener wouldn't hear a jump, copy-and-pasting the mountainous peak of an inhale from later in the conversation to mask the disruption. Over and over I replayed the tape, tweaking it this way and that. *She and her ex went wrong*, I heard through my headphones, *went wrong, went wrong*—inhale.

My habit of pre-editing was unusual among hosts; everyone else I knew at the station passed the raw tape immediately on to their producers or to interns for a first-round edit. My custom was a bit of a mystery to me: going to vulnerable, risky places was worth it in an interview, and often, it panned out; you never knew where a limit would lie until you hit it. Missing the mark could be seen as a sign of rigorous journalism, of doggedness—of success. But these moments made me self-conscious, and though there was no concealing that I'd made these edits—on the screen, the jumps appeared as vertical lines, even when I'd made them inaudible—I maintained my commitment to slashing when necessary. My producers abided by my inexplicable shame, never discussing my excisions (at least, not with me). Jenny, who was present for the real-time interviews, had once mentioned a fragment I'd cut, but after my awkward reply, she'd never done so again.

Though the day had started out merely cloudy, and it had been only drizzling when I went out to get lunch—my go-to was a turkey sandwich and pickle from the deli across the street, which I'd eat at my desk—by the afternoon, the sky had grown so dark that the whole office had, too. I hadn't checked my phone since I'd thrown it in the drawer hours earlier, restraint that surely, absolutely, would be rewarded with a message. I opened the drawer inch by inch, giving Theo a few extra seconds to contact me before I confronted the little screen; brushed the index cards aside; and lifted the phone with a dramatically trembling hand.

No message.

Through the window, lightning sheared the sky, followed by its thunderous shadow. How comically appropriate. I felt as though Theo had slit my belly with a scalpel and walked away with everything inside. I imagined Felix sniffing at the cavern where my guts used to be. I worried about Felix: he hated thunder and was probably barking uncontrollably. I hoped he had squeezed himself under my bed, his safety spot.

I turned back to my computer to send Jenny the edited Aldine tape. The window behind me cast its lightning-filled reflection onto the monitor, an annoyance; but given that the wall I faced was made of glass, it was better that I sat here, so that my colleagues couldn't possibly know how often I took breaks from editing to search up Theo's name or look at photos of him I'd scrolled through dozens of times before. I clicked through to my office email, sent off the file, and began prepping for my upcoming interview with the Young Adult novelist Joanie McIntyre, trying to immerse myself in *Foreign Lands*, her sole book of essays. McIntyre wrote often—in her novels, but in her essays too—about short, life-changing dalliances. I typed: *In essay "Dunbar Street," McIntyre writes, "the man who, in the week I knew him, transformed me." How does McIntyre think about intimacy—why & how can a brief encounter hold such weight? Is it about the encounter, in the end, or the way it puts her in conversation with herself?*

I checked my phone again. Still nothing. I cued up a recent recording of Theo and me chatting while walking Felix in Fort Greene Park, which I played through my headphones as I leafed through McIntyre's work. (This tape is one of the few I still have.) To anyone beyond the glass wall, I must have looked as though I were listening to music, or perhaps to one of McIntyre's previous interviews. The glass was surprisingly soundproof, a fact I sometimes lamented—recording my colleagues' conversations wasn't possible without leaving my door open, an obvious sign—but now I was grateful for the quiet. The clarinety sound of Theo's voice washed over me; every so often a phrase or exchange would stand out, distracting me.

THEO: Do you pee in the shower?
ME: Yyyyessssss.

A pause in the conversation—in the background, a child screaming, "I want *goldfish!*"—as Theo, I remembered, raised his eyebrows at me. Smirking.

THEO: I knew it.
ME: How? What was it about me?
THEO: Because I hear you saying *Pssssss* when you're in there.
ME: *[Laughter]* Oh my God.
THEO: Detective work.
ME: Do you want me to stop?
THEO: No.
ME: Good. 'Cause I like it.
THEO: I bet you do.
ME: Come on . . . You do it too. . . .
THEO: I swear to you I don't.
ME: But you like it. Your feet communing . . .
THEO: With your pee?
ME: Mm-hmm.
THEO: My toes, they like it. So they tell me.

I paused the tape and checked my phone again. No text. I messaged my friend Maya, as if to convince myself this was why I'd picked it up:

Still on for dinner tonight?

She didn't reply immediately, so I tossed my phone into my bag and turned back to my book, reading the same sentence over and over again. I picked my phone back up and texted my sister Talia—

Phone call this week?

—then put it far away from me on my desk and ripped off my headphones and tried to concentrate on reading, my disobedient hand nonetheless jerking over to my phone to check it again every few lines.

By the end of the day, Maya had confirmed, and Talia had replied (phone call Wednesday night). Nothing from Theo.

The thunderstorm had waned briefly but returned with ferocity shortly before I left the office, crackling its way between the buildings and thrashing the pavement. I waited under the building's awning for ten minutes, hoping it would subside. It didn't. When impatience overtook my distaste at the idea of being soaked all night, I made a run for it, the wind whipping my umbrella inside out.

On the subway, everyone was drenched. The arms of my shirt, a white cotton button-down, had become translucent; my socks squished in my shoes. My hands were too wet to take out my book, and my pants were too wet to dry my hands. Those around me had given up trying to scroll on their phones and sat chatting or gazing vacantly. It had been years since I'd been on a subway car without thirty little screens glowing simultaneously. When an announcement garbled its way unintelligibly across the speakers, a few of us laughed. In the seat across from me, a woman in a knee-length cardigan grabbed one corner of her sweater, wringing it out like hair.

A stream of water trickled onto the floor. She caught my gaze and we shook our heads at each other, wide-eyed, *can you believe this weather?*, before looking away again. So what, Theo hadn't messaged—I had community!

At the other end of the car, a group of Showtime dancers blasted music and started clapping. A couple of obvious tourists clapped along as one of the dancers flung himself to the floor and into a head bridge. Closer to me, a young man stood shirtless, dripping, flanked by a guy and a girl. His friend and his girlfriend? Presumably he'd taken off his shirt because it was soaked; he was now holding it, balled-up, in one hand. He had a teenage body, pecs barely raised above the bones underneath, small pink nipples, stomach a shallow hollow. A necklace hung down below his collarbone, stuck unevenly to his wet chest. He was brazen, standing there half-naked, and he was getting away with it because he was a young and pretty boy. I examined my reflection in the window across the car: lines ran down from my nose to the corners of my mouth; puffed-up pouches sat beneath my eyes. Theo had probably realized that he was in another league entirely.

If I was single now, why shouldn't I seduce this college kid? I stared at his visible sternum, ribs branching out from it like tree roots. I could pin him to the floor with one hand and lick each individual rib and then, right as his penis started moving like a worm exploring the earth, get up and walk away.

My phone buzzed. I went rigid. But it was my mom:

Whatcha up to? Around for a chat?

I was relieved I was on the subway and could sate the query with texts—though as soon as my relief registered, there followed the familiar twist of guilt. I sent back an overlong reply about my day, how I had hoped to befriend my interviewee, a fantasy that had in the light of reality and professionalism presented itself as ludicrous.

> **Mom:** Who wouldn't want to be friends with you?! Her loss!!!
> **Me:** It's fine—it was wrongheaded of me anyway
> **Me:** Sigh
> **Mom:** No sigh! You are charming and beautiful and a brilliant interviewer and anyone you spoke to for your INCREDIBLE show would be beyond lucky to have you as a friend!!!

This text was followed by the jazz-hands emoji, the hearts-surrounding-smiling-face emoji, and, inexplicably, the coiled-snake emoji. I laughed. My mother's faith in my sisters and me veered into the grandiose. This was flattering, and gave me a hit of dopamine. But it was also unsettling in its delusion, which suggested that she didn't really know me, or that if she saw my very human limits, she just as quickly looked away. Not that I wanted her to stop. I sent a text promising to call her.

When I got out of the subway, the rain had stopped. The sidewalks shone; my boots flung water up onto the backs of my calves. I wondered if, when we met for dinner, Maya would think my boots were ugly, or if my loose button-down, which this morning had seemed to me effortlessly cool, would read to her as boring.

I'd known Maya since her family had moved to New Orleans in the second grade. Her first day at school, she'd worn a polka-dot shirt tucked into a short elastic-waist skirt with plaid leggings. I remember looking at the clashing patterns and thinking, "People are allowed to dress like *that*?" I only had two outfits at that age: my purple jumper and my denim jumper, always with a white shirt underneath. After I met Maya, sometimes I'd throw in a hair ribbon, a patterned shirt instead of a white one—never enough flair to get me noticed, but more than I'd ever ventured before. Being around her, both then and now, exposed the gulf of possibility between what I did and what I could do, who I was and who I could be.

The buildings' slick reflections glimmered in the streets. As car wheels zipped past me, spraying, I dialed my mom.

"Sweetheart!"

"Hi, Mommy." I had a fleeting urge to tell her I'd met someone a few weeks ago and fallen in love but that, tragically, he had all but broken up with me. But I knew she would blow past my concerns with her typical abrasive cheer: of *course* he would message! He would be a fool not to love me unconditionally—anyone would! No—from the beginning, I had sensed that revealing my relationship with Theo could be ruinous. It all seemed too delicate and private, like an idea for a radio story: if I spoke it too soon, it might evaporate. If it hadn't already.

Evaporate—or be devoured. As a child, I'd had trouble keeping anything from my mom. I'm not sure how I first intuited that sharing all my thoughts—granting my mom unconditional access—was fair payment for her care, but perhaps it had something to do with the pinky swear she initiated every so often: "No secrets." In the aftermath of spilling, I'd often feel sick, as though I had lost control, or given away something precious to me.

The physical separation of adulthood now served as a buffer against this impulse: without her there, imploring me to tell her more, to tell her what I was *really* thinking, I could protect the mental space I'd come to think of as mine. I didn't know what I feared she'd do with the information that I was in love, but the instinct to keep it private, to keep Theo to myself, arose as quickly and strongly as had the urge to divulge.

Instead, I asked my mom about her day. She had a leak in the upstairs bathroom, and the plumber had forgotten to come. If he didn't come tomorrow, she was confident the water would stain the dining room ceiling. She half wanted him to forget again, since it would give her an excuse to redo the room.

I idled outside the restaurant, listening to her describe her vision for the redecoration; Maya was always late and I knew she wouldn't yet be inside. "Oh, I almost forgot, I ran into your father on the street the other day," my mom said, and from the tone of her voice I knew she'd been waiting our whole conversation to divulge this detail. "He was alone, even though it was near dinnertime." She was digging for gossip about his marriage, which I didn't have and wouldn't give her if I did. Maybe, too, she was covertly checking if I'd talked to him recently, making sure that she had the most of me.

A low voice punctured the air near my left ear: "Excuse me, ma'am." I jumped and let out a squeal; Maya cackled.

"Every time!" I shouted, my heart still racing. "*Every* time." We hugged. "Hold on, I'm on the phone with my mom."

Maya leaned in and crooned, "Hi, Cecilia."

"Tell Maya hello, and say hi to her mother," my mom said. "But no more pranking my daughter!"

"Okay, Mom," I said, cringing adolescently. "I gotta go. Love you."

"Love you the *most*!"

I hung up. Maya and I entered the restaurant, made our way to the host's stand.

"What is this?" I asked, fingering her fur vest as we waited.

"Faux! Duh. I was thinking of dying it mauve. What do you think?"

"I like it as is."

"Of course you do. You'll be surprised how good mauve looks."

At the table, she told me that her mother had a new beau. Like my parents' marriage, Maya's parents' had ended when we were children; unlike my mom, though, Maya's had a new boyfriend every time we got together. "Personally, I think she needs to go to SLAA," Maya said. I asked what SLAA was. "Sex and Love Addicts Anonymous," she said, gawping as though I should have known. "You know, like for people addicted to sex and love?"

"Instead of alcohol or drugs."

"Or in addition."

"What does it mean to be 'addicted' to love?"

"Obsessed with it," she said. "Unable to function without it."

"How do you know about this thing?" I asked, and then added, in case I was being disrespectful, "this *organization*, I mean."

"I've been before," she said, rolling her eyes. "Half of AA is in it. I went because I couldn't get over Rodney—you remember? Just to a few meetings; AA is more my scene. But when I was there, like half the things I heard reminded me of my mother. Some of the things I *said* reminded me of my mother, which was the really disturbing part, but anyway. At least I'm doing something about it, you know? I'm not here to take her inventory, but it's clear she's sick and suffering and I wish she cared enough to help herself." She chewed the inside of her lip, eyes narrow and distant, clearly taking her mother's inventory.

"And you?" I asked.

"Actually, I've been having these crazy fantasies lately," she said, leaning toward me. "Do you remember, when we were kids, you were horny for Big Ben?" Sometime in middle school, I'd confessed to Maya that I'd developed an intense crush on Big Ben. My parents and I had traveled to London, and when I'd caught sight of Big Ben bursting above the skyline, I'd felt undeniably aroused. Looking back, this seemed less to do with its—"his"—obvious phallicism (I can't remember fantasizing about fucking the building) and more to do with his imposing but protective presence at a time when the bond between my parents was fracturing. It was more like the kind of crush one has in kindergarten: an amoebic pull.

"I've never told anyone about that but you."

"People have far weirder fantasies, trust me."

"I resent that."

"So have *you*, since then."

I shrugged. I still hallucinated half the nights I was with Theo, imagining in my liminal pre-sleep state that my mother was hovering above me, pressing her fingertip to my nose. "Tell me yours," I said.

"They're violent," she cautioned.

"Sure."

"So I was meditating the other day? And this image *flew* into my mind of hitting Vince"—her current boyfriend—"in the face with a rock. Or more like a giant boulder? And then his face was restored in my mind and I got to saw his head off with, like, a chainsaw. I made him normal again and then popped his head off like he was an action figure and attached a string to the bottom of it and it flew off into the sky like a balloon. When the bell dinged and I finished meditating, I was like, whoa."

"And?"

"Well, I realized I was really pissed at him," Maya said. "So I told him, 'I'm fucking pissed at you.' We talked about it."

"Pissed why?"

"It doesn't matter. Actually, I can't remember."

"And this helped?"

"Dude, *yes*. Whenever you start dating someone, imagine throwing a boulder in their face. So cathartic."

"Actually, I *have* been dating someone." Or, *had* been. I remembered how he'd sucked my earlobe like an artichoke petal and felt the approach of tears.

Maya didn't notice. "You have?" She grabbed my forearm, gave it an excited shake. "Dude! Yes! Fucking finally!"

"Come on, it hasn't been that long," I said, wishing she'd notice I was upset.

"Olive. It has."

"Rude."

"Are you fantasizing about defenestrating him yet?"

"That and more."

"Fucking in public? In a filthy bathroom stall?"

"More like . . ." And I described the tendon, the hollow above, how I wanted to wedge my tongue as far inside as it would go. The gap between his teeth, which I wanted to probe with my fingers, my tongue, any part of me that would fit inside.

"But I think it's over," I said tremulously.

"What? Why? If you push this guy away—"

"It's not like that," I said. "He hasn't texted me all day."

"Have you texted him?"

"No, but he always texts me first—it's a thing."

"Olive. Get over yourself."

"I'm serious. He's too good for me anyway. It was bound to happen."

"Shut the fuck up and tell me the whole story."

Over three shared plates of pasta I told her how we'd met at the food pantry, then gone on a run and fucked ("Sex on the first date!" she said. "I didn't know you had it in you"); how even then I knew I wanted to be with him forever; how in the time since we'd become inseparable, except not really because he worked constantly and we had to spend every third night apart, which was why I'd got into this mess of waiting all day for the text that never came. How I was the happiest I had ever been, except for the moments I was barfing with misery. How it was somehow over even though it had barely begun, even though he'd reassured me

Felix was *not* my soulmate, even though he'd heard me pee in the shower and told me he'd *liked* it—

"Olive!" Maya interrupted.

"What."

"You know what."

"I legitimately don't."

"Text the man! Text him! You've been dating this man for weeks and you need me to tell you that?"

I held my breath and sent Theo the kissing-cat emoji. Maya and I waited, staring at the phone, barely breathing, until he sent back a heart.

"You are so dumb," she said, then—finally—noticed I was crying and came around the table to hug me and call me her boo-boo banana.

"It's fine, I'm fine," I said.

"You're crazy," she whispered into my ear, making me laugh.

"Does love always feel this good-bad?"

"Always and unavoidably."

Outside after dinner, the streets shimmering with wet, everything louder because of the rain, Maya put her hands on my shoulders and said, "Lick his tooth gap already. Okay?"

"What if he's grossed out? After all this?" I dangled my phone in the air between us.

"If he's disturbed by you putting your tongue in his fucking *mouth*—"

"Defenestration?"

"Exactly."

I'd been sleeping for a couple of hours by the time the phone rang. My dream transformed the sound into a high school marching band. By the time I woke up, I'd missed the call: it was Theo. I went downstairs to let him in—the buzzer had broken, and instead of replacing it, our landlord had removed it—rubbing the sleep out of my eyes, swishing spit around my mouth to get rid of the staleness. He looked tired, his eyes half open. His kiss tasted like peanut butter.

"You're here," I said.

"Of course I am."

"I thought . . ."

"What?"

"When you didn't text this morning . . ."

"Didn't I?"

I shook my head.

"Why didn't you, then?"

"I figured if you didn't, it was because you didn't want to."

"Don't figure that," he said.

"So," I said. "You're here."

"I'm here."

"Come upstairs."

In bed, we murmured into the darkness.

ME: What's that on your boxers?
THEO: *[Laughter]* Sandwiches.
ME: Turkey? Ham?
THEO: Roast beef. With coleslaw.
ME: Milky or tangy?
THEO: Tangy.
ME: The best kind.
THEO: Which am I?
[Kissing sounds]
ME: Tangy. Definitely.

So, yes. I recorded us. And that night, once I was sure Theo was asleep, I let the pads of my fingers press against his tendon, taut as rope; above, the soft cavern of hot skin. He didn't stir. I propped myself up next to him and reached toward his mouth. My heart thunked in my throat. At the last second, when I could feel his breath against my fingers, Theo's eyelids fluttered and I pulled my hand away and feigned sleep.

4.

From Sharlene's Bar, June 10:

> THEO: So how'd you start running, anyway? You're really good—
> ME: —horrible. I'm so slow!
> THEO: You're actually pretty fast.
> ME: Slower than you.
> THEO: Just a little. And, so? You look like an—
> ME: —ostrich?
> THEO: —antelope. Or a gazelle, or something.
> ME: That's sweet.
> *[In the background, someone's shrill burst of laughter.]*
> THEO: Are you blushing?
> ME: No, liar. It's too dark in here for you to even tell.
> THEO: So . . . ?
> ME: With my dad. Like, twenty years ago, probably. This was after my parents got divorced and I'd go to my dad's place every other weekend and on Tuesday nights—
> THEO: With Talia and Romi?
> ME: No, they were out of the house already.
> THEO: I didn't realize they were that much older.
> ME: Mm-hmm. I was twelve when my parents split, Talia was in college, and Romi had graduated and was living in Houston.

[Clanging noises from the kitchen]
THEO: Anyway, so—
ME: Right. So my dad took up running as some sort of post-divorce midlife crisis thing—before this he'd told us the only C he'd ever gotten was in gym class. But he started going out every Sunday, and I'd go with him when I was over at his place.

I had the urge to play Theo a recording of a run with my dad (by the time we started running together, I'd used my allowance to buy a new, smaller recorder that I could duct-tape to my body, underneath my shirt) but stopped myself. I couldn't tell him about that recording without telling him about *this* one. One day, I would share my tapes with him, and we could cohabit an echo chamber of our own memories. I hoped that, when I did, he would recognize that my recordings were a way of being close to him, of honoring him—of loving him. But it was too early to test this theory, especially since I wasn't ready to stop.

THEO: Did you like running right away?
ME: I hated it at first, but pretended I loved it to spend time with him. Then there was a day I realized I'd kept going without thinking about every single step, counting down to the end—my mind had just been wandering. Like, running was suddenly easy. And since then—whenever I'm in shape, anyway—I've felt more natural running than almost any other time. Like my legs are built for it and know exactly what to do.
THEO: Me, too.
ME: I can tell. *[Pause while, as I remember, we smiled shyly at each other.]* So, you: running origin story.
THEO: Middle school. I had a ton of energy as a kid, I was always jumping on tables and breaking vases, and my parents didn't know what to do with me. They had me join the track team so I could run it out.

ME: Did it work?

THEO: Lucky for them, I loved it, and it kept me out of their hair for a couple of hours after school. But no, I continued to "express my energy" all over the place.

ME: You're still like that, a little. The adult version.

THEO: Tell me.

ME: Waking up before work to read medical journals, running ten miles on the weekends, volunteering at the food pantry that one time and never going back—

THEO: I'll go back!

ME: You probably barely fit it in that first time.

THEO: It's true.

ME: Energy overload.

THEO: You forgot to mention: forgetting appointments, getting lost in hobbies—

ME: Like collecting scraps of paper on the subway?

THEO: Not just scraps.

ME: What else?

THEO: You don't want to know.

ME: I do.

THEO: I'm honestly afraid to tell you. It's not cute.

ME: That makes it sound like you collect dead bodies or something.

THEO: It's not quite that bad.

ME: Now *I'm* scared! You have to tell me, or I'll imagine something horrible.

THEO: Like a button that fell off someone's shirt. Or a scrunchie with a few hairs still stuck in it. Water bottles with a little backwash still left in them . . .

ME: Where do you keep this stuff?

THEO: In the same place as the notes.

ME: You're trolling me.

THEO: I'm not.

ME: Ew! That's why you wouldn't let me see what else was in there!

THEO: See? I told you! I want you to still, you know, want to fuck me—

ME: Sorry, sorry. I do. But . . . Old teeth?

THEO: Sometimes.

ME: Fingernail clippings?

THEO: Too small.

ME: Barf?

THEO: Okay, no. That's too disgusting even for me.

ME: Thank God.

THEO: Are you too grossed out?

ME: Nah. As long as you promise: never barf. Or pee.

THEO: I promise.

ME: And will you wash your hands before you see me? Like, always? *[Silence while Theo sticks a finger in my mouth, followed by a squeal; laughter.]*

ME: I want to see it all.

THEO: It's under lock and key.

ME: Show me the scrunchies, at least.

THEO: Okay. Just the scrunchies.

Absorbed in thought, Theo was performing the gesture I'd noticed at the food pantry, pushing the tip of his tongue through the gap between his bottom teeth. I wondered if he tongued his teeth in this way while he was kneeling to fish a discarded hair tie from beneath a subway seat. I was relieved he was at least a little gross; it made it less likely he would leave me and more likely that, whenever I did tell him about my recordings, he would understand.

Theo glanced down at my leg, which was bent up on the couch we'd staked out in the back corner of the bar. My heart kicked up into my throat and I stopped talking, just looked at it along with him. It looked like a runner's leg, and I wondered if he liked it. Theo's elbow was perched on the back of the couch, his hand dangling toward me; silently, I begged him to slip his fingers into the crease behind my knee, wrap them around my calf. He looked back up at me and our eyes met.

"What are you thinking?" I ventured.

But Theo shook his head briskly, dispelling the train of thought. "Nothing," he said, like a knife.

That night, as I drifted off to sleep, I once again felt my mother hovering above me, convinced myself I smelled her rosy perfume, and awoke with a start. Only Theo was there. He lay on his back, as usual, mouth open, as usual. I propped myself up next to him. There was his tooth gap, devilish as ever. I reached toward it as I had the other night, asking myself if I would really touch it, but I had fingered his tendon on multiple occasions now, and was this really so different? Yes, it would be harder to feign sleep if he awoke; but as far as intrusions were concerned, the two were one and the same. I moved closer, half hoping he'd wake up and save me from having to go through with it—but he was completely still. Gently, I tapped my finger to his teeth and slid it down toward his gums, then back up and behind. His teeth were smooth, squeaky to the touch. The gap was not wide enough for my finger to fit through. I wanted to press hard enough against his teeth that they'd begin to separate, growing further and further apart until they broke his mouth open so wide I could crawl inside. I lifted my hand away and peered into the cavern of his throat. It was too dark in the room to make out its contours; the streetlight through the sheer curtains was faint. What secrets were down there inside of him, nestled between his organs? What didn't I know?

From Fort Greene Park, June 16:

ME: Favorite painter: go.
THEO: Favorites are too hard.

ME: I said, "Go . . ."

THEO: Okay. John Singer Sargent, Alice Neel, Frida Kahlo, Gustav Klimt. For starters. The Dutch Masters for technique. Lucian Freud. Balthus. Egon Schiele. Now—you go.

ME: Wow. Well, I've gotten a crush on a portrait before.

THEO: What!

ME: Once.

THEO: You have to tell me which, obviously.

ME: It's this one at the Met—I don't remember what it's called, or who it's by, actually.

THEO: Not allowed.

ME: I really don't remember.

THEO: Find it on your phone.

[Long pause: children shrieking. Someone chastising in Arabic. Children still shrieking. Wind crackling into the microphone.]

THEO: *[Reading:]* Ilya Efimovich Repin . . .

ME: Mm.

THEO: It's remarkable. *[Pause]* So this guy, hunched over his desk with all these papers, this writer—

ME: "Vsevolod Mikhailovich Garshin," apparently.

THEO: Have you read his stuff?

ME: Not one bit. I've avoided looking him up on purpose. No matter what I found out, it wouldn't live up to my fantasies.

THEO: Tell me more about your fantasies.

ME: Let's go home and I'll show you.

But what I thought was: *I want to cut you open.*

From my bedroom, June 23:

ME: Where do you want to go that you've never been before?

THEO: Egypt. Also the La Brea Tar Pits. You?

ME: Montana.

THEO: Why?

ME: I have to think there's a quality of silence I've never heard before.

THEO: So loud it hurts your ears?

ME: Like a deprivation tank. An overwhelming rush of—nothing. Am I being unfair to Montana? I mean it in a good way.

THEO: I know.

[Through the window, the overwhelming rush of too many somethings: teenagers yelling and laughing. Music blasting briefly, from a boom box strapped to a bike, maybe, speeding by. A baby's piercing wail from upstairs. A couple's argument in the street: "But you said—" "I didn't!" "You—" "No, you—"]

THEO: What do you think they're arguing about?

ME: Let's say our interpretations at the same time. One, two, three—

[At once:] **THEO:** She's cheating. **ME:** He's cheating.

[Laughter]

ME: Can we just—not?

THEO: Not what?

ME: Cheat.

THEO: So you want to be *boyfriend-girlfriend*?

ME: I mean—do you?

THEO: Do you?

ME: . . . yes.

THEO: Me, too.

[Delighted, maniacal laughter, like I might explode.]

I love you, I thought then, but it wasn't until he was fully asleep later that night—mouth open, soft snores leaking out—that I said it aloud, the first time in my life I'd said it to a man who wasn't my dad. I wondered how Theo would've replied if he'd heard. I wondered if I should tell him about the recordings before I told him I loved him for real. Theo's arm was flung above his head on the pillow, exposing his armpit's fine silk. I got my nose as close as I could without touching—he was ticklish and I didn't want to wake him—and breathed in a deep one. I knew his scent intuitively, and tonight as ever he smelled "like Theo," but now I had the chance to parse the elements without interruption: soil, sweat, a surprising undercurrent of anise. When I touched his teeth, I pressed harder than I ever had before, and I thought I must be imagining it, but there it was: they budged.

5.

I'd spent almost my entire adulthood without Theo, but now that I had him, I struggled to remember how I used to occupy myself. Though I had been, overall, resentfully single, I had managed to find pockets of abandon and even joy. I remembered taking the F train home to Brooklyn as recently as six months earlier, tipsy on saccharine happy-hour margaritas and the particular freedom of New York, blasting pop songs through my headphones as the train surfaced at Smith-Ninth, the sunset bursting into view. I remembered going to a movie or the Philharmonic alone and sinking anonymously into the darkness as though it were a womb; taking myself to dinner and covertly recording the conversations I overheard ("Is it too much to ask that she let me know *beforehand*?"); thinking, alone, in the total silence of early morning. I remembered going to the Met and having conversations in my head, as if I contained within my single self two very charming and intelligent people.

Now, my Theo-less pockets of time seemed senseless. I thought of Theo constantly, even when to all persons present I appeared to be focused on the conversation at hand, and spent the moments we were apart calculating the time until we would see each other again. Why would I want to go to the Met without Theo when I knew what it was like to go with him? He said things that surprised me, that made me laugh, that I disagreed with—things the charming interlocutors inside my brain would never come up with. When we finally stood in front of Ilya Efimovich Repin's portrait of Vsevolod Mikhailovich Garshin together, I pointed to the man's furrowed eyebrows, like a shelf over his eyes, which stare straight at the viewer. Less concern than invitation, his gaze burning through the paint. Theo, meanwhile, pointed out the brushwork, the fine detailing on the books and papers splayed across Garshin's desk. How could I appreciate art by myself now, knowing I was missing all that? Theo said *"Bless you!"* at the varying pitches of my sneezes; pressed his thumbs into the arches of my feet; scratched Felix's belly whenever he revealed it, paws in the air; outlined, with his tongue, the crevices of my ear. We talked like adults but played like puppies. I asked him if people farted during surgery and he said, "Of course. Just like you farted in your sleep last night." (I claimed it had been Felix. "You think I don't know what your farts smell like by now?" Theo said.) When one of us yawned, the other would lick their chin, interrupting. We'd spend minutes yawning over and over, passing the urge back and forth, until we each finally got it to crest. Over and over, I felt compelled to tell Theo about my recordings—we'd been together long enough now that withholding could be construed as dishonest—but each time the urge rose in me, I swallowed it just as quickly. I still couldn't bring myself to take the risk; in fact, the longer I waited, the scarier it became. Theo, on the other hand, finally showed me his collection of subway finds, which he stored in a ratty backpack he'd also found on the subway, and let me add my own acquisitions: a purple glove with a coffee stain, a MetroCard with the words FUCK U OK? on the back, a half-eaten Ring Pop. And now: I was supposed to remember how to be happy without him.

So I felt ready for my trip home. It would be a distraction. Each summer, my sisters and I converged on New Orleans for our

Momstravaganza, during which we "surprise"-visited our mom to celebrate her birthday. Unfailingly, by the time we arrived, she knew we were coming; though she claimed to adore surprises, and seemed to seriously believe she did—she implored us, each year, to catch her off guard—she always wheedled the date out of one of us. She tried to be sneaky about it and, because she clearly enjoyed having us think of her as a surprise aficionado, we were sneaky back, never telling her outright when we'd be there, only planting semi-obvious hints.

Talia, Romi, and I had planned a few adventures for the four of us—a visit to my mom's favorite hair salon; dinner at Arnaud's, where we'd celebrated all of our birthdays forever—but not too much: though our mom claimed she preferred when we planned everything, she actually relished helming the schedule, choosing exactly what she liked and, most of all, taking care of us.

I loved going home, and not only because I felt more myself with my sisters than I did with anyone else; nor because being Jewish was actually special there, if only a little; nor because I thought New Orleans was the most beautiful city in the world, though I did. It was also because for a short time, I was released from the pressures of adulthood, which always subsumed me as soon as I returned to New York. While we were with her, our mom paid for everything, and we were never alone.

Yet now I had Theo, from whom my parting had been as wrenching as it was cliché. Though I'd claimed to myself that I wanted this trip, that it would be good for me—as though it were medicine—upon saying goodbye in the morning, then peering through the window as Theo exited my building and walked down the street toward the subway, I'd burst into comically overdramatic tears. Even now, looking out the airplane's window, the setting sun casting its orange glow across the ridged cloud floor, my craving for Theo registered as nausea. It made me suspect I would spill to my mom about our budding relationship so that, through speech, I could feel near him. Telling Talia and Romi could be fine, even satisfying, assuming they kept it to themselves, but I continued to feel wary of inviting my mother in. Divulging to even someone as tangential as Binita had unsettled me; she now felt entitled to ask "So . . . ?" every food pantry shift, and I felt obliged to answer. Binita wasn't my mother, of course. But maybe worse, my mom really knew me, and had access to parts of me someone like Binita didn't even know existed. The plane lowered over my city, swaths of land coming into view, some pocked with houses and roads and others raw with trees and still water. The sun bled a purple twilight, reflected in the small amoeba-shaped lakes. With a jolt, the wheels touched down.

Romi had arrived the night before, so I took a cab from the airport alone. My mom had insisted on picking me up, but I'd insisted even harder back—partly out of pride, and partly so I could have a short communion with New Orleans on my own. My sisters had more flexible schedules than I did: Romi was a full-time mom in Houston and could fly whenever her husband could solo parent or her in-laws were free to babysit; Talia, a therapist, had moved back to New Orleans after college and saw our mom most regularly. It was my suspicion that Romi and I had struggled more than Talia with our mom's overwhelming style of loving. Romi was the firstborn, an only child for several years and our mom's main focus until Talia and I came along, and I'd spent the most time with my mom actually *alone*, post-divorce, when my sisters were already out of the house. So maybe we needed, more than Talia, to get away. I was grateful that Talia lived here. It kept my mom in town: she'd often assured us that she'd move wherever we ended up living.

The weather was sweltering. Cicadas screeched, amplified to a deafening decibel by the humidity. As I lugged my suitcase up the front stairs, sweat rolled down my neck, plastering my hair to my skin. But I opened the door (we all had keys) to a house verging on cool, AC blasting, and the three of them in pajamas, splayed variously across the sitting room—Talia in the armchair with her legs draped over one of the arms, my mom and Romi leaning against each other on the couch—waiting for me.

"Ollie!" my mom cried, jumping up to hug me, the ends of her silk robe fluttering behind her. Talia and Romi rose up in her wake. From over my mom's shoulder I glared at Talia, who was covering her mouth, laughing. I hated the nickname Ollie—my mom had named me Olive; why couldn't she say it?—but she consistently "forgot" and called me it anyway.

"Hi, Mommy," I said, giving in to the hug and melting into her, almost swaying. As the hug extended beyond its due, I examined the front room, which looked new to me each time I saw it after some time away: the tall French windows with their heavy, patterned drapes; the piano, framed by paintings of flowerpots; and, covering almost the entire wall above the sideboard, photographs of us. In one, my sisters and I are pictured in the backyard, huddled around our favorite tree. I, sporting a nineties side ponytail—I'm probably eight—have wrapped my arms around the trunk, Talia is perched cutely on a branch, and Romi, about to leave for college, is striking a model-esque pose a bit in front of us. Already, she looks like a sorority girl, pretty in a shiny way; Talia has a much softer beauty, the kind you'd notice only after staring at her for a while, and that grows the longer you look. I've always thought I look more like Talia than Romi, but maybe I'm flattering myself thinking I resemble either of them. In the photo, the tree—thick and gnarled and perfectly climbable—looks like a fourth sister, absorbing our secrets, never judging. The last time I'd visited, I'd been dismayed to find that the tree had died and been cut down.

"Why do you still call her *Mommy*?" Romi asked, like she always did.

"I think it's sweet," said Talia, like she always did.

"Me too! I do!" said our mother, drawing Romi and Talia into our hug and kissing the three of us so aggressively we started to laugh and push her away.

* * *

The next day, before the salon, we made breakfast together: scrambled eggs on toast, our childhood favorite. (These days, we all skipped the ketchup, though my mom dutifully—relentlessly—put it on the table anyway.) My mom and I helmed the egg operation; I was on toast and table-setting duty, while my mom took care of the scrambling. Though she'd cooked for us unfailingly before the divorce, never requesting help (in fact, forbidding it, lest it distract us from our homework), something shifted after the split. She began letting me serve as her sous chef and, when she saw I had a knack for it, make our Sunday night dinners on my own. She taught me pasta with homemade sauce, then my grandmother's secret stew, and, by the time I left for college, a full roast chicken. (Brisket waited until a particularly dull spring break my junior year: all my friends were in Florida, but I'd felt too guilty. "That's so *sweet*," my mom had said when I'd floated the possibility of returning to New Orleans for the week, hoping she'd discourage me. "But only if that's what you really want!" I'd claimed that, of course, it was.) I took pride in my cooking, as she had; when I'd made a simple pasta Bolognese for Romi's family over the winter, Romi had taken a bite, then raised her eyebrows dramatically: "Shit! Were you always this good?"

Ostensibly, food was love—this was how my mother had framed it. "I feed you because I love you!" This particular morning, she'd asked if the eggs were up to standard, and we'd gushed over them, as always: they really were perfect, fluffier than I could ever get them when I tried to replicate her technique at home. "I'm so glad!" she had exclaimed, beaming. Her pleasure was genuine, but I had at times wondered whether there was an attempt to bind us to her through her cooking. *Food is sacrifice; now sacrifice back.*

Salon time. I'd opted out of an appointment, choosing instead to just "keep company": a ruse. While my mom was getting her hair colored, her head in the basin and gaze safely averted upward, and Romi and Talia sat side by side in styling chairs in the back, I snuck out to call Theo. I walked toward my dad's house, hoping I'd run into him by chance—on a Mom trip, I'd never visit him outright. Except for holidays, for which we'd developed an alternating routine reminiscent of the custody arrangement they'd maintained when I was young, I always booked separate trips to see each parent, and kept the Dad trips from my mom. All three of us did. It was less about animosity between the two of them (in fact, they'd get together for dinner once a season, presumably to talk about us, or perhaps just to brandish their easy cordiality) and more about my mom's struggle to share us with anybody else. If it hadn't been court-mandated when we were kids, I wonder whether she would've let us go to his place at all, and how she would've excused it, to us and to herself. Part of me was surprised she'd even gotten divorced, since it meant having to share us—but that same part suspected it hadn't been her decision.

The heat wound around me like a thick robe. Outside a café, teenagers hunched over a phone screen together, cackling. A lone saxophone rang out, tunelessly, from a corner. I turned onto a residential street and called Theo, pressing the phone to my ear as if it were his mouth. As the rings accumulated, my heart pounded, pleasurable and sickening.

"It's you!" he said. His throaty voice, his burst of a laugh.

"It's *you*," I said.

He asked me to paint the scene for him, and I held out the phone in hopes that he could hear the soft rustle of leaves in the breeze. When I pressed the phone back to my ear, a siren was wailing in the background on Theo's end of the line; I laughed. He hadn't heard a thing. I described the uneven pavement lined with colorful houses, gingerbread-esque, their front gardens exploding with jessamine and ferns and plants with leaves the size of bodies. In New Orleans, I felt held, the trees arcing over the street like giants' arms, moss hanging down like jewelry, sometimes creating such a canopy that light couldn't get through. In New York, I missed New Orleans's trees as though they were people. My bodyguards.

I told Theo I was passing by my granny's house—elegant like her, two-tiered and cream-colored with thin white columns, a chandelier peeking through its tall windows—but that I wouldn't go inside. Granny still lived in the house my dad had grown up in; after the divorce, he had moved around the corner. I hadn't yet managed to cross his path accidentally, and today, as ever, my father did not appear.

"Is she threatened?" Theo asked. "Your mom."

"If she found out that on her special weekend I'd seen my dad, or even Granny, she'd be . . . well, it's off-limits, anyway," I said.

"So you won't see him at all while you're there?"

"Not unless I run into him by chance, which could happen."

Theo asked me to tell him about Granny, so I explained Slug Lady, the game we used to play when I was young. This was on Friday nights, when we'd go over to Granny's for Shabbat dinner. Granny would lie on the couch, totally still and sluglike, and let me arrange her any way I liked. Sometimes I'd cross her arms over her body like she was hugging herself to keep warm. Sometimes I'd cross one leg over the other, sit her up, and hold out her arm with her pinky outstretched like she was at the fanciest party in the world. As soon as I broke down laughing, she would crack up, too, coming out of the pose and hugging me to her.

"I already love her," he said, and my breath caught. He hadn't meant to say "love," had he? Or was he hinting?

He asked what we were all up to today; I told him the others were getting their hair done at the moment. Color and coiffed bob for my mom; blowout for Romi; something as close to air-dried as possible for Talia, who was merely being accommodating.

"And what were you doing before I called?"

"Reading an article," he said.

"In the newspaper?"

"A medical journal."

"About?"

He read me the title: "'The cost-effectiveness of extended prophylaxis in postoperative ulcerative colitis patients.'"

"Is it good?"

"Very."

"Like, the writing?"

"That's not really the standard."

"Then how is it good?"

"Really comprehensive, meticulously researched. Et cetera."

"Do you know you do this thing while you read—push your tongue between your teeth?" I asked.

"Do I?"

"It's extremely cute."

"I had no idea."

"Don't stop, okay?"

"I won't."

"Promise?"

"Promise."

If you want, I could do it to you, I thought but didn't say. I flashed back to the night the previous week when I'd pressed so hard on his teeth it had felt like they'd budged apart.

I circled the block again and again. I asked what he'd done for dinner the night before: pizza with "an old friend." My insides twisted and I resisted asking who. He asked if I'd had any strange dreams, and I told him I'd dreamt I was giving birth to some four-legged mammal. That was funny, he said, because he'd had one involving a kangaroo, but he couldn't remember if he was watching the kangaroo, if he *was* the kangaroo, or if he was snuggled inside its pouch.

"Can I tell you something?" he said suddenly, in an urgent tone. My heartbeat kicked up into my throat.

"Of course."

"I did something. . . ."

My heart beat faster. He was going to tell me he'd applied to a fellowship in California and, if he got it, didn't want me to come with him. Or that he'd signed a lease for a new apartment not in Brooklyn, not even in Manhattan, but in the Bronx. Or that he'd slept with someone else—

"I got in trouble at work," he said. I stifled a relief-laugh. My limbs felt weak. "I took something from the hospital," Theo continued. "Which you're not supposed to do."

"A scalpel?" I guessed.

"No." He sounded scared. "Some discarded . . . tissue."

Pieces of a person's body? This was grosser than anything else in Theo's collection—closer to piss or barf than to someone's old clothes. But it was intriguing. I wondered what it smelled like, and what sound it had made when he'd dropped it into his backpack.

"I didn't know you collected stuff at work," I said.

"I usually don't. Just the subway. Or the sidewalk. But it was this fascinating older guy. . . . He would doodle these hilarious caricatures of people in the hospital. And then he died."

Now discarded body tissue didn't seem so bad. Frankly, I wouldn't have blamed Theo for taking home something even more personal. He had lost someone.

"I'm so sorry," I said.

"I rarely take patients' deaths so hard. I mean, it happens literally all the time. But this guy . . ." He let the sentence dangle.

"Did he remind you of someone?"

"No, not like that. Maybe the grandpa I wish I had, or something. But the tissue—"

"What's the problem? It's not like they need it."

"It's a biohazard," he said. "Just a thing you are super-not-supposed-to-do. Plus, obviously, it's weird."

"It's not *weird*," I said. "Caring about a patient is *weird*?"

"The chief called me into his office, alone, and told me if I do anything like this again, I'll be fired. He asked how I could possibly think this was an okay thing to do. I couldn't even come up with anything—I just stood there like an idiot, apologizing. If I lose my job—"

"You won't," I said. "But these people—they're *soulless*. If taking something they don't even need, at *all*, because you cared about someone—if that makes you feel better, how can't they understand?"

"The hospital doesn't work like that," Theo said, his pitch rising. "I should've stopped myself. I had this moment right before I took it when I tried to tell myself not to—*it's not like I can even save this stuff! It's going to rot!* But I couldn't help myself."

"How did they even find out?"

"Turns out the nurse who was cleaning up the room is absurdly meticulous. So they had a record of this missing tissue, and then—oh,

Olive, it was so mortifying, the little baggie fell out of my pocket during the next surgery. I want to throw up just thinking about it. I don't know how I'll go back to work tomorrow."

"I promise, *you* are the sane one here," I said. "Will you show it to me when I get home?"

"I really miss you," he said in answer.

I said I missed him more.

By the end of the weekend, we'd watched three movies and cooked three meals; gotten Sno-Balls; consumed our Arnaud's feast (fried oysters, cornbread, and fish, same as always), then moaned and clutched our stomachs to reiterate to ourselves that we had eaten; and dissected the details of each other's lives. Somehow, I managed to call Theo covertly three times over the course of the weekend, and texted him far more times than that. At last, it was our final night in New Orleans, which meant the next day, I would see him.

But before our reunion there was a flight to take, and before that was sleep, and before that was dinner. My mom and I cooked together again—coq au vin, which we plated on her fine china and garnished with chopped parsley. She got out the linen napkins and the heavy napkin holders and the cut crystal glasses for our wine, and the four of us ate formally at the dining table ("Mmm!") while mercilessly dissecting a cousin's wedding from two months before. The best part of any family event was always the debrief, and we savored it like a meal; this one we had saved for when we could really enjoy it. Romi thought the limited wine selection—just one red and one white—was ludicrous: "It felt like a college dorm room party." Our mom thought the bride's dress looked "like a bad cake." Talia was concerned about our cousin Shauna, who had lost a dramatic amount of weight since we'd last seen her.

"She looked gaunt," I said. "Did you talk to her?"

"Only for a minute. I was trying to see if she had that fuzz on her arms, you know, like anorexics do?"

"So did she?" Romi asked, swirling her wine and taking a sip.

"I frankly couldn't tell. I couldn't find a way to look without her noticing."

"No one looks at someone's arms while they're talking."

"Too obvious."

"Do you think she's sick, though? In a not-anorexia way?"

"Surely Aunt Frankie would have told us. . . ."

On and on we went. At times, as had happened when we were young, my sisters back-and-forthed with such agility that I had trouble inserting myself. As they spoke, I recalled an image from the wedding that had taken on nightmarish significance in my mind: my grandmother's glass of after-dinner milk next to her half-full wineglass, still on the table. The sight of the two liquids juxtaposed was grotesque. At the wedding, I'd thought ruefully about how that was going to be me in a few decades, but minus the widow status, the pile of children and grandchildren; just me and my wine-and-milk combo. But now I saw a different future. I imagined Theo with our child on his lap, a small boy in denim overalls who, at my invitation, laid his little palm across my belly, pregnant with his sibling.

My sisters were talking about the groomsmen's speeches, which had been exclusively about Dungeons & Dragons.

"The worst was that cousin of his," Romi said, and Talia started laughing.

"With the boom box? Oh my God."

"I can play the speech," I blurted before they could move on. This would be perfect. If I couldn't bring myself to share my tapes with Theo yet, at least my family would be familiar with their potential.

On my seventh Chanukah, my parents had given me a plastic tape recorder that I had used to record my conversations and surroundings almost every day thereafter. Romi had quickly soured on my red-and-yellow buddy, which I brought everywhere with me; after a few months, she had started demanding that I put it away. "I don't want every fucking thing I say on tape! For fuck's sake!" she had yelled at one point, startling me: I'd never heard her say "fuck" before. She was in high school by that point, so she must have been saying it for years, but never in front of me. Talia, for her part, hadn't seemed bothered so much as bemused by my habit. And I hadn't stopped recording. I felt a kinship with the recorder, as though it were a friend, whether it was my original plastic device or the sleek black rectangle I upgraded to years later. Listening back through the day felt as though we were combing over its details together. I kept all the tapes, neatly labeled and organized, in a box that still sat buried beneath piles of arts and crafts equipment in the closet of my bedroom in this very house. I assumed that at some point since I was seven, my sisters had figured out I'd kept recording, even if my parents hadn't, and that their earlier antipathy toward my habit had softened into understanding, even amusement. They would laugh at the recorded speech. They would love it.

"Play it, meaning . . . ?" Romi asked.

"I'll show you."

I went upstairs to grab my computer from my bedroom, then thumped back down the stairs—laughter from below, though I couldn't make out what about—and, once I'd returned to the dining room, laid it on the table to cue up the tape.

"What are you going to show us, some You Tube?" my mother said, pronouncing it as though it were two separate words.

"No, I'm playing the horrible wedding speech. Like I just told you."

Romi gawped at me. "You recorded it?"

"I recorded the whole wedding," I said.

The three of them were silent. Only Talia looked sanguine, unsurprised.

"Olive," our mom said.

Romi said, "You're still doing that?" She looked at my computer with the furrowed eyebrows and pursed lips of someone who's tasted something unpleasant. My mother squinted in my direction as though trying to puzzle through something. Talia looked back and forth between the two of them. Far from including me in the conversation, the tape had pushed me even further away. I outlined the flowers printed on the tablecloth with my fingernail.

"I still do it, yes," I said. "From time to time."

There was a long pause.

"I figured once you started interviewing people for work, you started *telling* people you were recording," Romi said.

"I do tell my interviewees when I record them," I said. It came out insistent. "Just not, you know, other people. But I don't do anything with the recordings. I mean, until right now, I've never done anything with the tapes I've made outside of work, other than play them for myself."

Romi looked at Talia. "It's a curious habit," Talia said.

Talia always saw through me. This had largely been a boon: when my parents had first split and I'd begun shuttling back and forth between their houses, Talia alone had sensed the depths of my distress. She'd insisted that our family dog, Irving, come with me, despite how desperately my mom insisted on keeping him for herself. (Irving had since died, and our mother hadn't gotten another dog, which infuriated me: had her fixation on Irving been only mimetic desire?) Now, though, I dreaded Talia's insights, and wished

I'd kept my "curious habit" to myself. Mercifully, for the time being, she said nothing more.

"How did you even have a recorder on you at the wedding?" Romi asked.

"The dress had pockets."

"Love a dress with pockets," Talia said, trying to soften the mood. I wondered how each of them would react if they knew I'd recorded Theo—whenever, that is, I finally told them I had a boyfriend. I had assumed Romi would one day find it funny, or kinky, and would demand to hear the tapes, but now that fantasy seemed misguided. Talia would probe. Our mother would be distressed.

"Ollie, darling," our mother said, "aren't you afraid of people finding out?"

"People are doing *far* worse these days," I said, my anxiety rising. "They take photos of other people in ugly outfits on subway platforms and post them all over the internet, and nothing happens to them." Or, I thought, press on their boyfriends' teeth in the night, pushing them apart. Telling Theo about my recordings suddenly seemed like a terrible idea. "Anyway, New York is a one-party consent state. It's legal."

"What, are you investigating your family members for fraud?" Romi said.

"What does 'one-party consent' mean?" our mom asked.

"Only one of the people in a conversation has to consent to it being recorded," I said.

"So wouldn't you have to ask, then?" Romi asked. "For them to consent?"

"No, the one person is me."

"As in, *you* consent to your own secret recording?" Romi asked.

"Right."

"Damn." She shook her head and aggressively forked a chunk of meat.

"Well, that's how it is," I said. "Most states are one-party consent. Louisiana included." I looked away from them and toward the large abstract painting on the wall. It had too many colors and too many angles and I'd always hated it.

I felt betrayed. It had always been the three of us fending off our mother together, but now Romi was turning against me? I sought out Talia's eyes, hoping for a life raft.

"What are you scared will happen if you give up this crutch?" she asked gently.

"It's not a *crutch,* it's a *tool,*" I said.

"What's the difference?"

"'Crutch' makes it seem like I'm compensating for something."

"Are you?"

"And what are *you* compensating for by treating me like one of your patients?" I snapped. "Isn't that the same thing as me recording things socially—taking your work outside the office?"

Talia twisted up her mouth and didn't reply. I felt a pre-crying flush.

"Are you recording us right now?" Romi asked.

"Maybe," I said.

"Olive!"

"Ollie, we're your family members, so our love is unconditional, but not everyone would be so understanding," our mom said. "You should be careful."

Was it possible that Theo would understand, if I ever told him now? Maybe he could accept me in a way that even my own family couldn't. Wasn't that what romance was about? You couldn't choose your family, but you could choose your partner. Maybe Theo alone could take my recordings for the nonthreat—frankly, the compliment—that they were.

"Do you even know that I listen to my recordings when I miss you?" I said plaintively.

"You do?" our mom said.

"Here she goes—" Romi said.

"Okay, you can keep doing it!" our mom cried.

"—and fin," Romi said.

"Too late," I said, and took the recorder out of my pocket and dramatically pressed the stop button. "No more."

"Tragic," said Romi, but our mom looked anguished, which satisfied me.

True to my word, I didn't keep taping them that night. Still, at bedtime, I set my recorder on the windowsill to record the barges' long symphonic moans alternating with the trains' shorter, more insistent calls. It wasn't like vehicles could indict me. In the darkness, I tried to make out the dogs on my bedroom wallpaper, marching along in horizontal stripes—my room had remained unchanged since childhood, as had Talia's and Romi's—but they were small dark smudges. My white dresser was easier to make out, standing where it always had, against the wall across from the foot of my bed. I'd opened the drawers when I'd first deposited my suitcase in the room, wondering if my mom had finally found another use for it, but no, it was still filled with old clothes of mine I'd neither decided to keep nor made moves to give away.

Down the hall, I heard my mom run her electric toothbrush and flush the toilet and creak the bed as she climbed in. My phone buzzed. Talia had texted in our group chat: "xxx." This was a now-common callback to our childhood, when one of us would knock three times on the others' doors as a signal to convene in secret—without our mother.

I snuck down the hallway toward the strip of light emanating from Talia's room, where Romi and Talia were already huddled in bed together, closed the door softly, turned off the light, and climbed in between them.

"Are you really so mad about the recording?" I asked.

"I'm not *mad*," Romi said, though she obviously was. "But do you still need to be doing that? Really?"

"I won't do it to you anymore," I said, pouting. "But I still don't think it's that bad!"

"It's not," Talia said.

"Romi thinks it is."

Romi sighed. "It's not bad, and you're not bad," she said. "It just makes me squeamish."

"Because why?"

"Privacy," she said.

"Do you not trust that I won't do anything with it?"

"It's not that!" Romi threw up her hands.

"What she said was it doesn't *feel* like you're respecting her privacy," Talia said.

"You, of all people, should understand that," Romi said to me.

"Why?" I asked, though I knew what she meant.

The two of them gestured toward the door—toward our mother.

As if I hadn't spent the whole weekend remembering, as I did every time I stayed in this house, opening the top right drawer of my dresser sometime after New Year's my freshman year of high school to find the underwear mussed. Until that year, I'd never kept a written diary; I had my recorder, which I'd use not only to eavesdrop but also to confide in. Under the tent of my quilt, I would whisper to my recorder my crushes, my frustrations, my fears. Sometimes I would record over these confessions the next day, blacking them out forever; other times I let them stand, confident that my hiding spot for tapes—underneath the old arts and crafts supplies in my closet—would remain a secret. As, apparently, it had.

The diary, on the other hand, had started as an assignment: as part of my freshman year English class, we were required to "free-write" for at least twenty minutes a week. Sometimes our teacher would build time for this into class, letting us write for ten minutes before we dissected that week's text. Always, when the time was up, I felt startled and cheated, like I'd barely begun. I started freewriting on the weekends, and then some days after school, until I was doing it every day. I wrote about how much I wished Talia and Romi were still at home; about how I was dying to kiss a boy (but the one who was dying to kiss *me* happened to be "gross"); about Maya's and my dreams for Mardi Gras: we hoped to be invited to the popular kids' corner of St. Charles, an event Maya was delusionally confident would happen, and which I knew would not. (I was correct.) And I wrote about my mother, who I still claimed in these pages was "perfect" and "the best mom ever." But why did I feel so sad in this house, like I was the "loneliest person in the world"?

I kept my diary in my underwear drawer, which I thought was private enough to be safe. When I opened the drawer that January to find the underwear mussed, I feared immediately that my diary had been found. I flung the underwear aside until I'd exposed the little book: the rubber band I kept religiously wrapped around it was gone.

My immediate thought was Romi. She and Talia had been visiting for the holidays, and while Talia would never go through my stuff, I suspected Romi might. As I stuffed the underwear back into the drawer, my fingers brushed against something sticky. I examined the offending pair, and indeed, a smudge of fresh discharge lingered on the crotch, as if the underwear had been worn.

With a guttural moan I threw the soiled garment into my laundry hamper. I would never, absolutely never, have put a worn pair of underwear back into my drawer. Someone had borrowed my underwear and replaced it without washing it—the same someone, I was convinced, who had read my diary.

Immediately I called Romi, even though it was late at night. She answered groggily but with a note of worry in her voice, asking if everything was okay.

"Is everything okay?" I repeated. "Is everything *okay*?"

"Olive, what the hell?"

"Why did you do it?"

"Why did I . . ."

"Read my diary! For F's sake!" I hadn't yet graduated to using full curse words. "And—and—"

"What are you talking about?"

"And—wear my—" I was still too repulsed by what I'd found to articulate it.

"Olive, I didn't read your diary," she said. "Or wear your sweater, or whatever. I'm sorry to say, but I don't have any motivation to read that."

"That's rude."

"Now you want me to have read it?"

"No."

"Okay then."

"But I want you to have *wanted* to."

She laugh-scoffed. "You tell me everything," she said. "What could I possibly find? And, like, have you forgotten I've already been a teenager? It's *boring*."

"You're being a real B right now."

"Sorry, sorry."

"Talia would at least not read it out of *respect*."

"She's definitely a better person than me."

Silence.

"Do you think she did it?" Romi asked.

"I have no idea. I really don't think she would."

"You could ask her, just to be sure."

We hung up, and I called Talia. I explained what I'd found, this time managing to describe the cold stickiness of the underwear. I said I'd been sure it was Romi, but she'd denied it convincingly. I felt sure that Talia hadn't done it, but otherwise I was at a loss. So: had she?

"I wouldn't do that," she said. "You know that."

"I know, I know." I sighed. "Am I crazy? Maybe I just left the rubber band off. Sometimes I forget stuff."

"And the underwear?"

"It could've just not gotten washed properly, or something. Like—residue."

"Maybe," said Talia.

"You don't think so?"

"I don't know."

"Then who?"

"Olive . . ."

The thought hit me with cold force.

"*Mom?*"

"I'm really not sure. It's possible."

I shook my head, though Talia couldn't see. "No. There's no way."

"You're probably right."

But the image of my mom in my underwear blazed in my mind. I yawned dramatically.

"I should go to bed," I said.

"I love you," Talia said. "Okay? Sleep tight."

I barely slept. All night I pictured my mom creeping into my room while I was at school, sitting on my bed with the diary open in her lap—in my imaginings, she was for some reason sucking on a lollipop, something I never in reality saw her do. And then the more offensive image would insert itself: her putting the diary back into the drawer and plucking out the black cotton pair of underwear. Taking off her pants and then her own "panties," as she called them. Pulling mine on, modeling them for herself in the full-length mirror. Gleeful that she fit into her teenage daughter's underwear. Pleased with how she looked.

It was months before I found another pair of sticky underwear. I'd said nothing the first time, but this time I pinched the pair between two fingers and brought it to the garden, where my mom was on her hands and knees in the dirt.

"What is this?" I said.

She wiped a gloved hand across her forehead, leaving a smudge of dirt in its wake.

"Panties?" she said, squinting at them through the sunlight.

"Look at them." I thrust them at her.

She removed her gardening gloves and took the underwear from me.

"What am I looking at, here?"

"They're dirty!" I said.

"So put them in the laundry and I'll wash them."

She was acting like I was insane. I started to cry.

"Olive, what is it? Throw them away and I'll buy you new ones!"

"You wore them!" I said. "My underwear! You wore them and now you're pretending you didn't!"

"Oh . . ."

She stood up and took me in her arms, pressing me to her, hard.

"I did try on your underwear. I frankly forgot. I had no idea you'd mind. I wondered if it was a style that would look good on me. I thought it was like—sisters, you know? Sharing clothes."

Guilt washed over me. She wanted to be sisters because she wanted to be close to me, because she was lonely, and because she loved me. What, really, was the big deal about her trying on some of my clothing?

"It's fine," I said. "You can try them on whenever you want. Sorry."

"That's so sweet," she whispered into my ear. "My little Ollie-Polly. You're the best daughter I could ever have dreamed of."

After that, when I found my clothes in disarray, I didn't bring it up. Instead, I started trying on her clothes, too—her dresses, her pants, her shoulder-padded jackets, her way-too-large bras. The only thing I could never bring myself to try on was her underwear—it brought me back too sharply to my moment of discovery. In my own closet, I kept a pile of secret, "safe" underwear she didn't know about. It was years before I told Talia and Romi the whole of it. They were at once aghast and unsurprised. We all decided that it wasn't great, but it could have been worse. At least she really loved us.

But apparently, all these years later, my recording habits were unforgivable. I looked Romi straight in the eye and said, "We're family. I don't get what you need to be so private about."

"Everyone needs privacy."

"Not *sisters*."

"Yes, sisters."

"It hurts my feelings," I said.

"Then why don't you tell us whatever you've been hiding all weekend?"

Taken aback, I didn't immediately reply.

"Oh, so only *you* get privacy?"

"What are you referring to?" I asked, my nerves making me formal.

"You think we haven't seen you grinning at your phone twelve times a day?" Romi said. "While *twirling* your *hair*?"

"I twirl my hair?" I said. "Not really."

"Literally constantly," said Romi.

"Not constantly," Talia said. "Just when you're in flirt mode."

"Spill," Romi said.

"Don't tell Mom," I said. "Okay?"

"Of course not."

So, in a low whisper, I told them about Theo.

The two of them hugged me and tried to snatch my phone from my hand to read his texts. I resisted until I didn't, shushing them periodically when their squeals and giggles threatened to awaken our mother. I dreaded the idea of her knocking, asking, "What are you talking about?," dreaded us having to protest: nothing, nothing, we're going to sleep! Other mothers seemed to love watching their kids commune privately; ours seemed affronted by our attempts to bond without her. I was endlessly grateful for Romi and Talia and had long been convinced that if it had been any one of us alone, without the buffer of the other two, our mom would have eaten her whole.

"Are you done yet?" I asked, tugging on the phone, and Talia said, "Yes, yes," releasing it, and Romi said, "But you have to tell us everything."

So I told them about the run and the kiss and the sex and the seeing each other almost every night, how I was finding it hard being away from him for this short spell and felt incomplete, like I was missing part of myself, even though I'd met him less than two months before. "You're the only family I've told about any of this," I said. "Practically the only people."

"Then it must be serious," Romi said.

"Too serious?"

"You always twist things so they look wrong. No, O. That's just love."

But I didn't tell them everything. I didn't tell them I'd recorded him, and I didn't tell them about the tooth gap either.

* * *

At the airport, Theo waited for me inside with the limousine drivers, holding a sign with a giant picture of a green olive, stuffed with a pimento pepper. His hair was disheveled, a piece of it sticking up in the back like it'd been pushed up by the car seat's headrest. He smiled when he saw me, showing the gap. My heart started to race.

"I'm more of a Kalamata," I said once I'd threaded my way through the crowd, gesturing to the sign and then to my dark hair. My heartbeat was still loud in my ears.

"But you taste as good as a green one." He nibbled my earlobe, then licked the bowl of my ear as though it were an oyster shell. Emboldened, I pressed my mouth to his and pushed my tongue through his teeth, praying he wouldn't recoil. He didn't.

"Is that okay?"

"Mm-hmm."

I kissed him again, flicking my tongue against the gap. He kissed me back harder.

"I missed you," I whispered into his mouth, and he said he'd missed me too. I hoped he meant it in the same way. I didn't just want him pressed against me, I wanted him wanted him wanted him, I wanted him to be all mine.

Part Two:
Metamorphosis

Part Two
Metamorphosis

6.

By August, the city had bloomed a bright, wet green, and Theo and I had been together for three months. Though we maintained the same sleeping rhythm—his place for a night, my place for a night, apart for a night—he now kept enough belongings at my place, and I kept enough at his, for me to be able to imagine, at times, that we lived together. Theo's apartment was incredible—high ceilings, tall windows, fancy molding. There was a second bedroom, which he used as an office; other inhabitants, presumably, had used it as a baby's room. To his apartment, I laid claim. I kept an extra electric toothbrush plugged in over his bathroom sink, a bag of Felix's food in the kitchen along with an extra set of his bowls, a stack of books on the nightstand on my side of the bed. In the living room, a few of Felix's toys; in the toiletry cabinet, a pink tub of fancy face cream. I hoped that Theo would see the cream and think of my skin, and that on the mornings he awoke to find I wasn't near, he would unscrew the gold top from the tub and inhale the scent of me.

Because we *didn't* live together, not really. That we kept sleeping apart maddened me, when I allowed myself to think about it; if Theo's lack of roommates hadn't made it obvious to me that we should always stay at his place—that I should live there—the grandeur of the apartment would have. But if anyone was going to suggest we sleep together every night, I wanted it to be Theo. What if I made the request and he said no? I definitely was not going to be the one to suggest we move in together, even though I thought about it constantly, craved his presence all the time.

Inspired by Maya's strategy of imagining upon her partner various bodily misfortunes, I tried picturing *really* being one with Theo, figuring that it might allow me to get it out of my system in fantasy. I could build a private, perfect world of union, one I could return to whenever I liked. I imagined melting Theo's and my bodies over an open flame until we were liquid, the pools of us swirling together to create one small pond. In the winter we froze over; in the spring we melted; in the summer, heat shimmered above us; when Theo thought a thought, it was my thought, too. I imagined opening my mouth as wide as a cavern and swallowing him in his entirety. But then his body was heavy inside me, his mind obscure—the opposite of what I craved. I wanted to be inside *him,* to be held, subsumed, almost crushed, with total access and yet inaccessible. So I imagined him in bed, on his back, with his mouth open as usual; I imagined prying apart his two front teeth, ripping his body down the middle. The sound of a metal zipper. Flesh tearing unevenly, blood spurting out. A squelching, throbbing symphony to welcome me home.

My desire to move in—if not sufficiently fueled by my longing for Theo and for the life his beautiful apartment suggested we could have together—was amplified by my deteriorating dynamic with Ava. My relationship had aggravated her into a level of hypocrisy I had rarely encountered before; no matter when Theo was in the bathroom, she fiddled with the handle, then knocked loudly. The previous weekend, after Theo and I had spent both days lingering lazily in the apartment, Ava had texted me from her room:

> Would you mind spending more time at Theo's on the weekends? I'd appreciate the consideration . . . it's a small space!!

I couldn't believe it, after Blob had half-lived in our apartment for the past year—after they'd taken over the kitchen when I'd hoped to cook, blaring trap music; after he'd spent hours napping on our living room couch during weekend afternoons when she was out. I wanted to crunch her finger in the garlic press. Instead I did nothing, just let her text languish without a response, which was the most direct aggression I could muster. When Ava and I passed each other on the way to the bathroom the next morning, we smiled pertly at each other, pretending nothing had happened in the electronic netherworld.

It wasn't until later that day that it occurred to me that I hadn't seen Blob in weeks. I hadn't heard Ava's performatively loud sex noises in a while, either. I'd been so wrapped up in Theo I hadn't even noticed. While she was apparently now the lonely one—and, before that, had been stuck with Blob, of all people—I had found perfection. Theo traced his thumb along my knuckles while we watched movies on his couch; said "Aww" along with me when Felix shifted onto his back and pawed at his eyes; showed me his latest subway finds and told me about his patients and his dreams, and listened to my interviews and my desires. At night, we would curl our bodies around each other as we drifted off to sleep: "Don't abandon me," I would whisper, and he would whisper, "Never." Prying his body open became my go-to fantasy; as I lay next to Theo or pressed his teeth at night, I would picture splitting him open and sliding into the hot cavern I'd revealed—though each time his teeth budged, fear took over and I yanked my hand away.

Much as I missed Theo when we were apart, I had my collection of recordings of him, to which I'd added two new installments since returning home from New Orleans: a walk in Fort Greene Park and a night of obliterating sex. (What a shame, when it was over, to return to myself.) My family's lukewarm reception of my recordings had made me long even more to share them with Theo. The closer we became, the more convinced I felt that he alone would understand. Perhaps he would have known about them all along, and would already love them as a part of me. Even my mom loved my recordings, now that she knew what they meant. But each time I felt the urge to tell Theo, I couldn't bring myself to do it. There was always next time, and by next time, he would care for me even more than he did now.

I finally called my mother to tell her I was seeing someone. She shrieked in oppressive excitement. "It's very new," I said quickly, picking at my cuticles, but she wanted to know his name—no, his *full* name ("He's not Jewish," I said—a fact that titillated me and made me feel independent), what he did for work, where he lived, when she could meet him.

"Soon," I said, then diverted her onto other topics: her garden, my sisters, New Orleans's unbearable heat.

On a Monday evening not long after, in the midst of unearthing a chunk of fudge from my ice cream while watching TV with Felix, I received the customary text from Theo about his schedule for the week: he had to work throughout the weekend, but was "ninety percent sure" that on Sunday night he would be home by seven o'clock. Ninety was the highest percentage he ever gave, so I recapped the ice cream container, shoved it back in the freezer, and jumped up and down with a little squeal. Felix perked up and jumped off the couch and came rushing over with his tail wagging, then put his two front paws on my thighs, tongue hanging out the side of his mouth, as I kissed his head.

I asked Ava to give me the apartment on Sunday night, a request I didn't take lightly and felt I couldn't make again soon. But Theo had said ninety percent, so I spent what Ava credit I had accumulated—I'd been obsequious toward her since the "small space" texts—claiming the apartment as my own. I blocked off the day, went to the Food Coop in the morning and then, all afternoon, baked bread and prepared roast chicken with carrots, onions, fennel, and potatoes. Through the door of the oven, I watched the layers of onion peeling apart from one another, contorting like limbs in the heat. To start, a light salad; to finish, crème brûlées in little ramekins.

Ten minutes before Theo was supposed to arrive, everything was ready. I had laid out a lacy tablecloth (Ava's) and two of the linen napkins I'd received from Romi as a birthday present the year I'd turned thirty. I didn't have napkin holders, but I'd tied each napkin with a bit of twine and placed it in the center of the plate. I was wearing a knee-length black dress and heeled booties, and as I waited for Theo I sat at my place, trying out potentially appealing positions. With both feet on the ground, I could sit straight up, elongating my neck, but with one leg crossed over the other, I was able to casually expose a length of my thigh. It was quiet in the apartment, save for Felix's steady sleep-breathing from under my chair. I fiddled with the silverware on the table, fanned the edge of the linen napkin out across my plate. My phone buzzed. My body went stiff. *You don't even know who texted you,* I reminded myself as I walked to the counter to check the message. But I did know: it was Theo, and yes, he was going to be late. Probably an hour.

I threw my phone with a yell at the couch, where it bounced off a pillow and onto the floor. Felix scurried out from underneath my chair and let out a piercing bark. I said "Shh" and reached down to pet him, but my heart was pounding with stupid rage. Why did Theo have *this* job rather than one that was less demanding, where he wouldn't be whisked away at the last minute, wouldn't be on call for twenty-four hours at a time, dealing with patients who were strangers to him? My fixation on his patients had intensified after Maya had, in a moment of particular obtuseness, informed me that surgery patients often developed "love feelings" toward their doctors. In one instance, a woman who'd undergone a simple vascular procedure became so obsessed with her doctor—standing outside his house, writing him emails, calling him day and night—that he eventually gave up trying to convey that her love was unreciprocated and moved his family to Spain. This story sounded apocryphal to me, but the internet confirmed that such crushes could indeed be side effects—if infrequent ones—of undergoing surgery, an experience that often left patients feeling some combination of vulnerable, grateful, and overwhelmed. I hated imagining the people who already got so much of my boyfriend's time and attention lusting after him on top of all that, thinking of some frail and tender ill person gazing longingly at Theo, *my* Theo, who offered in return the soft and calming expression he was so good at making, and that I wanted reserved for me.

I was starving, and grabbed a few crackers to tide me over, chewing furiously. I'd opened a bottle of red Burgundy a few hours prior, intending only to let it breathe before Theo arrived, but now I poured myself a glass and swirled it so aggressively that a bit sloshed out onto the table. I wished Ava were home to distract me, even if only with endless chatter about her one million stylish friends.

I'd been doing a good job, I thought, of keeping my jealous musings to myself: Theo knew I missed him when we were apart, but as far as I could tell he did not know that when I said *missed* I meant *craved with an intensity that bordered on pain*. Sometimes I texted too avidly during the day, my anxiety at his lack of response bleeding into a kind of anger. But usually when I was in these moods, I could catch myself, call Talia instead, tell her how much I was struggling to be apart from Theo and hear her say, "You *will* see him soon, and you *will* be okay," but also have her validate how hard it was, how much better it was to live together like she and her wife had been doing for years, how comforting it was to know the other person would be home every night, how Theo and I would get there, too, but also how she and Romi and I came from a mom who called at least one of us every single day, so was I really to expect myself to handle separation like it was the small deal others felt it was?

I called Talia now and explained the situation: Theo was late, and I was forlorn.

"Look," she said. "You slept in Mom's bed on and off 'til high school."

"College," I corrected, though I'd slept with her sporadically since then, too. Romi had slept with our mother until Talia was born; Talia had until I was born; I was the last, so I'd never stopped.

"So. That makes it harder, being apart."

"But Theo's not Mom."

"It doesn't matter."

I remembered my mom's stomach against my back, her arm draped across my waist, the warmth of her breath against the back of my neck. I remembered her soft, worn sheets, her quilt covered with dancing forest animals. I had loved that whimsical quilt, which she'd gotten after the divorce to replace the staid adult one she and my dad had shared. I pictured her hovering above me, finger pressed to the tip of my nose. I was still sitting at my place at the table and fingered the napkin I'd set out, picked at the knot of twine.

"When you slept with Mom, when you were a kid, did she ever do anything weird?" I asked Talia.

"Like wear my underwear?"

"Basically." I tossed another cracker into my mouth.

"What'd she do?"

Through a mouthful, I said, "Sometimes I'd wake up in the middle of the night and she'd be sitting up, staring at me." Crumbs sprayed across the table.

"That sounds right."

"Or even touching my nose."

"She's obsessed with your nose."

"Because it looks just like hers."

"She'd slurp the boogers out of it if she could."

"Gross." I ate another cracker. "So no? Nothing like that?"

"Not that I can remember. But she's different with you."

"I kind of miss sleeping with her," I said.

"But only kind of."

"So I said."

"That's the thing with merger," Talia said, using a therapy term she'd explained to me before: the attempted return to a state of parent-child oneness. "It's blissful—"

"Yes."

"—until it's nauseating."

But *blissful* was the word that hung in my mind.

The phone call had momentarily removed me from my misery. Once we'd hung up, I was plunged back into tormented waiting. By eight o'clock, I'd eaten half a box of crackers, but I made two plates of the now-lukewarm food and set them on the table. Small bowls of salad; little plates of bread; fancy glasses for the Burgundy. I admonished myself for my sullen mood, told myself I'd better still enjoy the evening, better wring pleasure out of it, given how much effort I'd put in. I sat back at the table, crossed one leg over the other, and took a sip of wine, trying to appear, to an imaginary observer, at peace.

My phone pinged with a message: Theo had arrived. I jumped up to buzz him in—our landlord had, finally, replaced our buzzer—unlocked the apartment door, and resumed my seat at the table. As I waited, Theo's footfalls on the stairs growing louder, I recrossed my legs so the dress hiked up my thigh. *Casually.*

He opened the door. He was wearing a dark blue suit, no tie: he'd changed out of his scrubs before coming over. So he'd intuited that this was a special occasion, that I'd put real effort into it, which made it even more hurtful he'd arrived so late. Whatever work interruption had come up, how could he have prioritized it over this—over me? His cheeks were flushed, maybe from rushing, his eyes bright.

"You look *great*," he said, coming over and giving me a hello-kiss.

"Bon appétit." I swept my arm over the table.

"Thank you," he said. "*So* much. I'm sorry I'm late."

"It's no big deal."

He sat at the table, slid his jacket off and hung it over the back of the chair. The top two buttons of his shirt were undone, and a tuft of chest hair emerged like a spray of flowers. I had the urge to pluck them. The meal looked amazing, he said, and smelled even better—

"Taste before you compliment," I said, and my tone, which I'd intended to be playful, must have registered as harsh, because Theo cocked his head.

"What?" I said.

"You're mad."

I shrugged. "A little." I was surprised to find that I was shaking. I bobbed my foot in the air, trying to soothe myself.

"That I'm late?"

"What else?"

"I can't control it," he said. "I wish I could."

"Do you?"

"Of course."

I nodded. I thought, stupidly, *You could quit*.

"It's hard for me, sometimes," I said. "Sharing you." I stared down at my plate: beige chicken, browned carrots, slimy onions and fennel. Suddenly, it looked disgusting and very dead.

"Sharing me with . . ."

"Everything," I said to the chicken. "But especially your work."

"Look, I'm really sorry." He paused, chewed the inside of his lip, thinking. "I thought you loved that I love my work."

"I do."

"Then what?"

I shrugged. "Nothing."

"Don't *nothing* me. Please."

"I wish we spent more time together."

"We spend *so* much time together."

"Not compared to other couples—"

"Other couples where one person is a surgeon?"

"—or to what I want."

"Which is what? All the time?"

"No."

He sawed at his chicken and then chewed it slowly.

"Really," he said.

I didn't reply. He cut off another piece of chicken, but instead of bringing it to his mouth, released his silverware with a clang.

"So you're asking me to pick between you and my work?"

"No," I lied.

"It feels like you are."

"I just wish it were different. Okay?"

"Well, it's not."

"Could you give me empathy? Is it that hard?"

"I was just *one hour* late and *rushed* here to make that happen—"

"I know."

"—and wore a *suit*, even—"

"I love the suit," I said. "I just wish I got more of you."

"I give you as much as I can," he said, which hit me with searing force. I twirled my fork in the fennel, watching it catch on the tines and coil around them like a snake, leaving a slick trail in its wake.

"Okay," I said.

"Can we just eat?" Theo said. "I'm starving."

We ate in silence. I sat straight and poised as a dancer, trying to simulate a version of myself that hadn't just heard the phrase, *I give you as much as I can.* What would Talia say about our fight? That Theo was being unfair, surely? Maybe she'd tell me I'd pushed him too far, asked for something that nobody could provide. Maybe she'd say that, okay, I was being a *little* like our mother. I watched Theo chew, noting, as I had before, that he didn't always close his mouth fully. I could see the paste that was once chicken and I wanted to enter the hole that was his mouth, to get bit, ground to a pulp; I wanted to spread myself over his tongue, then slide over it into the dark warmth of his throat. I wanted to wedge myself between his organs, curling myself around the hot pile of his intestine and clutching it to me like I sometimes did Felix.

"I wasn't abandoning you earlier," Theo said, startling me. He must have seen something on my face.

"I wasn't thinking that."

"Oh, you weren't."

I was silent.

"I promise, I wasn't," he said.

"Then what were you doing?"

"There was a crisis at the hospital," he said. "A surgery that did *not* go the way it was supposed to. At all."

"I'm sorry," I said without feeling. "That must have been hard."

His jaw clenched. "It was extremely hard."

I knew I was now supposed to ask for details about the situation: What was the crisis? Had the patient died? How did Theo feel now, and what did he need?

"I don't like being separate," I said instead. I couldn't meet his gaze.

"I know," he said. "But look—we're not right now."

I dared to look up at Theo. His expression was tender. So he wasn't repelled?

"It feels like we are," I said.

He pulled his chair around the table next to mine and put his hand on my thigh.

"What about now?"

"Closer."

He scooted his chair so it was flush with mine.

"Now?"

"Closer."

He stood and then lowered himself onto me, straddling me, his groin pressing up against my stomach. His weight was arousing and painful at once.

"I listened to your Sara Chandra interview," he said. I'd emailed him the link a few weeks prior, and had debated as the days passed whether to ask if he'd listened yet. Ultimately this had seemed too needy. Well, he had listened. At the revelation, my body went tense and alert. He was saying, *You were with me, even when you didn't know it.*

"You have a great radio voice," he said. He ran his fingers lightly up and down my arm. I shivered. "It sounds like you could start singing at any minute." His voice was so soft someone standing across the room wouldn't hear it. Even the recorder, sensitive as it was, shoved into a crevice of the armchair nearest Theo's seat, probably hadn't picked it up. He whispered: "I love it," and little hairs sprang up all over my body. *I love you,* I willed him to say.

"I love your voice, too," I murmured finally.

"You do?"

"It lives more in the back of your throat than other voices do."

"You like that?" He removed his hand from my arm, scrunching his nose.

"Yes," I said, trying to move my arm back into the orbit of his hand. "The way you say *L*s—"

"My mom hired a speech therapist to try to train me out of it. She said it sounded juvenile."

"I'm very happy that didn't work." I reached for his hand, interlaced my fingers with his. My legs were beginning to throb beneath his weight.

"And why?"

"I just am." With my gaze I consumed the delicate angles of his face.

My ears started to ring as I thought it—*I love you*—but apparently I had said it, said it with my very own mouth, because Theo started beaming in a beautifully unhinged way: "I love *you,*" he said.

"You do?"

He laughed. "I do."

We smiled giddily at each other. He curved his arms around me like I was his prey.

"I love you," I said into his chest.

"I love you."

On the count of three, we said it at the same time. I felt certain I would explode. I undid his pants and he rose and yanked them off (*I love you*); rolled down my underwear, peeling it off over my boots (*I love you*); shoved Theo down onto the chair, his erection blooming. Towering above him, I could see, over his shoulder, the recorder. Had something in me known, when I'd decided to tape this evening, that it would be momentous? I hadn't taped Theo in at least two weeks. Thank God, I thought, thank God. The next day, when Theo was on call, and during the week, when he worked into the night, I could listen to this evening over and over again. *I love you, I love you.* The next time his schedule changed, or he was late, or got called away, I might even be okay.

Felix cried in protest as I guided Theo inside me. The chair creaked precariously beneath us and Theo thrust wildly, almost hurting me, practically breaking me open, but I wanted to be broken, ripped like a new mother, annihilated. I stuck my fingers in his mouth and said, "Bite me," and he bit me so hard I yelped in pain. He stopped thrusting at once, pulled my hand out of his mouth and said, "Are you okay?" But I kept rocking back and forth until he joined me, then shoved three fingers into his mouth and then four and then my whole hand. Somehow his mouth fit my entire fist as though it had expanded to accommodate me. Theo was thrusting faster and faster. He spit my hand out of his mouth and brought his tongue to my ear, wending it around the rim of cartilage and into the little bowl, he shoved his thumb against my clit and pressed until I came, I pulled him toward me as he came after me. For several moments I kept clutching him against me, my head burrowed into the hot pulsing flesh of his neck. This was my moment to confess; we were so close, and telling him would only bring us closer. *Of course you have,* he would say. *You're a radio host, that's what you do, I knew it already and I love it and I love you.*

"I've been recording you," I whispered into his neck.

But he didn't say, *Of course you have.* He didn't say, *I knew it already.* He didn't say anything at all, just pulled away from me with a stunned expression, then swallowed heavily.

Watching his throat move, I was reminded of the first time we'd kissed, how right beforehand he'd seemed unable to speak, just swallowed as he had now, his Adam's apple rising and falling like an elevator. As he breathed, his body expanding and contracting beneath me, I remembered the first time we'd fucked, how he'd had me lie down on the floor with my limbs splayed, starfishing. Into the silence that stretched between us came the cold, sickening realization that I had made a colossal miscalculation.

"You what?" Theo finally said.

"I've been recording your voice," I said. "Recording *us,* I mean."

He felt stiff in my arms.

"Are you recording this?"

I was, I admitted.

"Can you get off?" he said.

Mechanically, I unlaced my body from his and stood to the side. He rose up next to me.

"Theo—" I reached out to touch his arm, but he snatched it away and returned to the table, pulling his clothes back on with terrifying swiftness.

"Please," I said.

"I need to take a walk."

"Do you need to pee or anything?" I said desperately.

He didn't answer.

"Are you going to come back?"

"I don't know."

And then he was gone.

An unquantifiable period of time passed in silence. Even Felix, sitting at my feet with his head pressed against my leg, seemed to understand that something irrevocable had taken place. Numbly, I went to look out the window, the streetlamps bulging round and bright into the black sky. They looked like tumors. I turned away, disgusted; there, in the armchair, the recorder still sat, lit and absorbing sound. I grabbed it and stabbed the stop button and threw it back onto the chair with a wail—which is when the sobbing began, athletic and grotesque.

Heaving, I made for my bed, Felix following behind me, whining to be carried. I scooped him up and curled around him, clutching his hot weight. *"Why?"* I cried, over and over, by which I meant why hadn't I listened to Talia and Romi and my mother, why had I seen fit to record him in the first place, to record anyone—but also why *hadn't* he understood, the way I'd so hoped he would?

My crying was so loud that, were it not for Felix's sharp and insistent barking, I might not have realized that my phone had begun to buzz. Theo was texting me. Abruptly I stopped crying and wiped my face.

Hey. I'm here.
Can you let me in?
Hello?

My phone rang: he was calling. I jumped up from the bed to buzz him in, Felix scuttling behind me, then rushed to the bathroom mirror. Mascara was streaked below my eyes; snot bubbled from my nose. Theo's footfalls grew louder on the stairs. Vigorously I washed my face, scrubbing the mascara away, leaving my eyes puffy and red-rimmed, bare and exposed.

The front door creaked open. "Olive?"

"Hey." I peered out from the bathroom.

"Damn," he said, referencing my face.

"I know."

He came over, put his hands on my cheeks, wiped underneath my eyes with his thumbs. His kindness was nearly too much to take.

"Why did you come back?" I whispered, begging him to say it: *because I love you.*

"I have questions."

"I'm really sorry," I said. "Like, *so fucking sorry*—"

"Will you let me ask my questions?"

"Okay . . . Okay."

We sat at the table, where the dinner dishes still sat, crusting over. I pushed mine away; the smell of the soggy fennel was revolting.

"Are you just recording when we're together? Or when I'm . . . alone?"

"Together," I said quickly. *"Together."* The thought of covertly recording him when I wasn't present had occurred to me, obviously. But if I had trouble justifying to myself the recordings I'd made of us already, those would have pushed my behavior beyond exculpation. Not to mention that it wasn't legal, and would have been risky to orchestrate. Given his reaction to the recordings I *had* made, I felt woozy with relief that I hadn't gone further. If, anyway, he was preparing to forgive me. Which I couldn't tell if he was.

"What kinds of things have you recorded us doing?" he asked.

"Conversations, mostly."

"Like . . ."

"Dinners, walks, that sort of thing."

"What was the first time?"

"The food pantry shift," I said. "Where we met."

He took a big inhale, let out his breath. "I wish . . . I'd known."

I blinked rapidly, swallowed. "Do you?"

"I don't know."

"It wasn't like I *meant* to do it," I said. "I started the tape as I was walking to the food pantry and kept it rolling throughout the shift. It just happened to be recording when we met. Actually, I'd recorded the same shift all the weeks I'd been before. I never told anyone there that I was doing it; I've never used the recordings for anything. But I did think about telling you."

"Why didn't you?"

"I just did."

"But why didn't you—before?" Before we'd said *I love you*, he meant.

"I don't know." I pinched at the underside of my thigh, forlorn. "I really wanted to. There were so many times—"

"But you didn't."

"I was scared," I said.

"Or did you *like* me not knowing about it?"

"No, I hated it," I said quickly. "I was desperate for you to know." But his question had startled me.

He twisted his mouth to the side, as if there was something he wasn't sure whether to ask.

"What?" I said.

"Nothing." I stared at him, chewing my tongue, a current of anticipation coursing through me. He squinted at me. "Have you taped us having sex?" he asked. "Before tonight."

I looked down, traced the outline of my knife on the table with my fingertip. "Once or twice." Flipped the knife over and back again. "Three times," I admitted. "Exactly three."

"Have you listened?"

I nodded.

"Is it hot?"

I looked up at him, jolted. He was staring at me intently. Whether he was aroused or angry, I couldn't say. My heart began to race.

"Very," I said. I clenched my jaw, kept staring at him.

"I want to listen."

It felt like my organs were melting inside of me, pooling viscously in my center. I had the bizarre urge to break out in laughter.

"Do you want me to send it to you?"

"No. We're going to listen together."

Immediately I got wet. I nodded.

"And then you have to send them all to me," he said. "And never do it again without telling me."

Suddenly I felt slapped, though this was what I'd wanted: to be close to him, secretless, floating together in a pool of our shared memories. "Yes," I said. "Okay."

We stared at each other. I gave a single, definitive nod.

"So?" His eyes were fixed piercingly on mine, his breathing audible.

"You want to listen . . . now?"

He did. As he stood, he asked, "Is it still on?"

I shook my head.

"Turn it on, and bring it into the bedroom."

His eyes seared my back as I walked over to the chair and retrieved the recorder. He held out his hand and I gave it to him; he examined it, though it was a complicated instrument and I wasn't sure what he was hoping to divine. We walked silently into my bedroom, Felix following. I turned the recorder on and placed it on the desk next to my bed. We took off our clothes, slowly and deliberately. Theo stood behind me, his body pressed against mine, as I searched for one of the sex files on my computer—"T sx"—and began to play it.

THEO: Hey!
ME: Hi!
[Kissing sounds]
THEO: How was your day?
ME: Ugh. You won't believe—

"Fast-forward to the good part," Theo said. I had played the tape many times, and knew exactly where to skip to: 10:37.

THEO: Are you ticklish?
ME: Very. *[Pause, squeal]* Ah! No!
THEO: What are you going to do about it?
[Uncontrolled laughter]
ME: Oh my—God—
THEO: Hmm?
ME: Just—fuck me—already—

Theo pushed me onto the bed and pressed into me like an anvil. I wrapped my legs around him; he ground his hips into me; I guided his penis with my hand and pushed into him until he was deep inside me.

"Do you still love me?" I asked.

"Yes—oh—"

"Say it, please say it."

He pressed his mouth right up to my ear and murmured, "I love you, I love you," his tongue flicking against my earlobe each time he said *love*—

"I love you—"

"I love you—" He thrust wildly, the bedframe creaking, the mattress thumping against the wall. I reached over my head to grab my pillow with one hand, pulled Theo closer with the other—he pounded with such force Felix started to cry, then came quickly and loudly, with an uncharacteristic scream.

After, I pulled the computer onto my bed, and he watched me send him the files.

That night, Theo fell asleep quickly. I still marvel at this capacity to leave behind the day and its attendant anxieties, sinking effortlessly into slumber, an ability or freedom that strikes me as distinctly male. I lay restless beside him. Several times, I began to touch sleep, then hallucinated my mother above me and startled awake again. At the foot of the bed, Felix lay on his side with all four legs intertwined in a bouquet. As I listened to Theo's snores—louder and more ragged than usual—my thoughts of relief (he had come back, he had forgiven me, he hadn't left, he still loved me) bled into panic about the sent files. About the limit Theo had set, the limit I had agreed to. That I would no longer record him in secret.

In my interview with Chandra, she had talked about the triangle of writer, character, and reader. I wondered now if life, like art, was built in threes: there was Theo, there was me, and there was the recorder. One could even argue that the recorder's role was really my own, a perfect mirror: there was the me on tape—the participant—and the me who listened—the observer. The tape we'd created tonight was defanged, somehow, by the fact that we both knew about it. If Theo and I were both knowing observers, if there was no deceit involved, wouldn't the triangle collapse?

I was too wired to sleep. I turned onto my side, gathering the corner of the comforter into a bundle and hugging it to me. Did I not want to be close to Theo, not really? Had my suspicions about myself before we'd met—that I wasn't capable of love—been, after all, correct? Or did I want to be close to him, to be one with him, but only so long as I was the initiator and had control?

I shifted onto my back, closed my eyes, stretched out my hand until I reached the soft comfort of Felix's fur. As had become my routine, I imagined prising Theo's front teeth apart, then his chin, his throat, his chest, his stomach. I imagined the uneven gash, the blood, and, beneath, his beautiful insides. A home for me to make mine.

I opened my eyes. There he was, still beside me, snoring away. Gingerly, I shifted onto my knees, then waited a beat to make sure I hadn't awakened him. His snoring continued unabated. I fingered his bottom teeth, squeaking my skin over the hard enamel. Against my hand, the tickle of his breath. I pressed his teeth, and, just as they always did, they shifted a millimeter. This time I kept pressing, so hard my arm began to shake, until they shifted apart a fraction more, then still more, until my entire finger slid inside. My heart was pounding just as it had the first time we'd had sex and, as then, I pictured the fierce muscle working hard to fill my body with blood. I pushed my finger in up to the knuckle, grazing Theo's tongue. He stirred; I pulled my hand out and lay down, my breathing shallow and brisk. Was I hurting him? But he was still sleeping soundly, his chest rising and falling like a contented child's, and soon he'd resumed snoring, the sound so familiar and regular I wondered if I'd been half-dreaming again. I sat back up slowly, silently, and touched my finger to his teeth; it slid all the way through the gap until I could feel again the thick muscle of his tongue. I looked down the bed: there was Felix, his legs still entwined; there was the persimmon-patterned comforter, bunched beneath him; there was my bedroom window, the trees visible through the gauzy curtain as dark stains in the night. Theo's teeth pinched my flesh. It was real.

I slid my finger back out, wiping Theo's saliva on my pajamas. I felt as wide-awake and buzzing as though I'd done uppers, or received an electric shock. I reminded myself that Theo had just panicked about my recordings and—kindly, unnecessarily—forgiven me. I thought, *I love him, and how could I do something like this to someone I love?* But wasn't this the most powerful and titillating thing I'd ever done? And, anyway, he was sleeping; I wasn't hurting him; he didn't know. And wasn't that part of the thrill? Maybe I had kept my recordings to myself for so long not only because I was afraid of Theo's reaction, but also because the privacy of my intrusion was what brought me pleasure. Like doing surgery on someone under anesthesia, rather than someone awake.

Beneath me, Theo's mouth was opened unnaturally wide, snores still tumbling out, head flung back on the pillow, face directly beneath mine like a funhouse reflection. It was easy to admire him from this angle: his delicate and beautiful face, teeth now yawning apart. I was, I realized, in the exact position I'd caught my mother in during those odd nighttime hours. I touched Theo's teeth again, with one finger and then both at the same time. How far would they budge? I hooked my pointer fingers around them and began to pull. The teeth separated further. My heart thudded, but my fingers continued straining. The gap widened still more, then became a gaping hole, and then, with a sound like tape being ripped from a cardboard box, Theo opened down his chin and neck and chest, all the way to his groin.

The slice was neat and bloodless, not the uneven gash it had been in my imaginings—as though his body had been waiting patiently to admit me. His tongue had not been split, but lolled to one side, as if the incision had politely circumvented it. Beneath me, his organs glistened. They were less red than I had imagined, most of them closer to pink or even brown. *Pink pasta*, I remembered him saying.

I could see his lungs still breathing, his heart contracting. I thought I must be dreaming, but when I lay my hand on his skin, it was soft and hot. Felix, who had sidled next to Theo's torso to peer inside, tipped his snout closer to Theo's innards, his nose twitching mightily, then dipped in, licking his intestines. Alarmed, I pushed him aside. I was awake, my boyfriend was split open beneath me, and I was the one who had done it.

Frantically I pushed Theo's skin and all the layers underneath back together, and as easily as they had separated, they rejoined. There was no seam, no mark at all to indicate what I'd done. My hands shook as I continued pressing along the tear all the way up to his jaw, which I shoved back into place with a soft click. Once he was fully zipped up, I lay back down, clutching Felix to me, shivering so hard I was nearly convulsing, and stayed awake until the sun rose, when I turned onto my other side and faked sleep.

7.

As I kept my eyes closed through Theo's departure, as I walked Felix and listened to him munch his breakfast kibble, as I texted Theo back the new three-word phrase in our vocabulary ("I love *you*!"), as I rode the subway to work and prepared for an interview the next day, I thought again and again, with a horror that bled into manic desire, about Theo's teeth, pushing apart under the force of my own fingers. His skin, cleaving without even a trickle of blood, right over his trachea, the hollow of his collarbone, his ribcage; right through his navel and along that slash of dark, curly hair. His organs, nestled and coiled, expanding and contracting. I pictured gliding my fingers along the pink pasta, dipping a toe into the soft wet matter—

Each time I caught myself in this ravenous imagining, I pulled myself back, reminding myself that on the very heels of Theo balking at my recordings of him I had split his body open. I fed myself stock phrases of chastisement: *What kind of person does that? Which are you: crazy or evil?* I made myself walk through the fight we'd had, how he'd forgiven me, how I'd sent him my recordings and then ripped him open immediately after. It was worse, far worse, than recording him; it was probably unforgivable.

But inevitably the image of his split-open body would return to me, organs pulsing and steaming, and along with it a hunger so powerful I wasn't confident I would be able to put it aside. For some time, maybe; but forever? Now that I knew what was possible? Wouldn't I starve?

I haven't mentioned this before, but often, on the nights Theo and I slept apart, I'd take the subway to his apartment and stand outside until I saw him in the window, even if it took an hour. Even if it took two. There were always errands I could do in Theo's neighborhood—the dry cleaner there, for example, was much better than the one on my corner—which enabled the fiction that I'd landed outside his apartment by chance. Now, as on those nights, I tried over and over again to reason myself out of my overwhelming urge. But overwhelming urges don't respond to reason. Just as my feet would march me to the subway over my mind's protestations (*stay home, stay home*), I feared, or maybe knew—it's impossible to distinguish retrospectively—that at some point, I would open him up again, no matter what my mind thought about it. And this time, I would go further.

I was in bed by the time Theo arrived the next day—because he had to work so late, we were sleeping at my place again, an unusual adjustment to the routine—and feigned grogginess as I went downstairs to let him in. When I opened the door, he pulled me in for a kiss so deep and genuine I almost pushed him away. His mouth was as tender as a ripe nectarine. When we parted, Theo put his hands on my shoulders and made his eyes soft with care. "The person I love," he said.

My stomach twisted. I leaned into him, kissing him with a forcefulness that almost made me forget what I had done. *I don't have to do it again,* I thought. *It's enough.* I had overstepped once, and I wouldn't again—not tonight, not ever.

Upstairs, we lay together like a braid. It wasn't long before Theo fell asleep. I wasn't at all tired: my body hummed as though supplied by electricity. I pressed my back into his stomach, trying to find enough comfort there to relax, if not fall asleep.

Time passed. Theo snored and then stopped snoring and then started again. He shifted onto his back, then onto his other side, then toward me again with his arm slung over my shoulder. Felix yipped in his sleep, then emitted a silent, awful fart.

Gingerly I extricated myself from Theo's limbs and sat up beside him. Curled on his side, he looked as innocent and peaceful as a little boy. I stroked his hair, smoothing it back behind his ear, and he murmured a soft "Mmm." I watched him until I was sure he was sleeping, his breathing heavy and rhythmic as it always was when he'd entered that underworld, then shifted him, inch by inch, onto his back.

His eyelids fluttered. I lay back down. He began to snore. I sat back up. I could pass hours like this, looking at his beautiful face, his delicate features, his dark thick hair, and I thought maybe I would, but I needed to at least test it, *see* if it had been real. Maybe it hadn't been, and I'd be freed from doing anything at all.

As I had the night before, I pressed my fingers to Theo's teeth. At first they didn't budge, and I felt simultaneously liberated and desolate—but then, bit by tiny bit, they began to shift. The relief of consummation enveloped me. I pressed forcefully, my muscles straining, until the gap was wide enough to fit both fingers through and pull his teeth apart. His mouth split open, down his chin and neck and torso, down the curling hairs that led to the waistband of his boxers, which was where I stopped, the bulge of his penis intact.

Felix raised his head, roused by the smell. I kept rawhides in my desk to distract him while I was working; now I reached over and, as quietly as I could, opened the drawer to extract one. Felix sniffed it and then took it into his mouth, gnawing it with force.

I turned back to Theo, holding my breath to see if Felix's chewing would wake him up. He didn't stir. If his face was beautiful to behold, his insides were—are—transcendent. I was, as I'd been the night before, as moved as I'd been at the symphony, while singing familiar songs in synagogue, when looking at a pine-ringed lake. I imagined this was how Theo had felt at work when he'd first started. I stroked my fingers along his intestine; it was silky and slick. I wanted to lick it. Instead, I brought my fingers to my mouth and closed my lips around them. I had expected Theo to taste metallic, but there was instead a stringent bitterness.

I balanced on one knee, hand pressed against the wall, and lifted the other foot up and over Theo's body as though climbing into an inflatable pool. For a few moments I hovered my foot above the pulsing puddle of his organs, then quickly, before I could lose my nerve, dipped my toe into his intestine. It was tender and warm. With little effort I pushed my foot in up to the ankle. It squelched loudly. My breath caught, and I froze—but Theo's eyes remained closed. Felix, somehow, hadn't barked, as if he understood this behavior to be on a continuum with the masturbatory scenes he'd witnessed. His head was still flat on the bedspread, but his eyes were open, watching me, marbles revolving in their sockets. Without removing my foot from Theo, I reached over and petted Felix's head, then shifted my weight to the foot inside Theo in order to sweep the other one in next to it. Still, Theo didn't stir. In the pool of his torso, my feet looked smaller than normal, as though they'd contracted to fit the space available, though this apparent shrinking didn't register as any kind of tension or crunching or pain. It was feelingless, in fact—natural, biological; the only sensation was that of his organs against my skin. I sank my entire body inside him— each part seemed to grow smaller as it made contact with his insides—and lay on my side, fitting myself between what I thought were his stomach and his liver. One of his lungs, or maybe it was his diaphragm, pressed down on my head, his ribcage a crown. The opening was now above me, and I zipped him back up until the darkness was complete.

By now it was clear I wasn't dreaming. (With the benefit of hindsight, I can promise that I was not.) My guilt vanished temporarily as I marveled at my surroundings. When I'd fused the skin back together, the layers underneath (muscles and fat, I thought, plus some tougher tissue I couldn't identify) hadn't quite rejoined: there was a slight aperture between the two halves. I figured that sealing together the under-skin layers would involve the same procedure—pressing them together with my fingers, bottom to top—but decided to leave them slightly parted, so that it would be easy for me to unzip Theo when it was time to get out. My pajamas (boxers and an old T-shirt) had bunched beneath me in spots—not exactly comfortable—and I wondered if I should have removed them, but that might have awakened Theo. I hoped my presence wasn't restricting his breathing, but the movement of his lungs, inflating and deflating above me, seemed consistent. There was, as he'd once told me, a slippery fluid coating each organ; it felt slick and oily against the exposed parts of my skin. I listened to the thudding of his heart, muffled by the organs pressing against my ears. The tempo was steady and calm. He was okay. Maybe he even liked it, the feel of me inside him; didn't I like it when we had sex? Didn't pregnant people feel special, anointed, as though they could be holding the messiah? The observer part of me heard these thoughts and responded: *You're excusing yourself for something inexcusable.* But these protestations were halfhearted. The other part of me, the present and feeling part, had no desire nor intention to leave. Life among Theo's organs was squishy and warm. I fit perfectly, as though his body had been made for me, and mine for him. I could feel the reverberations of his heart, rhythmic through his body, shushing me, making me drowsy. I spent the following hours in the deepest sleep of my life.

A noise, or maybe a pressure, woke me. I felt slickness, heat, an insistent drumbeat that resonated throughout my body. I had no idea where I was; I tried to open my eyes, but they were sealed shut. I called out, but the sound returned to me, muted, as though I were yelling into a pillow, and a slick acidic liquid filled my mouth. I wrenched one arm out of its straitjacketed position and rubbed my eyelids unstuck. Wet, thick meat. Organs, I thought. Theo's organs. I had climbed inside his body, and now he was stirring.

Quickly I reached up through his neck to his jaw, found the gap, and pried him back open. I climbed out gingerly, as though trying not to creak on the stairs. As I did, his organs slid back into place. It looked as though I'd never been there. I zipped Theo back up. His eyes were still closed, his breathing sharp and fast. Had my head been pressing against his lungs too hard after all? Or was this his normal sleep-breathing? I could no longer remember. I was covered in a fine yellowish slime, but before I could slink away to the shower, Theo opened his eyes, then startled away from me.

"Holy shit," he said.

I stared at him, my head throbbing so forcefully I thought it might shatter. I could not now comprehend how the me of mere hours ago had found it conscionable to do what she—I—had done. Again I wondered: had I dreamed it? But Felix, who had sidled up to me as soon as I'd emerged, sniffing at me curiously, now took to licking my feet, feasting on the slime. I ran my finger along my forearm: the slime was sticky and real. I had no idea what Theo must think, awakening to me covered in it, my pajamas glued to me in parts: could he possibly guess what I had done? Had he seen me in my coming and going, or felt me inside of him, or, with our bodies merged, gained momentary access to my mind? I opened my mouth to confess—in case Theo already knew, in case he didn't—but he spoke before I could.

"I'm sorry," he said. "It just scared me, waking up to you staring at me like that."

Did he not see the slime? Maybe his eyes hadn't yet adjusted to the light, or—that was it—I was backlit by the early morning sun, creeping up into the window behind me and through the sheer curtain. My hair was plastered against my head, but must look to him as though I had pulled it back in a severe ponytail.

I apologized for scaring him: "I just woke up a minute ago," I said.

"I had a strange dream. . . . I think it was Thanksgiving, or something about eating a big meal. . . . I don't know, it's slipping away," he said.

For a brief moment they came to me: the dreams I'd had those nights I'd awakened to my mother hovering above me. Stuffing myself full of chocolate cake. Finding myself pregnant with a jellyfish. Vomiting up a stream of marbles. I felt queasy.

"I don't think I had any dreams," I said to Theo.

At a vigorous slurping noise, we both turned toward Felix, who was now licking between my toes, rooting out the slime.

"Why is he licking like that?" Theo asked.

I had a desperate urge to tell him, but it just as quickly vanished. If he believed me, I would lose him. Of course, he wouldn't believe me: he would think I was inventing things, if not insane. But the biggest deterrent was the horrifying truth that telling Theo would make real to me what I had done.

"Maybe they're sweaty," I said. Felix had always licked my feet after I'd gone on runs; I used to think of it as "Going to the Felix Spa."

"Mind if I shower?" I asked.

"Sure," Theo said. "I don't have to be in for an hour."

I climbed off the bed, hardly believing I was going to get away with this. I glanced down at the comforter—it might be stained, but from this vantage point, at least, its pattern of interlocking persimmons made any irregularity difficult to ascertain. I turned toward the door.

"What, no kiss?" Theo said to my back. And then, like a dagger: "From the person I love?"

I turned back around, then gestured to my mouth: "I have horrible morning breath," I said. "I'll give you one as soon as I shower and brush my teeth. I promise."

"Since when do you care about morning breath?"

"Trust me." I made a gagging motion, then closed the door behind me.

In the bathroom, I stared myself down: the film of slime gave my face a ghastly sheen. When I was young, from time to time I would look at myself in the mirror and fall into a vertiginous trance: there was a person in the mirror, and that person was me. Those sharp lines were my sharp lines. That dark hair was my dark hair. A riddle. The feeling revisited me as I stared at my reflection, waiting for the water to warm: there were the sharp lines of my face, but I looked like no one I'd ever seen before.

8.

On the subway to work, I stood gripping the oily pole even though there was a free seat—a small punishment. As though that, or anything, could absolve me. For as I'd confronted myself in the mirror, the thought had soon presented itself: I didn't look like no one I'd ever seen before.

I looked like my mother.

The cold, sick feeling I'd experienced after realizing she'd read my diary had descended again. My mother had climbed inside of me. My little self, filled with her bigger one. Her daughter, who was not supposed to be the vessel, but the one contained.

The nights I'd caught her "admiring" me in the darkness, she had been about to split me open. Either that, or she had just exited and zipped me back up, and, like Theo, I hadn't noticed the slime. I'd only seen my mom in the night like that a handful of times, but perhaps she'd done it far more often than I'd caught her. Her breath on my face, her fingers on my nose: had she used that as her portal? As Talia had said, she was obsessed with my nose. Had she stuck one finger in each nostril to open me up? Or pushed my nose upward, making me look like a little piglet, until it began to tear?

My chest tightened at the knowledge that I'd done the very same thing to someone pure—to someone I loved. But it was different, wasn't it, climbing inside your partner rather than your daughter? Weren't you *supposed* to invade your partner's space, become one with them—the exact thing you were supposed to give up, as a parent, as your child grew? Finding your soulmate, your "other half," meant recreating the bond you'd had with your mother as an infant: the two of you together were meant to make a whole.

Yes, I thought, melting into your partner was different entirely. It was, at least, a different flavor of wrong.

I wondered, with a shot of terror, whether my mom had climbed inside me when I was home for her birthday the month before. Surely not, since there were other people in the house—but why else had I had such bizarre dreams? She had shared my bed whenever she'd visited me in New York; had she done it then? What about Talia and Romi—had she ever done it to them, or, as I suspected, were her ministrations reserved for me? Some part of me felt that if she *had* crawled inside my sisters, I didn't want to know it. I wanted to be as special to her as Theo was to me.

Though I had managed not to confess to him, I felt desperate to blurt my secret to somebody. Maybe I was looking for someone to pardon me; maybe I just wanted to relive my climb. I was dying to do it again. It felt hollow and despairing to be so distant from Theo, now that I knew what was possible. To be housed was sublime. The train car was full of strangers I could confess to, though as I scrutinized them one by one, each was revealed as implausible: the young mom scrolling on her phone while absent-mindedly murmuring "Mm-hmm" to her babbling son; the elderly man with tzitzit and payes, rocking back and forth over his open prayer book; the teens in backpacks, goading each other and yelling "Ohhh!"; the middle-aged woman with a slack face and varicose veins and four shopping bags nestled between her feet.

If I told Talia, would she excuse me? I was, after all, only trying to get close to Theo, and she herself had told me many people in relationships tried to do this in their own way. And Theo had still slept, hadn't he? Perhaps his strange dreams were his way of accommodating me. Didn't everyone in a relationship accommodate their partner in some fashion? One friend of mine had a husband who sleepwalked every other night, interrupting her slumber. By another metric, that might be considered more disruptive.

Maya would agree, I told myself. If I confessed, she wouldn't judge; she'd receive the news with curiosity, perhaps even excitement. "Speaking of raunchy," I pictured saying, "I climbed inside Theo last night."

"Like, you put your fingers in his mouth?" she'd ask. "His asshole? Good for you."

"No," I'd say. "I unzipped his body and climbed inside."

At the words, I shuddered. I definitely couldn't say it, even to Maya. Discretion wasn't one of her assets. She'd tell someone from home who'd tell someone else who'd tell my mother. Who would herself react in one of two ways: trying to bond with me over our shared behavior, or taking it as an invitation to resume her own climbs—if she'd ever ceased.

If anyone was climbing inside anyone, it was going to be me inside of Theo. Full stop.

It was an interview day at work, and my guest, the essayist Madeline Bernstein, was coming into the studio. My anxiety usually ratcheted up before face-to-face interviews, which required layering eye contact and proper posture onto the extant challenges of covering the necessary material, listening carefully, and responding as such. But today my preoccupations had made me almost forget that I had an interview scheduled at all, so that when I walked past Jenny's desk and she said, "She'll be here at noon, the dossier is on your desk," my immediate reaction was to raise my eyebrows in surprise, which I then attempted to cover up, emitting an idiotic

"Whoop-dee-do!" (Jenny, clearly unconvinced, gave me an exaggerated wink.)

Bernstein was mostly a personal essayist, though she'd written about the arts here and there and had started off as a journalist. Her personal essays were, I thought, her strongest work. She managed to mine her experiences with an unsparing and yet uncritical eye—more curious than judgmental, and, for that curiosity, all the more perceptive. She was in her sixties now and had been writing for three decades to much acclaim, though in recent years the culture had lost some interest in her work, owing, it seemed to me, to the fact that her essays took more of a psychoanalytical approach than a cultural-critical one, focusing on her personal history and relationships rather than the larger sociopolitical structures in which she was situated. This mode was no longer in vogue; yet it captured my interest in a major way, and I felt that it was important to create room for it still.

I was already in the control booth when Jenny escorted Bernstein in. She was wearing all black and was much slighter than I had expected—probably, I realized, because she had an enormous head. With her signature hairdo, the spherical coif of a certain generation, it looked even larger, so that as I'd watched her television interviews in preparation for our conversation, I had naturally imagined a medium-sized body appended to it.

We shook hands; I thanked her profusely for coming; she promised that it was her pleasure. I gestured to the seat across the table, fitted with its own microphone. Once Jenny had situated herself in the control room, fiddled with the dials, and given me a thumbs-up, I asked Bernstein what her usual breakfast consisted of so Jenny could adjust the levels.

BERNSTEIN: Peanut butter on toast. It fortifies me in case I forget to eat again until dinner.

ME: Does that happen often?

BERNSTEIN: Not often, no. Only when I'm in the final phases of a project and get really lost. But my husband chides me when I forget, which is so irritating I've taken to lying. "I had a whole raw chicken," I'll say.

At the word "husband," I thought of Theo, and my stomach lurched. I emitted a forced laugh. Jenny gave another thumbs-up: we were ready to roll. I started by asking about one of my favorite essays of Bernstein's, which had come out some fifteen years prior and traced the development of her writerly impulse alongside her personal maturation. Bernstein's mother had always struck me as similar to mine—loving but overbearing, generous but intrusive—but the prospect that her mother had also climbed inside her in the night seemed unlikely.

Still, her mother's impact had been potent. Bernstein's writing, which her mother had painstakingly edited throughout her daughter's career, had been affected as much as anything else. As with my Aldine interview, I'll reconstruct this one from memory.

ME: Let's start there, with your mother's edits on your schoolwork. What were they like?

BERNSTEIN: She has a strong sense of grammar and logic, and would fix mistakes, inconsistencies, that sort of thing. She is very sharp and, unlike many women of her generation, went to college—City College. Anyhow, her edits were excellent. But they were more corrections than prompts.

ME: Which made you feel—how?

BERNSTEIN: Well, like I couldn't create something on my own. And for a long time it didn't occur to me that I could have my own voice, or write to please an audience who didn't happen to be my mother.

ME: When did that start to change?

BERNSTEIN: It wasn't until after college, when I started to work for *New York Magazine* as a fact checker. After a couple years there, they started offering me little front-of-book pieces, which were small enough that I thought, "Okay, I don't need to send these to my mother." Which sounds ridiculous—of course I did not need to send my professional work to my mother! But she'd always held my hand, and I had this nagging fear that if she didn't, I would fail. Nagging—but not *quite* loud enough for me to actually listen to it. So I started practicing not sending my work to her for edits. And it went totally fine. I got edits from the person I was supposed to get them from: my editor! And the feedback was never what I'd feared—"This is horrible; who let you in here?" So that's when it started: the belief in the value of my own voice on the page. And not just the belief in it, but the pleasure of it: private, personal, mine.

ME: Is that still an important part of writing to you—that sense of "mine"? That control?

BERNSTEIN: Oh, yes. I still feel almost rabid when I say it: "mine." And really, how can it not be? Writing is such a strange form of communication. If we talk in person, like we are now, your language builds on mine and vice versa. Writing is different. Sometimes as I'm writing it feels like I'm in a small, dark cave that no one else knows about.

ME: Dark?

BERNSTEIN: In a good way—comforting. There's no interference. The cave is quiet. At some point my work is done, so I come out of the cave and leave it on the stoop of my reader and flee. First I'm alone; then, the reader is alone. What happens then is out of my hands, but in the act of creation, I've retained total control.

I knew something about dark caves. I pictured blurting my secret to Bernstein—"Last night I unzipped my boyfriend's body and climbed inside!" His organs, slippery and warm against my skin. I could tell Bernstein each detail and get to relive everything. If I was looking to one-up my attempt to befriend Eleanor Aldine, this would certainly do it. She'd ask what it felt like. I'd get to say, "Spectacular."

And how would she reply? "Well, if that isn't essay material! If you don't write it up right now, I will! It sounds grand. I may have to try it for myself—"

Distracted, I hadn't noticed that Bernstein was staring at me, waiting for my reply. What had we even been saying? All I could think of was telling her about the silky, squishy warmth of Theo's insides, about their pulsing rhythm, about his skin pulled over me like a blanket. I wracked my brain again for the lost thread and came up empty.

BERNSTEIN: You look lost in thought.
ME: I'm so sorry.
BERNSTEIN: Did I bore you? Horror of horrors.
ME: Not at all. I just got distracted thinking about a personal matter—
BERNSTEIN: Happens to all of us. . . . But now I'm curious.
ME: *[Nervous laugh]* You don't want to know.
BERNSTEIN: Okay, okay. *[Pause.]* "Dark cave."
ME: Dark cave! . . . Dark cave. Yes. Thank you. The dark cave in which you write, alone.

I hadn't wrecked it. But I was still on edge and sweating nervously. I leaned in hard, talking fast and bubbly.

ME: But "alone" is hyperbolic, right? Like, when you stopped turning to your mother, you invited in other readers who you didn't have an emotionally charged relationship with—like editors? Or friends, or colleagues, or—I'm not sure how many people you share your work with—

BERNSTEIN: Correct. Great feedback reveals my work to me anew, helps me to understand more clearly what I mean to say. *And yet*, during that initial act of creation, when it's just me and the page in my little cave, there's a sacred sense of communion not with an editor, not with a future reader, not with a critic, but with myself. Writing gives me the sense, if not the reality, that I'm in my own little utopia. That if I try hard enough, I can achieve perfection. What else in life offers this possibility, however illusory it is?

ME: Is it illusory?

BERNSTEIN: You tell me.

ME: You tell *me*.

BERNSTEIN: *[Laughs]* Okay. Control. What's coming to mind is these two essays I wrote about the summer my parents and I spent in the Rockaways when I was young—have you read those two?

ME: Of course.

BERNSTEIN: Well, thank you. And did you notice that the tone of each piece is very different?

ME: The one you wrote first paints the trip in blush colors. It's peaceful, soothing. And then the other one—what was it, a decade later?

BERNSTEIN: More.

ME: Right. The other one, the tone is more desolate and lonely.

BERNSTEIN: Yes! Good. Neither essay was a lie: The pleasure was true, and the pain was true. But in each piece I wielded the same experience in a completely different way.

ME: Almost like you were taking back control.

BERNSTEIN: Yes, exactly. While I was on the trip, it had had *me*. In writing about it, *I* was having *it*, wasn't I? I demanded that the journey submit to my telling of it—and then, a few years later, submit again, in a totally different way.

ME: That's interesting, because when I read your writing, I rarely get the sense of aggression you've just described. It feels to me much more about curiosity.

BERNSTEIN: Bless you. Yes. It *is* more about curiosity—discovery. It's not like I know where an essay is going to end when I begin it, believe me! Writing is an uncertain, deeply revealing, and sometimes uncomfortable adventure.

ME: So then where does the control come in? Or does it?

BERNSTEIN: Maybe it's this: writing isn't only control, or the lack of it—it is creating a safe enough sense of privacy that true abandon is possible. Creating the conditions necessary to uncover sometimes unpalatable truths. One condition is that the process of discovery itself is private. It is not to be intruded on. When I start an essay, I don't *know* anything yet—and I don't have to know. *That* is the control. I can explore quickly or slowly, with as many discursions and false starts as it takes. The page is just for me.

As Bernstein and I left the recording booth about a half hour later, I got a whiff of my stress-sweat body odor: rank. I pressed my arms close to myself, trying to suppress the smell. I had never come so close to blowing an interview.

I apologized again for becoming distracted.

"Oh, please," she said. "But you've really gotten me curious."

"I invaded my boyfriend's privacy," I blurted. Great.

"How?"

I thought again about Theo's slick organs pressing into me. The rhythmic pumping of his lungs. His muffled heartbeat. My vagina began to throb. The tape wasn't rolling anymore, our interview was done, and I would likely never see Bernstein again.

"I—" I began.

But her face was too eager. I had the same sick feeling I got when I spilled to my mother.

"I looked through his phone," I said.

Bernstein laughed. "Talk to me when you've gone to see your boyfriend's dentist ex. As a patient."

She clearly wanted to tell the story, but I only laughed. My clit was still pulsing with the memory of the night before. As soon as she'd gone, the elevator doors closing around a perfect image—Bernstein in pert low-heeled shoes, red purse dangling from both hands against her knees—I hurried to my desk, crossing my legs firmly in my chair to try to make it stop. I opened the recording of my conversation with Bernstein and tried to focus.

Peanut butter on toast . . . in case I forget to eat . . . husband chides me when I forget . . . so irritating . . . I had a whole raw chicken. . . .

I skipped ahead, trying to find the bit where I'd zoned out so I could excise it. I undershot, then overshot: . . . *still an important part of writing to you—that sense of "mine"? That control? . . . Oh, yes . . .*

The feel of Theo's slime on my skin and in my mouth. The taste of it—tart, or sour, like an off-limits candy. Felix licking it off of me, his wet hot tongue. Yes, it was wrong, what I'd done, but it was, as my father would say, a sunk cost now. Impossible to undo and thus useless to worry about. So I might as well use the memory for my pleasure, true? Theo was healthy and well. I hadn't hurt him, and he would never know. Maybe the point of crawling inside him this once had been to feed my fantasies forever. Some women had previous lovers to dream about; I had Theo himself. It was, put this way, an act of loyalty.

My interview with Bernstein was still playing in my headphones, but I couldn't listen. I could think only of the sounds of the previous night: Theo splitting open, like packaging tape being ripped away; the squelches and slurps as I climbed inside; the soft rustle of his lungs expanding and contracting; the drumbeat of his heart. I wished

I'd brought a recorder inside him and gotten it all, wished I could listen again to that rhythmic pounding—

At once, I remembered my recorder, next to my bed. At Theo's request, I had left it there while we'd had sex the night before last, and in the tumult of everything that had happened since, I hadn't remembered to turn it off. I had never lost track of my recorder for so long before; the tape had been running for nearly two days. Which meant that not only my initial intrusion but the entirety of the night after had been recorded.

I ripped off my headphones and emailed Jenny that the file was good to go and that I had to tend to an emergency, then grabbed my bag and left for home. There was no logical reason I needed to intercept the tape—Theo had left the apartment before me, and moreover hadn't noticed the recorder all night; Ava would never be curious enough about me to snoop around my room—but my need to do so was primal. Because obviously I was never going to share this one with Theo, or with anybody.

Although, it occurred to me when I was halfway home, what if I did? What could the audio possibly reveal to anyone other than me? I couldn't think of a sound anyone might pick up other than that packing-tape whoosh. An unusual thing to hear in the middle of the night, perhaps, but no more so than any number of noises emanating from the street below. If Theo even noticed it, he would dismiss it with barely a shrug. The mind eats things it can't make sense of. Our frameworks of the world, of the people we love, aren't capsized by a quick sharp sound.

But once in the apartment—Ava's door closed as usual, stripes of sunlight unfurling across our "gallery wall"—I was nonetheless afraid to listen.

I walked Felix to procrastinate even though the dog walker had already taken him out, tracing a route so long and circuitous that he, panting, began pulling me home. Still anxious, I stalled in the kitchen, grabbing a piece of bread from the freezer and finger-feeding myself butter from the dish while I waited for the toaster to pop. Felix sat at my feet, staring at me, sporadically pawing at my leg. Automatically, my mind still flush with thoughts of the recorder, I gave him a finger to lick.

I heard Ava open her bedroom door. I hadn't known she was home. She worked from home some Tuesdays, I now remembered, panicking. I knew she had no interest in my recorder or anything on it. But just in case, I could listen to the tape with headphones. Maybe her rustling about the apartment would even give me a sense of calm—keep me tethered to earth, no matter what I heard.

"Hey," I called. "Don't be startled, I'm here."

"I'm never startled," she said as she came around the corner and into the kitchen. "What are you doing home?" She reached above me toward the cabinet. I ducked so she could open it. I envied how easy she was about physicality; in her position, I would've stuttered an "Oh—excuse me—sorry" kind of thing. She retracted her arm, to which was now attached a box of cereal. "Want?"

I shook my head. "I had a stomach problem," I said, explaining my presence in the middle of the day. "So I took the afternoon off."

"A stomach problem?" She grimaced. "Which hole?"

"Butt."

"I was heading out anyway," she said. "So the bathroom is yours."

"Where to?"

"Meeting Alandra at Blue Point." She raised her eyebrows at me. "Know it?"

I nodded, even though I didn't. Some coffee shop or other, who cared? I didn't know who Alandra was either.

"She's remote today, too," Ava explained.

So she wouldn't be here while I listened after all. My muscles went limp with relief. I excused myself to my bedroom as Ava gathered her belongings. The recorder was still on the desk next to my bed, obscured by a box of tissues. I crept toward it and peered with fearful elation at the screen: it had been running for forty hours and thirty-four minutes. While the file transferred, I lay in bed with Felix huddled against my side, his nose in my armpit, the rise and fall of his ribcage a balm. I remembered Theo's lungs, pushing down on my skull.

"Do you want this toast?" Ava called.

"Uh, no, you take it," I called back through the bedroom door.

"You sure? I'm going to throw it away...." Who cared about the fucking toast, for the love of God? Was she too moral to waste a single slice of bread?

"I'm sure! I don't want it!"

"Okay," Ava called. I heard the front door open. "Feel better! Text if you need anything." Which was kind, and made me feel bad for hating her, but she probably didn't mean it.

The door shut, and there was silence. At last, I summoned the courage to check the computer: the file had transferred.

I spent several minutes searching in vain for the spot in the tape I was looking for, maybe taking so long because there was so much to fast-forward through, maybe because I was scared and stalling. Finally I uploaded the file to my editing program so I could see the shapes of the soundwaves, scrolling through the peaks and valleys of speech until they fell away. There was a short span of flat nothing—me and Theo lying in bed together—and then the low, rolling hills of his snoring.

I lay the computer back on my desk, letting the sounds of night unfurl: Theo's slow snores; my own quick, impatient breaths; a rustling of the comforter as I moved fitfully. I shifted to Theo's side of the bed and peeled back the sheets. There it was: a smear of yellow. As I ran my fingers over it, I heard on the tape a louder rustling, presumably as I sat up next to Theo; a span of several long snores; and then, at last, the packing-tape tear. There were squelching and sucking noises as I stepped inside him, first one foot and then, a minute later, the other. A louder series of squishing gurgles followed, which I understood to be Theo's organs accommodating my frame. And then there was the sound of me zipping him back up, which I hadn't been able to hear from inside: not a violent sound like the opening, but a long, soft slurp. What followed, from Theo, was a primal moan.

A queasy wave swept over me. Theo was in pain. It was impossible not to hear it. I kneaded my thighs with my hands. Another moan, more guttural than the first, and another still. As I kept listening, I wondered with one part of my mind: Was it possible Theo was aroused? The second part of my mind chided the first—wishful thinking; self-absolution. But as the tape kept playing, I couldn't ignore it: Theo's moans straddled pain and pleasure, grew louder and more insistent with each iteration, and finally, there it was—the ecstatic scream he'd emitted the previous evening when he'd come inside me.

9.

I next saw Theo two nights later. He was supposed to sleep over, as usual, but in an effort to postpone the terror of our first private post-climb encounter, I invited him to join my happy hour plans with Maya. She had, by this time, broken up with her boyfriend, and chided me over text for spoiling our one-on-one: "What, I can't get you alone anymore? Are you one of Those People?"

> **Me:** Did you not want to meet T?
> **Maya:** Oh, he's just "T" now, doesn't even need a full name
> **Me:** T . . . heo
> **Maya:** YES I want to meet T
> **Maya:** heo
> **Maya:** But when will we carry on our affair, mon amour
> **Maya:** Will you still massage me
> **Me:** Of course

Maya was my only truly old friend and was the first friend Theo was meeting, a momentous step. It occurred to me that I probably should have introduced him to Maya *before* climbing inside his body. Well, too late. Everything was free-floating these days, anyway: people had babies before they got married all the time.

At least Theo and I had said "I love you" first. Other than the addition of this phrase, our text exchanges had felt sickeningly ordinary since the morning of the climb. I kept thinking of a friend who, planning a surprise party for her husband, told me it had made her alarmingly aware of how easy it would be to have an affair. In the same way, I was disturbed by how *me* my messages read, as if I hadn't just pried open Theo's body and slept beneath his muscles and skin.

Me: How was work?
Theo: Pasta city
Theo: You?
Me: Interviewed a legend and managed not to vomit
Theo: But did you pee your pants?
Me: Only a little
Theo: Hero
Theo: Oh, I gotta run
Theo: I love you!
Me: I love you!

I thought of my mom, who had always acted like everything was perfectly normal. Had this torturous performance torn her up then as it did me now? Had she ever questioned herself? She had called me several times since I'd realized what she'd done, but in an unprecedented move, I hadn't called her back. Unfortunately, I discovered that I missed her. But if we spoke, what could I say? What would Theo say to me if he knew? That he'd been wrong to take me back after I'd told him about my recordings, that he should have left me that second, that I was as unhinged as he'd secretly always feared?

I met Maya at a bar on a boat docked off Brooklyn Bridge Park that appeared every summer and disappeared again each fall. I'd discovered it the summer before, the same way I'd discovered many things: on a bad date. Ditch the guy; keep the place. When I arrived, Theo was running a few minutes behind, and Maya had staked out a spot way at the bow, uncharacteristically timely. It took only a moment of scanning to locate her: red suede sleeveless dress; black boots; hand on her hip, perfectly at ease, even though she was standing alone and not even looking at her phone. As I neared, I saw she was holding a purse in the shape of a wolf; over her left breast sat a falcon brooch.

"Aren't you hot?" I asked, fingering the suede.

"Do you need *these*?" Maya wiggled my sunglasses on the bridge of my nose. It was true, the sun was descending, but the sunglasses completed my late-summer look—white cotton dress, denim jacket tied around my waist—an ensemble that, as usual, now that I'd seen Maya's, registered as plain.

I hugged her, the brooch stabbing me.

"Are you okay?" Maya eyed me suspiciously.

"What?"

"You're stiff, like a Stepford."

"I'm normal."

On -*mal*, a pair of hands reached around from behind me to cover my eyes and I shrieked. Maya cupped her ears dramatically. "*Jesus.*"

"It's only me," Theo said, removing his hands and laughing nervously. He'd changed into a simple Henley and jeans, which hung off his hips like a waterfall. Arousal twisted between my legs.

"She's being weird," Maya said.

"Says *she*," I said, gesturing to her wolf bag.

"So: you're Theo?"

"The one."

Only a few conversational beats later, the two of them were already deep in a faux-fight about the relative emotional manipulation of soapy television dramas and satirical sitcoms. I felt like a third wheel. In such circumstances, I employed an old trick with minimal to moderate success: I pretended that the space across from me was occupied by a friend named Barney, with whom I could share knowing glances when anything absurd or otherwise objectionable occurred between the "real" bodies present. Theo said that he thought satire couldn't be considered manipulative or sentimental because, as a viewer, you had to "reach the conclusion yourself."

"That's ridiculous," said Maya. "Being manipulated to laugh is still being manipulated! Maybe you're more comfortable being made to laugh than to cry." I squinted at Barney. He rolled his eyes.

"Maybe," said Theo.

"Literally every piece of art is manipulative, if by manipulative we mean designed to provoke a reaction."

As they spoke, Barney and I examined Theo's face and neck, looking for signs that I'd ripped him apart. Neither of us could find any. *I climbed inside him,* I thought with disbelief. Barney nodded; he understood, and didn't judge. *He doesn't know,* I added, as if Barney needed to be told. It was obviously a betrayal, what I'd done—but, I reminded Barney, it wasn't at all on par with what my mom had done to me. Theo was my partner, not my child. I lingered on his chin. It was remarkable: there was no trace. I wondered if there were effects I couldn't see; Theo seemed to me the very same as he had before. Had any two people ever been so close? (Well—yes.) I moved nearer to him, until his arm was flush against mine. Could I also climb up into his arm, between his biceps and his triceps? Down his thigh, so I could lick his tendon from the inside? Up his neck and into his skull? Could I read his brain from in there, or nestle myself between its folds?

"You've heard of her? Isa Genzken?" Maya asked, yanking me back into the conversation.

"No," I said, ashamed to be caught daydreaming, and embarrassed she'd heard of an artist I hadn't. Barney communicated to me that he hadn't, either.

"Oh," she said, clutching her chest, "her stuff is—" She turned to Theo. "How would you describe it?" So he'd heard of Isa Genzken, too.

"Vaginal?" he said, and Maya threw her head back laughing. I wanted to rip off her falcon brooch and stab her in the neck with its beak.

"She's most famous for her giant rose sculptures," she said to me. "*Not* very vaginal, actually," she added, looking at Theo and raising her eyebrows. "More phallic, if you think about it?"

"Maybe," he said agreeably.

"And I mean *giant*—dozens of feet tall," Maya said.

"Oh—like the one that used to be at MoMA?" I asked. My excitement over knowing some piece of what they were talking about made me feel like a middle school dork, trying to fit in. "In the Sculpture Garden?"

"Exactly," Theo said, appeasing me, but Maya was too deep in her monologue to notice.

"She finished the first one in the nineties, I want to say?" she continued as if I hadn't spoken. "There are a handful in cities across the world. They're all metal, sometimes with a silver stem, so the only colors are the pink of the petals and the green of the leaves right underneath. The silver stem against a silver building—well, you have to see it."

I had just told her I'd seen it.

Maya said, "She also does two-dimensional stuff—"

"As in, paintings?" I asked.

"No. Not paintings." Maya fixed me with a pointed gaze, her brooch gleaming. "Adhesive tape on aluminum panels. Different kinds—caution tape, packing tape, gaff tape—all crisscrossed. They're crazy. Hard to look at without feeling anxious or uncomfortable. So, case in point: manipulative."

"Is that really a better word than *evocative*?" I said. "'Manipulative' sounds sinister." Silently, Barney cheered.

"Didn't you just interview a manipulator?" Maya asked, refusing to let the bit lie.

My interview with Bernstein was still in production, and would air the next week, while one I had done with the young adult novelist Joanie McIntyre, whose most famous series centered on the story of a girl fleeing persecution in Eastern Europe to build a new life in America, had aired the day before. I looked out at the Lower Manhattan skyline, orange against the inky sky. The buildings' reflections stretched into the water beneath, a row of Narcissuses.

"By your metric, everyone I interview is a manipulator, I guess," I said.

"Why did you have Joanie McIntyre on, anyway?" Maya asked. "Didn't she write the *Lillian* books, like, ten years ago?"

"My show isn't concerned with news," I said, something Maya knew. I was both flattered she'd listened and irritated that she was goading me. Was she getting me back for inviting Theo, or baiting me out of envy—or was she simply being herself, blunt in a way that was sometimes refreshing, sometimes annoying? I couldn't believe I had considered, even briefly, divulging to her that I'd climbed inside of Theo. It was my secret knowledge, and she didn't deserve to be included.

"It's about the middle of the process, not the end of it," I said. "Making space for artists to talk about the confusing part, where they don't know what their project is going to turn into, or when." I was talking on autopilot, reciting the mission statement of my show as though pitching it to an advertising executive.

"I know, I know," Maya said. "I was *teasing*. Your show is incredible"—a compliment that surprised me into blushing. But then she turned to Theo: "Olive knows how to get people to open up, even if they don't seem to want to."

"That's the name of the game," I said, though the way she'd phrased her comment had sent my heart racing. "What would be the point of a conversation that stayed on the surface? Who would listen?" From there, I babbled: interviews were all about performing duality for the listener, who was invisible but necessary; no one would agree to being interrogated if the audience wasn't there; interviewees offered up intimacy as the price of publicity...

As my mouth continued to eject this speech as though I'd rehearsed it, Maya's words echoed in my mind. I had, by now, listened to the full tape. Theo had, throughout the night, screamed not once but twice. I was shocked it hadn't woken me, even though I'd been inside him. Of course, I'd told myself that his arousal, if that's what it really was, excused nothing—but I also had to wonder, did it? Regardless, standing next to him, feeling the heat of his body, smelling the deodorant that would forever be marked as his, I knew one thing: my longing to enter him again had not abated.

The night went on. The sun set; alcohol infused our bloodstreams; our voices rose toward higher decibels. When Maya seemed as though she might leave, I brought up her recent breakup—which I knew she wouldn't be able to resist talking about—to delay as long as possible being left alone with Theo. Though sharing him with her had left me feeling exasperated and insecure ("phallic"? Really?), I needed her now. Once home, I would have to either withstand my desire to climb inside Theo without acting on it, letting it devour me, or else submit to it.

But eventually, Maya did leave. I agonized, the whole cab ride home, about what to do once Theo and I were on our own—how, that is, to resist my craving, really my *need*, to climb again—zoning out of our conversation about Maya to the point that Theo said, "Hey, you there?" I was there, I claimed, and yet my mind sped along, faster than the buildings and trees spinning by my window. I had already committed two abuses: the action itself and the recording of it, which, since I hadn't sent it to Theo, explicitly violated a rule we had agreed upon.

But by the time we'd said hi to Ava and chatted about the boat bar (of course she knew about it and had been far more times than I), by the time we'd taken Felix out and brushed our teeth and gotten into bed, by the time we'd said "I love you" and kissed goodnight and turned out the light, thoughts of whether to resist had left my mind. He was there, and he was sleeping, and he was mine. I unzipped him and climbed inside.

10.

By a month and a half later, I had developed a routine. I rationed myself to one climb a week, to maximize my gratification—no need to build up my tolerance—and diminish risk, all while, most importantly, keeping my guilt minimal, or as minimal as was possible given what I was doing. Fridays were my night of choice: not only did we usually spend them at Theo's, but they felt like a consolation prize after I'd hardly seen him all week. (It also felt fitting to climb on a night that was holy to me and my people, but not to Theo and his.) In the event that Theo's dreams got strange, or that I disrupted his sleep in any way, he would have Saturday to recover. That is, if he wasn't on call. In those cases, I improvised: Wednesday, Thursday, even Monday if required, depending on when we were sleeping at Theo's or when Ava wouldn't be home.

But as far as I could tell, Theo wasn't negatively affected by my entrances—if anything, he seemed enlivened. Since I'd started, he'd kept up his usual running schedule with no ill effects. And our sex was increasingly rabid, a shift I couldn't tell who was driving. I was certainly aroused by my secret nighttime entrances, but so, too, seemed Theo: when I listened back to the recordings, he often moaned in pleasure, even when he fell short of coming—the latter of which I'd learned to recognize from inside him. Although I'd slept through his orgasms on my first climb, once I'd felt one while awake,

I couldn't imagine how I'd done so: the thrusting of his pelvis, which tossed my lower half up and down, was as close as I'd come in years to going on a roller coaster.

Even so, every morning after I'd successfully executed a climb, I felt the same rush of shame and self-castigation I'd experienced the first time. I would pledge to myself never to do it again; I could, I reminded myself, forever revisit in fantasy the experience of being inside him. Calling up my climbing memories during sex or masturbation was no different, really, than remembering an old lover spanking you with a hairbrush while your new boyfriend tenderly kissed you. The latter didn't mean you were going to cheat, so the former didn't mean I'd climb again. And I did have *some* measure of self-control: several days would pass with total normalcy, just sex and spooning in bed and walking Felix and eating eggs—total normalcy, that is, except for a steady undercurrent of desire to crawl inside Theo again, which grew day by day from a trickle to a rush to an absolute roaring need, crowding out every other thought or feeling, until I had no choice but to meet it.

I quickly abandoned the idea of confessing my behavior to anyone, if I'd ever been serious about it. The more compulsive my climbs felt, the more shame followed. The only one who knew was Felix. Before I executed each climb, I gave him two rawhides: one was probably enough to occupy him, but it was good to have backup. I'd thought about putting him on the floor while I was otherwise "involved," but I figured being sent away from the action would upset him more. Theo and I had gotten into the habit of putting him on the bed not only when we slept but also when we had sex. Otherwise, he would sit there screeching, periodically putting both paws on the side of the bed and peering at us with his tongue dangling, fishy breath wafting over us, begging to be included. This was considerably more distracting than what he'd do once he was situated near us, which was to lick Theo's toes or mine. In fact, there was something comforting about Felix's rhythmic licking, about his involvement in the act more generally, as though he were our observer and guardian. If at first I'd worried that, upon my disappearance, Felix would cry or bark, as I continued my climbs, these fears subsided: every time I emerged, he was munching peacefully.

No one else knew. When I talked to Romi, I told her only the happy milestones: that Theo and I had said "I love you"; that Felix now slept with his head resting on Theo's leg as often as on mine; that Theo knew about my recording habit, and—guess what—he didn't mind. With Talia I shared my struggles, but transmuted them into the realm of the normal: the deeper Theo and I got, the less I could stand to be apart from him, but acting out my excessive need for him invariably led to a shame spiral. (The furthest I went was to admit to Talia that I'd stood outside Theo's window, watching for him, on our nights apart; she gently asked whether that made me feel better, and how long the relief lasted.) When I got dinner with Maya—who I now made sure to see alone—I divulged only that I'd used a variation of her strategy of fantasizing harm upon her boyfriend. "What did you fantasize?" she asked. "Crawling inside him," I blurted before I could think too hard about it, then laughed, as if it were a joke. She laughed with me.

But the person I was most determined could not find out was, of course, Theo.

To this end, I came up with a series of rules, over and above limiting my climbs to once per week, to ensure that I would never be caught: I would wait until Theo had been asleep for at least half an hour to even *think* about opening him up. I would stay inside him for only a short period of time, and wouldn't ever let myself fall asleep inside of him again. (Even still, one morning after a climb, Theo told me he'd woken up to use the bathroom in the middle of the night and I was nowhere to be found. "Where were you?" he pressed, at which I began to panic, blinking rapidly. "Are you okay?" he added with undue tenderness, which almost undid my reply: I couldn't sleep, I claimed, and had wanted some candy, so I'd gone out to the bodega. He seemed convinced.) By a few climbs in, my hair had grown brittle and my skin flaky, so I committed to using leave-in conditioner and moisturizing my whole body twice a day to avoid it seeming like anything had changed. I would always, always shower before Theo awoke, even on days when I didn't climb inside him, so the change in routine didn't make him suspicious. This shift, when I first made it, required some skillful explanatory maneuvering, as waking up at ungodly hours of the morning to shower before my boyfriend left for the hospital was, if you didn't know the reason, objectively insane. I told him I'd fallen so far behind on my reading for work—true, but only because I was so preoccupied with my new habit—that I needed the morning hours between when he left and when I did to catch up. Waking up so early was painful, but necessary. On one visit, I tried using a wetsuit, which would obviate the need to shower afterward, but putting on and taking off the wetsuit in Theo's presence without waking him was an ordeal; why did no one ever talk about how loud wetsuits are? Besides, I missed the feel of his organs pressing silky and wet against my skin: after a few weeks I'd discovered I could strip my sleepwear without waking Theo, allowing me the full tactile pleasure of being inside him, his organs flush with my flesh.

All of these rules put an enormous strain on my sleep, but who can care for the body when there is a higher power to serve? On each entrance, I noticed new things about Theo, and felt I had never seen or understood someone so fully in my life. On my second climb, for example, his texture was just as I remembered—slippery—as was his tannic smell, but this time the finer notes of his scent revealed themselves to me: a slight sweetness, almost rot, sharpened by bright copper. On my third climb, or maybe it was my fourth, I tried to penetrate his neck, hoping that I could climb all the way up to his brain. My head got stuck around his collarbone, but still, I was closer to his brain than I ever had been, and could hear its faint stuttering sparks, a Morse code I wished I could decipher. (The next climb, I tried to open Theo upward instead of downward, toward his skull instead of his torso, but he was like a duffel bag: the zipper only went one way.)

I still hadn't confronted my mother about her own climbs into me. If I broached the subject, she would either lie that it had never happened—I was delusional!—or convince me she'd done no wrong, even twist her behavior so it looked flattering and sweet. What if she was so persuasive I gave her permission to continue? I had resumed calling her sporadically so that she wouldn't suspect something was up and try to ferret it out of me, but I kept our conversations superficial and brief. In any case, I kept reminding myself what I was doing was different, if I permitted myself to think this way at all. Mostly I put it out of my mind.

I held up my relationship with Theo as proof that nothing was awry, for we were thriving. The Olive who climbed was my shadow self, which fed my real self, the one Theo saw and knew and loved. Since our confrontation about my secret tapes, recording had become fully integrated into our life together: we would tape our dinners, which Theo said he listened to on his way to work; our walks with Felix; our phone calls, when Theo got home unexpectedly early on one of our nights apart; and, most of all, sex, which we'd listen back to together, fucking to the tapes of us fucking, taping all the while, creating a mirror hall of moans and grunts and screams that had a grainy audio quality I adored.

So I had kept my promise to let Theo know whenever I was recording, and to send him all the tapes I made—except, of course, for the tapes of my climbing pursuits, which were the only ones I still made furtively. I excused this by telling myself those tapes were part of a *different* secret, not the recording secret, and since my entrances hadn't been explicitly forbidden, these tapes were not, strictly speaking, a violation. At moments I fantasized that someday I could tell Theo about my penetrations, but then I would flash back to how wrongly I had predicted his reaction to the recordings. Risking another such brutal surprise—risking, again, losing him—was not an option. Of course, he had come around on the recordings in the end, which meant perhaps he would come around on my climbs, too; perhaps he could love them as much as he'd grown to love taping ourselves, as much as he'd grown to love me. And yet it was too much to hazard.

Secret it remained, then. At first I recorded only from the outside, as I had the first time, placing the recorder inside a cracked-open dresser drawer so that it wouldn't be visible to Theo. But I couldn't shake the fantasy I'd had, while listening back to my interview with Madeline Bernstein, of recording inside Theo's body. I could bring my standard recorder with its built-in microphone, but I wondered if more specialized equipment would give me even better sound. I had last recorded underwater, so to speak, when I was a child: I had covered my red-and-yellow tape recorder with a plastic bag and brought it into the bath with me to see if I could tape the sound of my farts. My efforts were semi-successful (imagine a muffled "bwomp"), but now that I worked in radio, I knew that sound traveled faster and with greater pressure underwater, and that it was best captured with a hydrophone, not my recorder's standard built-in microphone. However, as I scrolled through model after model of hydrophone online, I realized that the inside of Theo's body must not be strictly "underwater" since, after all, I was able to breathe while enclosed. Instead, the better option might be a contact microphone, or a piezo microphone, which senses sound via vibrations in solid objects (like, say, organs) rather than in air. I began researching equipment anew, spinning down a rabbit hole for hours until, finally, I decided that no choice would be perfect and the important thing was to commit to some model or other before I lost my nerve or gave in to my guilt, whichever would come first.

The contact mic arrived on a Wednesday in a box that looked innocuous enough, as all cardboard boxes do. It was still sitting on the front stoop when Theo and I arrived at my building after dinner—we'd gone out with a couple of his friends from work—and I picked it up with what I hoped was convincing nonchalance.

"What is it?" Theo asked, examining the shipping label.

"Just some audio equipment for work." I put the box under my arm and rooted in my bag for my keys.

"Why'd it come here instead of your office?"

"I must have put the shipping info in wrong."

When we got inside, Ava's bedroom door was closed, but her light was on. Why she hadn't taken my package in when she'd arrived was beyond me. I went into my bedroom and tossed it onto my desk, dreading Theo asking if I wanted to open it, but he didn't, seemingly having bought my explanation, so unsuspecting that I felt for a few moments that I might be a monster, and committed afresh to stopping my climbs once and for all.

But by the time Theo had left for the hospital the next morning, my resolve had, as usual, evaporated. I opened the package. The equipment was swaddled in bubble wrap, which I tore off with abandon, setting the mic on my desk to admire it: the key to my next phase. I planned to bring it with me on my climb the following night, which left me two full days to practice using it: we were sleeping apart that night. Since I was going to record inside Theo's body, the most reasonable test would be to record inside my own body first, so before I took Felix out for his walk, I squatted on the floor and gingerly pressed the microphone into my asshole. I'd stuck my finger up there before, but the microphone was bigger, circular and cold, and I let out a sharp gasp, which Felix echoed in bark form. I contracted my asshole a few times, doing a Kegel exercise of sorts, which sucked the contact mic farther up into my anal tract until it felt nestled, if not exactly comfortable. Once I'd connected it to my recorder, I rose inch by inch until I was fully upright, then pulled my underwear and jeans up around the wire and put the recorder in my back pocket.

I thought the walk around the block would be painful, the cord chafing against my asshole with each step, and it was, but as you might imagine, it was also arousing.

Early on Friday, before I left for work, I packed the mic and my recorder, which I'd wrapped in cellophane, leaving only its two built-in microphones exposed. Feasibly, the cord would be long enough for me to leave the recorder outside of Theo's body—it had been long enough to reach out of my anus, up and over the waist of my jeans, and into my back pocket—but would be a dead giveaway, in the event that he awoke while I was inside him, that something was horribly amiss. I pictured fusing Theo's skin back together from within, this time the cord inching up along with my fingers, from the base of his torso all the way up to his mouth, until it unfurled right through the gap between his teeth. Imagine waking up in the middle of the night to find a cord hanging out of your mouth! Even in the impossible event that he went back to sleep, enabling me to climb back out, and then awoke in the morning to find me reading for work as though everything were normal, how could I possibly help him make sense of his horrible midnight discovery? If I responded too casually ("You've never woken up with a cord in your mouth before?"), he'd think I was deranged. If he was too concerned, we'd need to go straight to an emergency room. The only feasible tactic would be to insist Theo had been dreaming, but what if he knew for a fact that he'd been awake?

This logistical challenge aside, based on what the contact mic had captured from within my body, the microphone only picked up the sound of the object it was pressed up against, not the ambient noise of multiple systems at once. Plus, the audio was tinny. But listening to my muscles contract rhythmically with my steps had been so exciting, I couldn't possibly give up the chance to listen in detail to the movements of Theo's organs, one by one. My plan was to first capture sound via my recorder's built-in microphones, then switch to the contact mic, which I'd move from organ to organ over the course of my stay.

All that day, I mentally rehearsed climbing inside of Theo while holding my equipment, worried that I would lose my balance and either drop the gear or fall, waking him. I planned to stow the recorder and microphone in my left armpit as I unzipped and then climbed in, pressing my arm against my body to secure them; once I was fully inside, I would nestle the recorder into the nearest space I could reach, leaving the microphones as exposed as possible.

When night came, and the requisite half-hour of Theo-snores had passed, I gave Felix his rawhides, then peeled off my pajamas and shoved them, as usual, underneath the bed. I'd left my work backpack on the floor next to my side of the bed and reached into it gingerly, turning on the recorder through the cellophane and tucking it under my arm. I unzipped him as slowly and silently as I could; crouched beside him; lifted one foot and then, once I'd safely balanced myself on my now-smaller appendage, the other into his open, pulsing torso. As had become my custom, I lowered myself to my knees, then shifted onto my side, curling myself into Theo's entrails; this time I nestled the body of the recorder between Theo's stomach and liver and pressed along the underside of his skin, pinching it together as though sealing dough, until he was fully intact once more.

According to my rules, I would stay inside for only half an hour, or what felt like it; the recorder could have told me, but I couldn't read the screen through the cellophane. Although normally I had to fight drowsiness once I was inside Theo in order to ensure I'd get out before he awoke, on this visit adrenaline coursed through me so avidly it would have been impossible to sleep. Once a small while had passed, I plugged the contact mic into the recorder and pressed it, sequentially, against every organ I could reach. At a certain point I sensed my time was up. I emerged and zipped him back up, then shuffled to the bathroom with the equipment.

I'd meant only to unwrap the cellophane, wipe down the recorder and mic, and store them in the toiletry cabinet, but once I'd cleaned everything off I couldn't help myself. Despite the idiotic risk, I pressed the recorder to my ear, turned on the shower for sound coverage and, at the lowest possible volume, played back the tape.

Even over the water pouring out of the showerhead, I could tell that the equipment had picked up far more than I could hear on my own. The sounds from the built-in microphones overlapped but were distinguishable, like sheets of trace paper that had been layered one on top of the other: there was the gurgle of Theo's stomach and intestines, the shushing of his lungs inhaling and exhaling, the hush of my own breath. The shift once I'd switched to the contact mic was stark: there, unimpeded, was the thick thudding of his heart, each time echoed by its slightly softer shadow. Next was his diaphragm, which on this part of the recording didn't shush as much as squeal:

the contact mic was picking up the stretching of the muscle rather than the movement of air above it.

I listened all the way through, the room filling with steam, before I finally stowed the recorder in the cabinet underneath the sink and stepped into the shower. Once inside, I lay on my back in the tub, the water cascading onto my stomach and face, causing the slime to slough off onto the white acrylic of the tub. I ran my finger through the yellowish water, rippling it like a boat's wake, replaying the sounds of Theo's body in my mind before inching backward in the tub until the water from the showerhead poured between my legs.

After that, on my off nights from Theo, I played back only the recording I'd made from inside of him. I listened to it on the subway, as I walked Felix, and even at work as a break from editing interviews. I figured that once I'd grown tired of this particular tape, I could always make another, but I also felt I had been graced with unlikely luck in not getting caught the first time. Anyhow, I wasn't *near* tired of it yet. On each playback I heard new nuance—how his heartbeat sped up slightly on his inhales, for example, and then slowed on his exhales—or, if I didn't, reveled in the familiarity and routine of the sounds, as though I were a teenager listening to a favorite pop song over and over again, or an infant absorbing a lullaby.

On a Friday in mid-September, sitting at my desk at work, I was listening to the recording for the umpteenth time—pretending to focus on my computer screen, twisting a lock of hair round and round my finger, picking apart the gurgles of Theo's stomach, wondering if he had been hungry or full—when my cell phone rang. It was my mother. I paused the file and, without removing my headphones, answered on speaker.

"Mommy"—thank God my office door was closed—"I'm at work. What's up?"

"I'm here!"

"'Here' as in my workplace?" I gave a panicked eye-sweep of the floor through my glass office wall.

"In New York City, honey."

My stomach lurched. Keeping things light on the phone was easy, but how would I feel when I saw her? How much could I pretend? Beyond all that, she was interrupting a climb day, as well as Theo's first completely free weekend in weeks. I'd been looking forward to it since he'd told me. Showing up unannounced like this was batty, even for her.

"Mom, I wish you'd warned me. I have plans this weekend already—"

"Can you move them for your dear darling mother? I have to meet this Theo, sweetheart. It's been months already and I have no idea what he even looks like." My mother couldn't have found Theo's call schedule—could she?—though perhaps she'd somehow intuited it. We had planned to go to the Philharmonic on Saturday, but there was no way we could get my mother a ticket so last-minute, and certainly not one next to our seats. A different mother would say, *Keep your plans, I'll see you in between!* Or, perhaps, *I'll come to the Philharmonic and sit wherever; it doesn't matter if we're next to each other; we wouldn't be talking, anyway.* I felt the sinking conviction that we would not be going.

"Why didn't you tell me you were coming?" I said. "So I could plan something?"

"*Sweet*heart, if I'd tried to schedule it, you would've pushed it off 'til next year." She was sharper than I'd given her credit for. A small saving grace: she'd made plans for that night with her friend Marsha, a college roommate she saw whenever she was in town. Normally she would invite me to join ("invite" here translating to "insist"), but now there was Theo, and she wanted their first meeting to be "pure," unimpeded by any distractions. To that end, she had made a reservation for three for brunch the next day at Balthazar: "It's where celebrities go, honey, isn't it?" I had to agree. "You, me, and Theo. Eleven A-M. Okay?"

"I have to check Theo's call schedule," I said, even though I already knew it was open. Beyond the Philharmonic, he and I had planned to go running and then volunteer together that Sunday for the first time since we'd met. Theoretically my mom could come with us, but she really wasn't a food pantry (or exercise) type of woman. I messaged Theo apologetically, informing him of my mom's surprise visit, the attendant surprise-brunch, and our dashed plans.

"I just texted him," I reported to my mom. "Where are you staying?"

"Oh . . . I usually stay with you, so I figured . . . Will that not work? I want as much Ollie time as I can get!"

My stomach felt twisty, as it did every time I thought about saying no to her.

"Theo is staying with me," I said.

My mom erupted in nervous laughter.

"I didn't realize you slept together every single night," she said.

"We do," I lied. "I'm sorry."

"Would you want to make an exception, to spend some quality time together?"

Would she force me to say that I didn't want her to stay with me? I could claim that Theo was letting someone else sleep at his place, but then she'd ask him about it, and prepping him on this lie seemed like more drama than he deserved. He'd also wonder why I didn't want her to stay with me, and I'd have to make up another lie to obscure the first. I could say he didn't have a cell phone, so I couldn't change our plans last minute, but I'd already said I'd texted him. Besides, that was absurd. I could claim all of Theo's stuff was at my place, but that would lead to a conversation about whether we'd moved in together without telling her.

"Felix is really used to having Theo there," I said dumbly.

"Felix," she said.

"My dog?"

"I know who Felix is."

I bit hard into my tongue, willing myself not to offer my place, and didn't unclench until she said: "I'll book a hotel right after we hang up."

My stomach churned with a sour mixture of relief and remorse.

"You know I love you?" I said.

"I love you too, honey. The most."

"Sorry," I said.

"Don't be silly!" she said in high-pitched singsong. "I'll call hotels right now. I'll see you tomorrow."

By the time we hung up, Theo had texted back. He fanned my apology away: of course he'd come to brunch and whatever followed, he couldn't wait. But unfortunately, he'd have to meet us there; he'd gotten slammed at the hospital and didn't know when he'd be able to leave, so he was going to sleep at his place.

> **Me:** I thought you weren't on call?
> **Theo:** I'm not
> **Theo:** It's a total emergency
> **Theo:** I'm really sorry
> **Me:** Okay
> **Theo:** Truly. I am
> **Theo:** I have to go now, sorry, I love you
> **Me:** Love you too

Yet again, Theo's work was ruining everything. If he arrived at brunch before me, my mom would know I'd lied. She'd be livid, but rather than telling me, she would transmute her displeasure into the toothiest, most cringe-inducing smile I'd ever seen.

Even worse, I wouldn't get to climb tonight. If being deprived of a climb on a normal night was uncomfortable, on a night like this—when I was filled with anxiety and desperate for an outlet—it was unbearable.

* * *

I left early for brunch the next morning, hoping my mom would arrive last. I'd asked Theo if he wanted to meet beforehand and travel there together, praying he would say yes, but he said he wanted to do some work on an article that was due soon, so he would see me there. If I'd presented it as a request rather than an offer, he probably would have said yes, but I hadn't wanted to appear needy. There was nothing to do but hope that everyone would arrive in the correct order.

As I walked from the subway to brunch, I recorded to calm myself, promising myself I'd stop the tape as soon as I got to the restaurant, and meaning it. It was a busy Saturday in SoHo, the streets jammed with tourists holding shopping bags from Uniqlo and Zara and Forever 21, my recorder picking up shoes clacking on cobblestones and the intermittent underground rumble of the subway and conversations in Spanish and Chinese and Hindi and an Eastern European language I couldn't identify. It had turned into an unseasonably hot day, but I'd dressed for fall, so as I walked the heat clung to me like a sleeping bag and I sweated so copiously I thought it must be audible, squeaking drop by drop out of my pores.

Distracted, I realized too late that I'd taken a wrong turn. By the time I got to the restaurant, my mom and Theo were already inside and seated, him laughing so hard he slapped his leg. They were across from each other, Theo facing away from the door and my mom toward it, but she was too engaged to notice I'd come in. She wore a gauzy black top, tapered at the wrists and waist, that she'd worn to dinners out with my dad when they were married and had continued to wear when she saw him post-divorce, presumably as a reminder. She'd let her hair dry naturally and it framed her face beautifully. She looked at ease, as she always did in social situations, her hands moving balletically as she spoke. The hands that had delicately pried open my nose, my chin, my throat, my chest so that she could climb inside. I felt nauseated and cold.

I switched off my recorder, approached the table and put my hands on Theo's shoulders.

Upon registering my presence, my mom broke into the overlarge smile I'd foreseen.

"Ollie!" she cried, jumping up to hug me. As she clutched me to her, I was overwhelmed by the competing desires to shove her away and dissolve into her embrace. Finally I patted her back a few times, signaling that it was time for the hug to conclude.

She pulled away and studied me. "Ollie, are you all right?"

"Of course," I said.

"You don't look well."

"I guess I'm overheated from the walk."

"You look pale, not flushed." She touched her hand to my forehead. I could feel Theo's eyes on me.

"I'm fine," I said, resisting the urge to bat her hand away.

"Drink some water," she said, removing her hand at last and handing me a glass. Obediently, I drank.

Theo rose and, though I offered him my lips, chastely kissed my cheek.

I sat next to him, facing the empty chair—Barney's chair. I scooted a hair closer to Theo, but it didn't make a difference; I was the clear third. My mother commented on Theo's handsomeness, as I'd known she would; he blushed and looked down, as I'd known he would.

"Theo and I were just talking about laughing," my mom relayed, a description so vague as to be aggressive.

Theo clarified: "Your mom asked why I cover my mouth when I laugh."

"A lot of people do that," I said.

"Ollie, listen to his answer."

I pursed my lips and turned toward Theo. I wished we were alone.

He opened his mouth and, with his tongue, indicated it—the space between his teeth. My heart started to pound.

"I've always been self-conscious of it," he said. "Even as a kid. In pictures, I always smiled with my mouth closed, even though my parents kept telling me to smile 'with teeth.'"

"I didn't know that," I said.

"Can you believe it?" my mom said. "He considered getting—what was it?"

"Adult braces," Theo said.

"Don't ever," I said. My mother raised her eyebrows and I realized belatedly that my tone had been too intense, that it clashed with their casually playful mood. "You look perfect," I said, attempting and again failing to achieve nonchalance, and then added: "to me." *And apparently,* I thought, *to my mom.*

She insisted on all three of us sharing, a gesture that felt to me overly intimate for their first meeting, but to which Theo cheerily assented. As we reached across each other, serving ourselves or sometimes eating straight from the communal plates, my mom and Theo exchanged fluid, easy banter. Ostensibly they were both doing this for my benefit, yet I felt extraneous, like an audience member. As a child, I'd felt like my mother's awkward shadow whenever we left the house. This sense revisited me now as I watched the two of them converse. I telegraphed my distress to Barney, who suggested that I distract myself by observing the diners near us, as though I were an anthropologist. A few tables over, in a coveted booth, a young woman with severe angles and hair swept up in an equally severe bun sat across from a man whose meaty back occupied the space in a solid, almost violent way. She was so ethereal that as she masticated the food with her visible jaw muscles, I looked at Barney with surprise: *So she eats*. Barney widened his eyes in agreement, then cocked his head toward a different table, smirking. I thought he must be grinning about the diners' shirts, ugly on their own but made even uglier by their juxtaposition, one patterned with neon flowers, the other dark gray with strands of some shiny material woven in to make it shimmer. On their other side was a couple, both dressed in all black, staring at their phones; I guessed they'd been together at least a year, probably five. Another couple: the woman sat erect, her legs neatly crossed one over the other, laughing a tinkly laugh, her plate untouched—an early date, then. I wondered whether Theo and I had been that obvious.

"She did a *very* powerful segment on how her classmates didn't get enough sleep," my mom was telling Theo. She clamped a pair of tongs around an escargot shell and gracefully forked out the garlicked snail. As she closed her lips around the blob of meat, I remembered, just last month, envying the chicken Theo was chewing. Perhaps, without consciously realizing it, I'd decided to climb inside him right then. Perhaps I'd harbored the knowledge of my mom's climbs somewhere in me all this time, and had known I'd do it to Theo, if given the chance, from the moment we'd met.

I scrutinized my mother. I wondered when she had climbed inside me for the first time, and whether it was something she'd been dreaming about for long. I wondered if she'd felt guilty and tried to stop herself from doing it again. But perhaps she'd thought about it as her right from the very beginning. Did she think about my insides whenever she looked at me? Was she thinking about her climbs at this very moment, just as I was thinking about mine?

My mom went on: "One student said he didn't sleep more than three hours a *night*." They were talking about my mortifying high school radio exploits. I'd roam the halls with my recorder, making vox pops about my classmates' sleep habits, favorite classes, and pets, which only my family would listen to. This in addition, of course, to the secret recordings I'd started making back in elementary school, and never stopped.

"I would pay good money to hear that," Theo said.

"Thankfully, there is no trace of it anywhere," I said.

"Are you sure about that?" My mom raised her eyebrows. I had to offer a little smile. She'd saved everything I'd ever done—including, I guessed, the things I'd tried to get rid of. I was sure she thought no mom could have loved her child more, and maybe she was right.

"Please, yes," said Theo.

As my mom regaled Theo with grandiose claims about my early radio skills, I wondered if she'd willfully or unconsciously forgotten why I'd become obsessed with radio in the first place, or if she'd never known. Throughout middle school, when my parents were fighting a lot and my sisters were already out of the house, I would listen to *Fresh Air* as a sort of comfort food. Terry Gross managed to probe without prying, her voice like soft fabric. I wanted her to interview me, to listen to me in that way. I wanted her to notice every feeling I had, and to honor each as though it were sacred. Only once I grew up and began to conduct my own interviews did I realize that I might not want to be a subject after all.

"I'll text them to you," my mom was saying to Theo, meaning my old radio stories. I balked. Where did she think she was getting his number from?

Not me, it turned out: already she was handing over her phone and Theo was inputting the digits.

My mother had—to my frustration if not my surprise—come up with a detailed itinerary for the rest of the day that she'd failed to share with me. Once the table was empty but for our oil-slicked remnants and she'd signed the check (Theo had tried to pay, but she had swatted away his hand), my mom said she'd bought timed tickets to the Museum of Natural History, where she wanted to see the gemstones.

She checked her watch. "We'd better hurry."

My anxiety pinged. Felix needed a walk, but my mom wouldn't want her plan interrupted. I explained the situation and suggested we all walk him together. "I can show you Fort Greene Park," I said. I silently pleaded that she wouldn't suggest she and Theo visit the museum on their own while I went home.

She pouted. "You couldn't get a dog walker?"

"It was too last-minute—you only told me yesterday that you were here." Strictly speaking, I hadn't tried.

"Felix really can't wait?"

I glanced at Theo, who had grown almost as attached to Felix as I was. I was relieved to see him raise his eyebrows.

"He can't wait," I said firmly. "But I promise, it will be fun—it's a really lovely park." *Really lovely:* I felt like a real estate broker. It was hard to predict when my mom would want to caretake and when she'd want to be cared for, when she'd want to play parent and when child. Romi had shared that when our mother stayed in her guest room, she fell right in with Romi's kids: did Romi have a sweater she could borrow? Hand cream? And could she make a turkey sandwich with mustard and swiss? In this case, I sensed that my mom wanted me to coddle her as penance, and would be flattered if I acted as doting tour guide.

"Okay," she said. "What a lucky dog Felix is!" She smiled so hard that I could see her gums.

"He's really lucky," I confirmed.

In the park, we let Felix off his leash, and he pranced ahead of us. (After a tussle—could we go to the Museum of Natural History after the park? Make it a short walk?—we had decided to postpone the visit until the next day, so we could really, as I put it, "relax and enjoy it." This afternoon, we would go instead to the nearby Brooklyn Museum, which I expected my mom would think was "fine.") I showed her around Fort Greene Park, explaining that Frederick Law Olmsted, who'd designed Central and Prospect Parks, had also designed this one. I pointed out the area where I took free yoga classes once in a while, and where Theo and I had gone to a soul concert a few weekends before. I did not mention, though I wanted to, that afterward, Theo had pinned me against a tree and stuck his hand inside my pants. Perhaps, if my mom and I got a moment alone, I would. Felix led us around the park's west side and I gestured to the farmer's market below.

"Ooh, Ollie, let's get stuff to cook for dinner tonight," my mom said. I'd made sure to use my most saccharine and peppy tour-guide voice, and it had worked: her mood had shifted. Mine had not. She'd not only worn my underwear, read my diary, *climbed inside me,* but she'd interrupted—and was continuing to interrupt—my precious weekend with Theo. This was supposed to be our Philharmonic night. I'd already sold the tickets over a listserv of people who worked in radio, but the phantom of the plan taunted me.

"Theo, did you have something tonight?" I asked, figuring I'd give him the out, even though I knew he was free, and pleading he'd take it.

"Nothing," he said. My chest tightened. I reminded myself that he was probably participating for my sake, not because he enjoyed my mom's company. "We can cook at my place, in case Ava's around."

"Who's Ava?" my mom asked.

"My roommate." I had mentioned Ava multiple times before, and wanted to add petulantly, *I've told you this already,* but in front of Theo, I pretended I was above such adolescent behavior.

My mother fell behind, taking photographs on her phone as Felix led us further down the path. Ahead of us, a young couple flirted as they strolled, one woman looping her arm around the other's waist. I was desperate to be alone with Theo. One of the pair pulled the other toward her and kissed her neck, causing her to throw her head back in giddy laughter. I glanced back at my mom; she was facing away, phone held above her head, zooming in on a high-perched bird. I tugged Theo in for a quick, covert kiss, then released him.

A child walking with her mother chirped excitedly as she passed us, looking back and forth between Theo and me. "Can I pet your dog?"

I gave my cheery assent, enjoying the misperception that Felix belonged to both of us. The girl reached her hand over Felix's head, which made him cower, so I taught her to put her hand under his chin, palm up, for him to sniff first. She laughed as his wet nose tickled her fingers.

"He likes you," Theo said to the girl, pointing out Felix's tail, swishing back and forth. As we walked on, Felix lifted his leg near a sidewalk tree. From behind me, the girl's voice: "That dog is going pee-pee!" I laughed, and Theo did too—covering his mouth, although my mother was still several yards behind.

She caught up with us, panting: "You walk so fast!"

"Sorry," I said. "I didn't realize you weren't with us."

"Don't be silly! You don't need to apologize," she said tightly, as though she hadn't demanded it. "Did you hear that little girl? She sounded just like you!"

"Me? How?"

"Narrating what everyone around you did: 'The cat is licking itself,' 'Mommy is cooking,' 'The tree is standing still.'"

"'The tree is standing still'—really?" I found this charming and, despite myself, felt a shoot of tenderness break through my ire.

"I swear it. Narrating everything."

"Like what else? Would I narrate myself?"

She said I would, and in the third person: "Olive is getting dressed in her blue jumper." I laughed. "You looked *so* cute in that little jumper."

"Do you have a photo?" said Theo.

"Of course, at home," she said. "Plenty. I'll text them to you when I get back."

The tenderness evaporated. Now that they'd exchanged numbers, I figured I should start a text thread with both of them, making sure I wouldn't be left out. On the other hand, if I left it alone it was possible my mom would forget entirely. Spontaneously, she threw her arms around Theo and me and cried, "I'm so glad the three of us are all together!"

"Me, too," I said, cringing into the space above my mother's shoulder—but as quickly as she'd pulled us to her, she sprang away.

"Ow!" she whined, dramatically.

"*You* hugged *us*," I said, unable to help myself.

My mother reached her hand into my pocket and pulled out my recorder.

"It's off," I said quickly, looking at Theo. His expression was sanguine—or was it? His eye contact hardened so slightly I could have been imagining it. Maybe he was issuing a challenge: *you wouldn't dare record me without asking first, not after everything we've been through, would you?* And it was true: I wouldn't. I hadn't. Except for the climbs, of course, but I shrugged away that guilt as I usually did. It was a different secret.

"You're recording me?" my mom said. "That's so sweet! You want to remember!" My mom held the recorder up to her mouth and crooned, "I *love* you, Ollie—"

"It's off," I repeated. "I'm not recording anything."

"Then why do you have it?" she asked. I felt Theo's eyes on me and couldn't bear to meet them.

"I was recording earlier, before we met up," I said. "For B-roll."

"What's B-roll?"

"Interstitial tape—background noise."

"Like what?"

"Can I just show you an example later?" My tone was tart and my mother gave an exaggerated wince of offense. "Sorry," I said. "I'm just tired. Do you mind if we get the groceries and head back?"

We walked to the farmer's market in silence. I was fuming and guilty. I knew that later in the day, whenever my mom and I had a moment alone—even if it was just while Theo went to the bathroom—she would tell me how "hurt" she was that I had "snapped" at her in the park. Had she, this entire interchange, been angling for a confrontation? Conflict could be more intimate than kindness. She couldn't know about the fight Theo and I'd had about my recordings, but if she'd been even the littlest bit attuned to me the way she always claimed to be, the littlest bit responsive to my body language, she would have backed off.

At the farmer's market, we reverted to superficial conversation about what to buy: tomatoes, of course, they were still perfectly in season and we could do a caprese; the brussels sprouts and the potatoes, which looked fresh, but not the onions, which must have been a bad batch; fish? Was it good here? I assured her it was. I still couldn't meet Theo's eyes, though his presence in the periphery was bright and hot as a flame.

We returned Felix to the apartment; I introduced Ava and my mom (I got a text later: "Olive, your mom is the *best*"); we went to the Brooklyn Museum; we retrieved Felix and the groceries and took them over to Theo's for dinner. *Now* this, my mom said, *is a neighborhood,* and though I didn't want to care, the implication still stung. Theo gave her a tour of the apartment and she looked meaningfully at me—impressed by his taste? Hopeful I'd live with him one day?—then peeked pruriently into his bedroom and raised her eyebrows. I stared back hard.

As I poured a glass of wine for each of us, as my mom and I cooked, as the three of us ate and chatted about something or other inane, I tried to bear a chipper smile and a fluttery laugh while, inside, I willed time to hurry by so that Theo and I could be alone. For obvious reasons, my mother's sillier habits incensed me more than usual. Like when she told a story neither Theo nor I could follow about someone we'd never met, which became increasingly arcane: "I've lost the thread," I finally said. "Could you explain it again?"

"I'm just thinking aloud," she said huffily—the same phrase she'd used throughout my childhood, anytime I'd struggled to follow her circuitous speech. "I'm just thinking aloud," to my mind, was a tautology: subjecting me to an unprocessed stream of thoughts was exactly what I was objecting to.

As her story went on, I plastered an attentive expression on my face while, mentally, I excused myself to imagine what might happen after she left. Theo would ask why I'd been carrying the recorder around, if I really hadn't taped the day in secret; he would ask me, point-blank, why I hadn't yet sent the recording of that evening we'd fucked, if there was any other tape of him I hadn't shared. I'd considered isolating and sending the pre-climb part of that tape, but doing so had felt too much like committing to a lie.

Or maybe I'd wanted Theo to notice. The thought of him sternly demanding to know—*Well, is there?*—unnerved and aroused me in equal measure. I could casually say that I'd forgotten to send the tape of that night—which would mean, at last, sharing the audio with him. *There's something else you should know,* I might say. The thought made me queasy; yet buried at the heart of this nausea was a seed of thrill.

11.

At last, my mom had gone, though not without opening the door while Theo was in the bathroom ("Mom, you have to *knock*!" "Ollie, it was a mistake, my goodness!" Theo, when he exited, was blushing scarlet). As she hugged me goodbye, she said softly into my ear, "I'll really miss you tonight."

The urge rose in me to placate her—*I'm so sorry, we really do almost always sleep over, last night was a rare exception, Theo had to work late*—but I swallowed it.

"You picked a great hotel," I said. "You should get a massage while you're there."

She pulled away, her face blanketed with cheer.

"Well, enjoy, you two lovebirds! I'll see you in the A-M."

I took Felix for a walk while Theo began the cleanup, then took up a place next to him at the sink, hand-drying the dishes. He'd looked up and smiled at me when I'd returned, then rubbed his foot against Felix's side—tender gestures that suggested he wasn't as angry at me as I'd suspected. But he hadn't leaned in for a kiss, as he usually did when we reunited, even after just a short time apart; and now he stood silently at the sink, scrubbing at a fork with a sponge, then picking at a stubborn bit of dried food. Come to think of it, his smile had been a little tight, maybe better described as a grimace. I stared at his nimble fingers, the nails rounded just so.

Surgeon's hands, delicate and strong. He was as meticulous with the fork as he must be with his patients' bodies—as he was, in bed, with mine, his fingers tracing my nipples, kneading the flesh of my ass. Was it possible I'd imagined his upset earlier in the day? His jaw was set, his eyebrows furrowed, which could mean either barely repressed rage or intense concentration on the task at hand. I'd seen this expression during our fight about my recording habits, but I'd seen the very same expression when he was bent over a medical journal, scribbling notes.

It was suspicious he hadn't said anything about our day yet, hadn't ventured a single comment about my mom, but maybe he was waiting for me to go first.

"So what'd you think?" I asked.

"Of?" he asked, with bite. Verdict: angry. I said I meant of my mom. He said she was "awesome."

I thanked Theo for entertaining her with such grace. "You don't understand what a service you did," I said, struggling to dry a particularly heavy pot without dropping it. "That made her feel so good—so cared for."

"It wasn't an act; she's great."

Surely he could tell there was tension between my mother and me. Even if, like most men I'd known, he was less attuned to such dynamics than even some of the denser women I'd met, he would, in a normal mood, ask me how *I'd* felt about the day. As I struggled to figure out how best to respond, I remembered his raised-eyebrow look when my mom had suggested we postpone Felix's walk for hours. He hadn't seemed to particularly enjoy her barging in on him in the bathroom, either. Theo didn't—he couldn't—have purely flattering thoughts about her. Not unless he was trying to punish me.

"She's great, but she's also *a lot,* don't you think?"

"Well, she cares a lot, if that's what you mean. I wish my mom cared half as much about me." That, he probably meant.

Still, I said: "Are you mad at me?"

He asked what I thought he might be mad about.

"Having my recorder with me earlier, obviously."

"You said you weren't taping anything, and I believe you." At last he looked at me. His jaw was still set. "Am I wrong to?"

"You're right to."

"Okay. Then I do."

He turned back to the sink. He was scrubbing hard—*furiously* was the word that came to mind. Finally he shut off the water with force and put his palms on the countertop, then looked over at me.

"*Why* did you never send me the recording of the night you agreed to send me them all?" he said. "How can I believe you haven't been recording without telling me, when you haven't even sent me that one?"

I didn't respond.

He threw his palms toward the ceiling. Soapy water from his hands dripped down his forearms. "Silence. Great." He wiped his hands on his pants, leaving dark smudges.

"Why haven't you mentioned it before?" I asked, stalling in a way that felt fumbling and transparent. "You've known for a month and a half I didn't send you that one. Why haven't you ever brought it up?"

"So this is my fault?"

"Were you waiting for me to send it? As a test, or something?"

"For fuck's sake. I was giving you the benefit of the doubt! I thought maybe you *forgot*!"

"What if I did?"

"I really don't think so anymore."

"Why not?"

"Because I'm not *stupid,* Olive!"

An icy prickle rushed across my skin.

"What do you mean?" I asked.

"What do you mean, what do I mean?"

"Like, what do you think I'm hiding?"

"I don't know," he said. "That's what's scaring me."

Theo was standing very still, except that with his pointer finger he scratched at a callus on his thumb, quick sharp movements that seemed likely to draw blood.

I wish I could say I weighed my options, that confessing was a rational choice I made. But the words came out in a rush, as though a long-dormant volcano were erupting at last.

"I didn't turn the recorder off after we—had sex," I said. "We went to sleep and it was running all night. *That* part was an accident." Theo nodded. He hadn't remembered to turn it off either. "But while you were sleeping, I couldn't sleep, and—well, I unzipped you"—I could feel the threat of nervous laughter and pushed it down—"and then the next night I did it again, and the recorder was still running, and that time"—I could stop here, but what was the point?—"The next night . . . I climbed inside."

Theo stared at me with fury.

"You're making shit up to get out of having an actual conversation? Really?"

"No—"

"You unzipped me? What does that even mean? What the fuck actually happened?"

"I'm not making it up," I said. "I swear." The impulse to laugh had vanished with the realization that he wasn't going to join me there.

In a flood, I explained everything: how I'd fingered his bottom teeth, my favorite part of his body; how they'd started to separate;

how as they did, his body had split right down the middle. How I'd nestled myself inside, closed him back up, and slept there until the morning. "Remember how you'd dreamt of being really full? Like Thanksgiving or something? That was me inside you," I said. "Or how Felix was licking my foot that morning? Like, licking it a lot? That was because of the slime from your body—"

Theo shook his head with his mouth open, livid.

"I don't know why you're doing this to me," he said. "I can't believe you."

Did he mean that he couldn't believe the story I was telling him or that he couldn't believe what I'd done, which was beyond the pale? The possibility that I wouldn't be able to convince him I wasn't making it all up, that I wasn't *crazy,* brought me close to tears.

"I promise, I'm telling you the truth," I said.

"You opened up my body. And climbed inside."

"Please believe me," I said, so despairingly that he sobered. As resolute as I'd once been to never let Theo know, now I felt he *had* to. That his seeing me, his loving me—the *real* me—depended on this union of my shadow and daytime selves. "Look, it's something that my mom did to me growing up. Which doesn't justify it," I added quickly. "I know it sounds impossible. But it isn't. You've probably seen miracles in the operating room, right? You know even science isn't always, I don't know, scientific?"

"Okay," he said, reaching into his pocket.

"What are you doing?" I said, panicking as he slid his phone out. "Are you calling the police?"

"What? No!" he said. "I'm calling your mom!"

I lunged for the phone; Theo snatched it away from me. *"Don't,"* I said.

"If what you're saying is true, she'll confirm it, won't she?" He was probably thinking that calling to "confirm" my "story" would be a way of covertly alerting my mom to the situation. Of getting her to "help" me. I grabbed for the phone again and Theo raised it above my head, too high to reach. I leapt for it like a kid trying to grab his jacket back from a bully.

"Give it to me," I said.

"I can't."

"She doesn't know I know," I said. "I just realized she'd been doing it. Like . . . an unearthed memory." I didn't tell him that what had unearthed the memory was my own residence beneath his skin.

If he told her, would she demand he put me on the phone or, worse, show up at my apartment to discuss it? Would she apologize and beg me to forgive her, or would she try to bond over our shared passion? Would she want, even more than ever before, to enter me? I jumped for the phone again and broadly missed. "I'm begging you: don't call her," I said.

Holding the phone high above his head, he thumbed the screen, looking for her number.

"If you have to call someone, call Talia," I said desperately. Even if, as I suspected, she didn't know about our mother's climbs, I thought she offered the best chance out of everyone I knew of confirming that it was something our mom was capable of.

"You're only saying that because I don't have her number."

"I will give it to you," I said. "Really. Look." I slid my phone from my pocket, dangling it before his face. I located Talia in my contact list and sent her information to Theo. His phone dinged with the incoming text. He looked at the screen skeptically, then with surprise: I had really sent him her number. His posture softened, as though this development had helped him see me clearly again, the fog of my disclosure having temporarily lifted to reveal the person he loved.

"Okay, I'm calling her," he said. His finger hovered over the screen, but his tone was unconvincing, and he didn't tap her name.

"I really wish you wouldn't."

"Because you're lying for some reason, and as soon as I call, I'll know?" He was speaking in questions, I noticed, not statements—which meant he was giving me an in.

"Because it's true," I said. "And you're the only one I want to share it with."

Theo slid the phone back into his pocket. Maybe he was only placating me, his insane girlfriend, but I still felt relief. Was he a little bit curious?

"Let me show you," I pleaded. "Listen to the recording with me."

"What will that do? What you described could sound like anything."

"Then what?"

Theo lowered his hands to his hips and squinted at me. "If you really were inside me, what does my spleen look like?"

"I don't know what your *spleen* looks like," I said, "because I don't know what a *spleen* is! I bet it's not even in the part of your body I've been inside!"

Theo moved closer to me, looking unusually commanding.

"Or is it because you've never seen it?" Had he always been this tall? His expression had shifted: now he was looking at me with the same intensity as he'd had just before he'd asked, when I'd first divulged that I'd recorded him, whether the tapes of us fucking were hot.

"Do you want me to prove that I climbed inside you or that I read an anatomy textbook?" I wanted to grab him and pull him against me. Instead, I stayed still, maintaining an impassive expression. I had two options, as I saw it: I could desperately list all the organs I *had* learned to name, describing how they'd looked and felt in great detail—the pink sponge of his lungs; the paler coil of his intestines—the equivalent of submitting. Or, now that I understood his game, I could play along.

"I do have a way to prove it to you," I said.

"I just told you how, and you blew it."

I shook my head slowly, eyes locked on his. "No," I said in a low voice. "Get on the bed."

We undressed more slowly than usual, watching each other as we peeled off our clothes and dropped them in little heaps. As we'd made our way to the bedroom, my bravado had dissipated: I was about to perform my penetration under Theo's watchful gaze. About to do what had until now been my private ritual.

But as Theo dropped his pants and peeled off his boxers, I noticed that his dick, to my amazement, was beginning to stiffen.

"You like this," I said, gesturing to it.

"My body betrays me."

"Does it?"

He didn't respond.

I told him to lie down on his back. He did, hands behind his head, feet flat on the bed. Still standing, I rearranged his limbs as though playing Slug Lady with Granny: I unlaced his arms from above him and gently lay them at his sides; I lowered first one leg and then the other straight in front of him. He looked delicate and fragile, hipbones protruding toward the ceiling, abdomen dipping between them, creating a little bowl that the sharp line of his pubic hair cut through. I felt sick with guilt and desire.

"Okay?" I whispered.

He nodded.

I lifted Felix to the bed to sit at our feet, gave him his rawhides. Theo watched silently. I lowered myself to sit next to him. A thin layer of goosebumps had broken out across his skin. Tenderly I ran my palms over his forearms, up toward his shoulders, down over his small nipples, the ridges of his ribcage, his stomach. He arched his back in response to my touch, pushing himself into my hands. I cupped his sides like I was holding him in. His breathing was rapid, like it was when he was nervous—or aroused.

"I don't have to do it," I said.

"Do it." His voice was throaty.

I shifted so that I was looming over him. He licked his lips, cleared his throat.

"Are you nervous?" I asked.

He pursed his lips and gave a quick nod.

"Are you?" he asked.

"Of course."

"That it won't work this time?"

That hadn't occurred to me. Rather than striking me with fear, it seemed absurd, impossible. It had happened many times, and it would happen again—unless there was a caveat, a clause in the climbing-inside-your-boyfriend contract, that said it would only work if you were unobserved. Like how when your eye is twitching, it stops as soon as you point it out to anyone, then resumes once they've looked away. Still, no; this was not my worry. I was subsumed by the more elemental fear of being watched in the act. As clear as it was that he'd become, against all logic, thrilled by the fantasy of what was about to happen, I couldn't imagine Theo would still be attracted to me once he'd seen me rip him apart.

I gestured to his mouth. "Open wide," I said.

He did, then closed it again: "Wait."

"Do you not want me to do it?" Relief washed over me.

"I do. Just—tape it."

Whether he was stalling or genuinely wanted a record of my breach, I wasn't sure. I hadn't dared to take out the recorder prior to his request, even though executing a climb without documentation distressed me: it would be a gap in my files, which until this point I'd maintained with pristine fidelity. Was a climb even real if it went unrecorded? Still, it had struck me as an impossible ask, on top of everything else. Now I gratefully retrieved the recorder from my overnight bag and set it on the table.

I pressed it on. The seconds began ticking by on the little screen.

"It's taping," I said.

Theo unhinged his jaw as though looking to swallow me.

"Not *that* wide," I said. "As though you're snoring."

He hardly blinked as I pressed my finger to the gap between his teeth; his only movement was a slight undulation of his tongue. Slowly, as they had every time before, his teeth began to separate. Theo's tongue retracted like a turtle into its shell. I pulled my hand away.

"Does it hurt?" I asked. "Should I stop?"

He shook his head. I continued. As before, the gap opened enough for me to fit both pointer fingers inside, and I pulled them apart; his chin split neatly with that packing-tape sound, then his neck, his chest, his belly. Theo's eyes widened dramatically, the pupils skittering back and forth. Quickly I zipped him back up and asked if he was okay. He swallowed a couple of times and nodded. "Keep going," he said, reminding me of the first time I'd had sex, in college, and had urged the boy to keep pushing despite the ripping pain. Just as he had reluctantly obliged, his erection softening perceptibly in reaction to what must have been a grimace on my face, I now gingerly continued, prying Theo back apart and then climbing inside, one foot and the other, and then my entire self.

As always, as I shifted into fetal position, his organs parted to accommodate my frame. Usually I laid my head beneath his ribcage and zipped him back up right away, but this time I kept my head up for a few moments, craning to look at Theo's eyes, still opened obscenely wide above the gash I'd made from his mouth on down. "Ready?" I said. He nodded once, and I slipped all the way inside.

After I'd zipped him up around me I counted to sixty using the "one-Mississippi, two-Mississippi" method. The seconds passed with agonizing slowness. Theo's heart beat faster than it had on previous entrances, which made perfect sense: he was awake and afraid. His diaphragm pressed with unusual force against my skull, creating a crick in my neck. I was desperate to open him back up, to relieve myself but also Theo of any pain or discomfort—desperate, too, to hear from him what it had felt like, what he had seen. What did it look like, from outside, when I opened him up? And when I climbed inside—how much did I actually shrink to fit inside him, and even then, how did his torso manage to accommodate me? Was there anything about housing me that felt good? A part of me was hopeful that he was enjoying it—that the sounds I'd heard emanating from him on the recordings were, as they'd seemed, an indication of true pleasure.

By thirty-Mississippi, I was starting to feel drowsy, as I always did. His heartbeat, even at this quickened pace, had a resonant thrum that lulled me as powerfully as barbiturates. My arms were pressed against my sides and I pinched myself to keep awake. I wondered if, when Theo had asked me to record, I should have offered to tape from inside him. It had all happened so fast that it hadn't occurred to me. Wouldn't he want even more to know what he sounded like inside? But that would've been one more thing to admit, and the fact that he hadn't left me yet was already a miracle.

At last I reached sixty-Mississippi. I reached up and unzipped him and climbed out, covered in slime, his organs slurping back into position. I took a moment to admire them, perfectly nestled together once more, then met his eyes. They were opened wide above his split-apart mouth, a gruesome and compelling vision. I zipped him back up and he was whole, with not a single mark on his skin. I curled my hand around his ankle and asked him if he was okay. He nodded, put his hand on his throat.

"That was the fucking craziest thing."

So maybe he *was* going to leave me, because watching me crawl inside him was as repellent as I had feared.

"Does your throat hurt?" I asked, trying to remind him I could also be tender.

"No."

"Why are you touching it like that?"

Theo raised his hand and looked at it with puzzlement, as if it had acted of its own accord. Felix began licking me vigorously. Theo's gaze shifted toward him.

"He's licking . . ." he said.

Which reminded me of the point of this whole exercise: to prove to Theo that what I'd claimed was real. That my climbs had really happened, that I wasn't *crazy*. For as frightened as I was of how Theo must feel about me now, I was also relieved. He had to trust me.

"Can you see it?" I asked. "The slime?" I held my forearm out to him. He ran his finger along my skin, then looked at the glistening tip.

"You've got me all over you," he murmured.

Could he be flirting?

"Now you know how it feels," I said, testing.

He licked his finger and then my own.

"I taste good," he said, just as I did when I kissed him right after he'd been between my legs.

"Did it hurt?"

He said that it had, but in a way that was so intense it was also pleasurable, like he was being obliterated: "like how people say it feels when they—you know."

"When they get fucked up the ass?" I said.

He laughed.

"When they have anal," he said. "Yeah." We'd talked about this before; neither of us had much interest. I figured when your whole profession revolves around assholes, they lose most of their allure.

"What did it feel like when I unzipped you?" I asked.

"That was the part that hurt most," he said, and my stomach filled with cold, heavy lead.

"I'm really sorry."

He shook his head. "Like I said, in a way that I liked—"

"But I should never have done it without asking you—"

"You shouldn't," he said matter-of-factly. "Obviously." My skin prickled.

"How come you let me do it again?" I asked softly.

"You think I believed you were *actually* going to do it?" he asked. "I thought it was impossible."

"But a part of you also thought it was possible," I said. "Right? The part that . . ." Here I gestured to his penis, reminding him that, imagining me entering him, he'd felt not only fear but also desire.

He shrugged in assent. "I've seen medical miracles, like you said."

"So then why?"

"Well, it's different if I *say* you can do it, isn't it? If I'm *awake*?"

"Was it to reassert control, then? Or something?"

"Control, yeah," he said. "But also, look . . . You didn't ask, but it turned out . . ." He curled his fingers underneath my thigh.

"It turned out . . ."

"I like it." He stroked my thigh and I started to get wet.

"What did it feel like when I was inside you?"

"Kind of like I was full?" He lifted his eyes to the ceiling, tonguing his tooth gap, thinking. "Not my stomach," he clarified, "so much as my whole self. Filled up and—comforted? It was almost too much, but it wasn't . . . it's hard to explain."

"I get it," I said.

"But *how?*" he said.

"How—"

"I still don't understand how you fit your entire body inside me."

"But you saw it."

"I *saw* it, but I can't explain it. It was like an Escher piece. You just—fit inside me. Even though it was impossible."

"Well, it isn't *impossible*—"

"How isn't it?"

"It's always felt to me like I'm shrinking," I said. "Like as soon as each body part makes contact, it gets small."

"Maybe," he said. "It was hard to see from this angle. I could only see whichever parts of you were still above—you know, in the air—"

"Out of the pool," I said.

"*The pool?* Wow. You have your own lingo already?"

I shifted uncomfortably. "Maybe it could be *our* lingo?"

"How many times have you done this?"

"A lot," I said. "I don't want to lie to you anymore—"

"Olive! Fuck!"

"Could we go back to the part where you're curious?"

"Could we go back to the part where I trusted you?"

"I'll tell you everything," I promised, feeling desperate. "*Everything.* I've climbed inside you six times, okay? Seven, counting this one. What else do you want to know?"

"Have you done this to anyone else? Before me?"

"No. God, *no*."

"Really."

"It would never have occurred to me." I reached my hand out toward his on the bed, but didn't grasp it. "You're the only person I've ever wanted to be this close to." *Or ever will*, I thought. He was, if I was flattering myself, my muse.

His expression softened slightly, before hardening again. Like he didn't want to give in again so easily, after he'd given in—given up?—so much.

"Have you recorded them?" he asked. "The climbs. Other than tonight."

"Yes."

"How many?"

"All of them."

His eyes blazed. "Olive—we'd been over that! You said you weren't going to make secret recordings anymore! You *promised*!"

"I had this thought, like . . . there were two buckets of secrets. . . ." But as I began to explain that in my mind, the climbing and recording buckets were not fungible, it did strike me as inane. "It doesn't make sense," I said. "I'm sorry. I'll send them all to you."

"Now," he said.

Once again, I pulled my computer onto my lap and sent him all the recordings.

"Déjà vu," he said.

"I promise, this is it."

"If you say so."

"What else could I possibly hide, at this point?"

"Olive, with you, I never know."

I could keep apologizing, or I could take a gamble.

"You like that," I said.

He didn't assent—not verbally—but he stared at me, hard, in a way that suggested he did.

"I don't like *pool*," he said, which I took to be a peace offering. He wanted to make up lingo with me, which meant he was still in.

"That's fine," I said. "What do you like?"

He let his eyes roam over the ceiling.

"Body," he said finally.

This struck me as rather literal, but he was, after all, a doctor.

"Body," I confirmed.

We looked at each other.

"Can I ask?" I said.

"What?"

I had more questions about what it was like with me inside him—his *body,* I said pointedly. He nodded.

"When I closed you back up, could you see the difference? Was your stomach bulging or something? Or your torso, or whatever?"

He said it wasn't. "Maybe slightly, but barely." I rested my hand on the taut drum of his belly, the curly hairs guiding my eyes downward, and he let me. I felt again a twist between my legs. "I mean, it really looked just like it looks now. A little raised, but no more than any time I've had a big meal."

"It's flat," I said.

"Okay, flat then." He lifted his hand and I hoped he'd put it on top of mine, but instead he pressed it to his forehead. "This is absolutely batshit," he said.

"They say it's impossible to know what a relationship is like from the outside, and every relationship is different, right?" I said. "So maybe a bunch of people are doing this too and we just don't know and never will." Except me, who knew about my mom. "Or maybe other people aren't, like, *climbing inside* their partners, but they're doing something else that would seem equally unbelievable to everyone else.

"What about love doesn't defy the laws of biology?" I said, hoping to appeal to his scientific side.

"Everything," he said. "Love is basically all biology. Getting us together so we can procreate."

He had used the word "procreate," a decidedly unromantic word—yet the fact that he had gestured toward even the vague notion of having children together gave me hope that, despite my incursion, or perhaps because of it, we were growing closer, and would last.

"What I mean is—love makes us temporarily insane," I said. "I've interviewed Esther Perel. I know."

He shook his head, bewildered.

"Every day since we met has felt surreal," I said. "Even way before this happened."

"Right."

"So maybe it's just—the latest act. In our surreal play."

"What could the next act be?"

I looked at him in disbelief. "Is this not enough?"

He shrugged.

"What, then?" I asked. I had no idea what he was going to say, a feeling that thrilled and sickened me in equal measure.

His face assumed the calm, smug expression of clarity. "Don't you know?" he asked.

I shook my head.

"I have to do it to you."

Let *him* climb inside *me*? I recoiled, rustling the bedspread. Of course, the possibility of this reversal should have occurred to me, but my need to be consumed had been, well, all-consuming. Being left on the outside, alone, was a cruel prospect. I imagined Theo splitting me in the night and wondered if I would ever sleep again.

"But you're inside me all the time," I said to Theo. "Almost every hole I have, you've been inside of."

"You climbed inside me," he said. "Now I want to climb inside you." His tone was decisive and set.

Please don't make me do this, I thought, but managed not to say a word. Still, my dread must have shown on my face, because Theo asked, incredulously: "What are you afraid of?"

Everything, I thought. I was afraid that there was no part of me he loved as much as I loved his teeth—nothing he had really ached to explore. I was afraid that, even if there was an access point, he wouldn't find my insides as majestic as I found his; that he would be less interested than he was in his patients' bodies; that he would find something there that even I didn't know about.

"What if you don't like what you see?" I asked. "Inside me?"

"Of course I'll like it; I'm a surgeon."

"That's not what I meant."

"What could I possibly find out that I don't know already?"

"I have no idea."

"So?"

"That's what scares me."

He traced my forearm with a delicate finger.

"I haven't left yet," he said. "Have I?"

His kindness startled me, bringing me close to tears.

"How will you get inside me?" I asked.

"How did you figure it out, with me?"

"It wasn't a question," I said. "It was always your teeth."

"It..."

"The first thing I loved," I said. "Liked, I mean." Wanted. *Craved,* bordering on *needed for sustenance.*

"So it was your relationship to my teeth . . ." he said quietly, as though to himself. "Not my body itself, but my body through your eyes."

"Something like that," I said. Only someone who'd loved his teeth as I had could get in through that gap—which brought to mind my mom, who we were supposed to meet the next morning.

"Oh my God," I said.

"What?"

"My mom," I said. "Is in town."

Theo started to laugh.

"I cannot believe we're still in the normal world right now," he said. "Like, we still have *plans* with your *mom* tomorrow morning?"

I checked my phone for the time: 3 a.m. We were supposed to meet her in seven hours at the Museum of Natural History.

"What will we even talk about?" Theo said. "The weather?"

"Ask her about gardening," I said. "It's what I always do."

He looked at me tenderly.

"She really did this to you?" he asked. "When you were a kid?"

I nodded.

"Are you sure?"

"I am."

"How?"

"I just am."

He laid his hand on my leg.

"I feel ambivalent about it," I said before he could pity me.

"Because you do it, too?"

"A little bit that. And also—although it's a betrayal, of course"—I gave an embarrassed smile—"it's also . . . flattering?"

"You feel special."

"In a way." I picked at a cut on my knee that had just begun crusting over. "Maybe I'm excusing her to excuse myself. Or maybe it's as simple as: she's my mom, and whatever else she is, whatever else she does, I know she loves me.

"But promise me . . ." I added.

"What?"

"You will *not* bring this up."

"You really don't want to talk to her about it?"

"I don't. At all."

"Then I won't."

"Good," I said. "Thank you."

"This doesn't mean I've forgotten," Theo said, his expression growing sly.

"Forgotten . . ."

"Now I get to climb inside you."

My chest tightened with anticipation. I couldn't bring myself to ask whether I could keep climbing inside him in the meantime.

"It's on you now," I said. "To figure out how to open me up."

12.

I hadn't been on the Upper West Side in months, and was comforted as usual by the sensation of one hundred Jewish grandmothers surrounding me. My first apartment in the city had been on West Seventy-third Street, where I'd taken the small room a thirty-something couple was renting out. I was still so young—in my early twenties—that they seemed to me another species. As I sat mostly celibate in my little cell, trying to drown out, with aggressively cheery pop songs, the sounds of my roommates' laughter or lovemaking, I imagined the old women across the street and down the block looking out for me, comforting me, protecting me. When I ran into these women at Fairway or further up at Zabar's, they were as vicious as anyone my age, shoving their shopping carts through the crowds; but in my private imaginings, far away from the reality of them, they all had hefty bosoms upon which they invited me to lie.

Theo and I had taken the C all the way up from Clinton Hill, an hour-plus-long ride that gave us a vital preparatory buffer before re-encountering my mom. Theo had slept soundly after the climb, but I'd barely slept at all, obsessed by the thought of him climbing inside my body while, passively, I watched. The fact that he didn't seem to immediately know his access point was a bit insulting—was there no part of me he lusted after with irrevocable force?—but perhaps, I thought, it spoke well of him that he hadn't objectified me in this way. But then, who *didn't* want to be objectified by their lover? Wasn't there one part of my body that drove him absolutely insane?

Maybe there was, but he was keeping it to himself.

As we walked down Central Park West from the subway I spotted my mom, characteristically punctual, standing outside the Museum of Natural History in a black sleeveless jumpsuit and big sunglasses. She did not look like a mom. I didn't point her out to Theo, just interwove my fingers tightly with his.

She saw us and brightened, waving both hands wildly. "Ollie! Theo!" she called as we neared. She kissed my cheek and then gathered Theo into a hug, causing him to release my hand. Her nails, I noticed, were a lurid coral.

"Great color," I said, taking one of her hands in mine to examine it. I wished she'd chosen a pale pink, or that I'd painted my own nails something even brighter.

She wriggled her fingertips jazzily. "Went to the salon this morning," she said. She redirected her finger-wriggling to Theo. "You like?"

He liked.

I took his hand again. "Let's go inside," I said.

After a long stay in the hall of gems and minerals, which my mother gushed over to a grating degree, I ushered her and Theo past the mollusks and the giant cross-section of a sequoia to my favorite part of the museum: a diorama showing a soil cross-section, hugely magnified. I positioned myself between them in front of the glass case and the three of us examined a worm the size of my arm, nestled underneath a foot-long fallen leaf.

Theo ran his finger over the glass, tracing the length of the worm. "Are these the kinds of creatures you see when you garden?" he asked my mom. I wondered what he was feeling toward her now: was his politeness entirely false? Or did he still feel some sympathy toward her—even some affection—despite what I'd divulged?

"These and more," my mom said. She really was beautiful. Theo looked at her as she spoke and I willed him to look back at me. She told him how, when she and my dad had laid new sod in the backyard one year, I'd led Maya in peeling it back to find the worms slithering underneath.

"I didn't know you were a bug girl," Theo said. I curled my arm around his waist. I wanted to split him open then and there.

He didn't soften, as though he was embarrassed to touch this way in front of my mom. Feeling rejected, I retracted my arm and used my radio trick to maintain a normal, unwavering tone. I told him I wouldn't go as far as peeling back sod anymore, but there was a reason this was my favorite diorama. Something about the magnification of the insects—by a factor of twenty-four, I knew from having read the wall text countless times—helped reignite my childhood fascination with forms of life I could hardly see, let alone access the consciousness of.

My mom told Theo that beyond peeling back sod, Maya and I would exchange bug stories—"Something I admit I found grotesque," she said.

"But you *garden*," I said with too much bite.

"Ollie, it's not like I can explain it."

Theo asked what kinds of bug stories, a bald attempt to dispel our tension, probably for his own comfort. Or was he feeling bad for my mom? I said I couldn't remember exactly, but one might be inspired by a millipede I'd seen inching its way across the sidewalk, jagged where a tree root had burst through. I'd tell Maya that the millipede seemed afraid of the crack, cowering before it—

"How does a millipede 'cower'?" my mom said.

I didn't answer. I said I would tell Maya that the millipede decided to try to jump the crack but fell onto the tree root, splatting to its demise. I'd describe in detail the millipede's radiant blobby guts strewn across the bark of the tree.

"See? Grotesque," said my mother.

"You might prefer a story about a bug princess," I said.

"Go on."

"She's a caterpillar who wears a tiny tutu. Because she's vain. That's it." My mom opened her mouth to reply, but I interrupted: "I think we've seen enough of the forest floor. Let's go."

"Where next?" Theo asked with artificial brightness.

"You choose."

His favorite exhibit was the blue whale. We wended our way to the atrium and, though I'd seen the whale many times, I was stunned once more by the size of it, hanging suspended from the ceiling. The museum had projected the lights in such a way, dappled and moving, that it looked like we were underwater, and the three of us lay on the floor, gazing up at the whale's belly as though from the bottom of the ocean floor.

"Did you know this is the biggest animal in the world?" Theo asked.

"Of course," I said. "Actually it's the biggest animal ever to have existed, they think."

"How big do you think its poops are?" asked my mom.

"Bigger than mine lately," I said reflexively, then winced. Not only did this divulgence demolish the sliver of space I'd inserted between us, but also, though I'd been curled up next to Theo's intestine as recently as a few hours ago and would do it again immediately if I could; though he knew my mother had climbed inside me; performing scatological analysis with her in front of him was a different matter.

"Honey, are you blocked?" my mom asked. "Have you tried magnesium? It's my new thing, I *swear* by it—"

"Tell me later," I said brusquely, turning my head toward her and opening my eyes wide. Though she wasn't one to take a hint easily, and I feared she'd keep digging ("How small *exactly*? Logs or balls? Are you skipping days?"), she got my message, letting the discussion wither.

After we'd brunched, Theo and I went back to my place to walk Felix before meeting up with my mom again later in the day. The subway was delayed, and, when it finally arrived, packed, so we stood pressed up against each other near the door, my breasts pushing against Theo's chest.

"I like that," he whispered. I slipped my hands into his front pockets and he moaned softly into my ear, then licked it. A woman on my right looked sidelong at us, pursing her lips, and I removed my hands gingerly. Theo looked to be on the precipice of laughter.

"So—debrief?" I suggested.

"She's overwhelming," he said, and I flushed with satisfaction: so he *had* seen her for who she was. "But she gets away with it because she's charming," he continued, and I bristled. "She's basically obsessed with you. She thinks you're the coolest person on earth."

"No, she wants to *own* me. Eat me alive." I gestured meaningfully to my belly, reminding him of what she'd done. As if he could forget.

"Can't it be both?"

I shrugged. I wondered if he thought she was more charming than I.

Theo squinted his eyes, like he was considering whether to say something. Was he envious? His mother hadn't paid him enough attention, whereas mine had paid me too much. Maybe to Theo, that seemed the better bargain.

"What?" I prompted.

"It's just—I would never talk to my parents about poop."

I laughed, relieved he wasn't going to extol my mother for her love, and relieved, too, that she had taken my hint at the museum and dropped the matter of my excretions.

"But you're a *poop* doctor," I said.

"I'm really a cancer doctor—"

"You know what I mean."

"We just don't talk about it."

"What would happen if you were at dinner with your parents and were like, 'I am so constipated'?"

"I don't get constipated."

"Seriously!"

"It's actually nauseating me to think about telling them that."

"Did you ever see your parents naked?"

"Never. You?"

"Not my dad, but my mom—all the time. I'd touch her boobs, just play around with them."

"When you were a little kid?"

"Yes . . . and older."

"How old?"

"High school?" The truth was that I'd had my mom's breasts in my palms as recently as the previous year, but from the look on Theo's face, I knew I'd been right to hedge.

"Maybe it's just a Jewish thing," I continued. "All my Jew-friends love talking about poop. Everything about bodies. There's not much off-limits."

"Clearly," he said. He chewed his lip, probably thinking about the evening before, picturing me sinking beneath his skin. "Can we . . ." He looked around the subway car, checking if anyone was listening. Was he going to ask whether he could climb inside me as soon as we got home? Would the protective comfort of strangers all around us make him bold? Sweat broke out along my forehead and upper lip.

"Can we . . ." I repeated.

"Can we listen to one of the tapes when we get home?"

I felt a giddy rush.

"Of course," I said. "How is that even a question?"

Maybe this meant I could keep climbing with no interruption. Could I climb right after we listened, or while we were listening—or even tape us climbing and listening simultaneously, like we did when we were fucking? I was about to present these options to Theo when I realized there was something I hadn't yet conveyed.

"I forgot to tell you—"

Theo groaned.

"Another secret?"

"No, no. Listen." I leaned toward him and stood on tiptoes to whisper into his ear: "I made one of the inside of your body."

"Fuck, really?" He grabbed my arms with surgeon-boy excitement. "We're listening to that one first. *Obviously*."

After we'd walked Felix, I cued up the tape of his insides, which I'd heard so many times by that point that I could sing along as his stomach made a particularly loud gurgle, as his heart rate increased and then decreased again, as his breath stopped for a moment before resuming.

Listening through Theo, though, was new. Watching him lean toward the computer, captivated, mouth slightly open and eyes blinking, whispering every few minutes, "This is so cool," I felt I must be witnessing something akin to his first experiences as a surgeon or, even further back, his brushes with wonder as a young boy. When the tape finished, he wanted to listen again: "So much better than what you get with a stethoscope. Unbelievable." By the time it was done, we had run out of time to take the subway to dinner with my mom. To arrive late to our final dinner would be seen as very rude indeed, so I called a car as I threw on a dress.

In the backseat, Theo cupped my thigh with his hand, pressed his leg flush against mine. I pressed back. I had the urge to fuck him—normal sex, missionary, his body crushing mine, the moans or maybe screams he'd let out when he came—a fantasy that reminded me there was one final thing I hadn't yet told him.

"It's not a secret," I added quickly.

"What, then?"

"You couldn't hear it on that tape, because it was inside you," I said. "But on the other tapes, you can hear . . ."

He widened his eyes at me and gestured fervently: *spill it*.

I leaned so close my mouth touched his ear.

"You came," I said. "While I was inside you."

He stared at me.

"Except there was no semen. But you made the same sound you make when you come," I said.

We both glanced toward the driver, who was speaking rapidly over the phone about weekend plans to "get fucked up."

Theo laughed. "Holy shit."

I started laughing, too.

"Why are you laughing?"

"Why are you?"

"I don't know."

Finally our hysterics faded.

"Can I keep doing it?" I chirped, barely breathing as I waited for him to respond.

Theo chewed the inside of his lip.

"We'll see," he said.

It felt as though, all at once, my organs had dropped into my feet. The spot between my legs twisted with desperate desire.

"We'll see . . . when? Based on what? Are you sure? You did say it felt good—like being full—"

But Theo shook his head. Not only would he climb inside of me, he said, but I would not enter him again, secretly or otherwise, before that point.

His climb would be the next. End of story.

Throughout dinner with my mom, I was barely able to listen to the conversation, so caught up was I in obsessing about Theo's ultimatum. How could I get him to climb inside me as close to immediately as possible so I could resume my entrances? Whatever fears I had about his climb, they were nothing compared to the prospect of being denied my own. Should I brainstorm portals with him? Entice him by talking incessantly about how marvelous climbing was? Use reverse psychology, pretending I didn't care at all?

I was so distracted that when my mom leaned in toward me while Theo was in the bathroom to ask if I was angry at her, I was caught off guard.

"What? No. Why?" I said.

"You've seemed—off," she said. "Plus, not wanting me to stay with you . . ." She let the sentence dangle.

"I have a boyfriend," I said slowly, as if explaining things to a child. "That was going to have to change. Did you think you could sleep with me forever?"

"Is that all?" she pressed, but Theo was returning to the table, bringing our duet to a close.

As we ate dessert, I tried to act normal, leaning in and sharing bites and laughing as though I were neither squirming to get away from my mom nor obsessing about Theo's climb. But Theo must have spent the meal thinking about it, too, because as soon as my mom paid the bill and we'd said our goodbyes—the hugging and kissing going on for so long, my mom clinging to me and then Theo, whom she kissed too close to his neck, that her cab driver threatened to leave if she didn't get in—Theo asked for the recorder, assuming correctly that I had it on me. He turned it on and, in the solemn tone one reserves for matters of ceremony, outlined the terms of our agreement: I would not climb inside of him, at any point, for any reason, until he'd climbed inside of me. "This will serve as a formal contract," he concluded.

"Amen," I said dumbly, then reached for the recorder to turn it off.

He snatched it away. "Now we each say our names, and that's our signature."

"What happens if I break the contract?" I asked.

He met my eyes with a hard, hostile look.

"You're not going to break it." His voice had the sharp edge of a military officer's.

I nodded.

Theo spoke his name, and, with no choice but to surrender, I spoke mine.

Part Three: Merger

13.

By the time the leaves began to turn, Theo still hadn't entered me. Each morning, I awoke with a nauseous kind of hope that this would be the day. But when night fell, that hope transmuted into a cold, thick melancholy. I would lie in bed beside his sleeping form, insomniac.

Whenever we were alone together, my heart raced with the possibility that he was about to do it, a feeling indistinguishable from the sickening thrill of our early relationship. Those early questions—whether and when we would fuck, whether and when he would leave, how much more I could reveal without sending him running—had been revived, if supplanted by this throbbing new one: when would he open me up, and how?

To scratch the itch, I contemplated opening Felix, with whom I was in some respects more intimate than I was with Theo. I'd wondered sporadically, since I'd begun my climbs, how his doggie insides would compare to Theo's human ones. Would I feel the familiar transcendence on splitting him open? Would my body shrink enough to fit inside him? Was Felix even accessible to me, and if so, what would my portal be? He wasn't my object of sexual desire, obviously, but neither was I my mom's, and she'd had no issues.

But this is where I always stopped myself. Though I had excused opening up Theo because he was my partner, how could I forgive myself for doing it to Felix, who was entirely dependent on me, who couldn't even talk? If it hurt, or if it frightened him, he wouldn't be able to say.

The longer Theo waited, the more desperate I became. If at first this was because I was aching to enter him again, as the weeks passed, I began to crave his reciprocation. I imagined the relief of feeling him tearing into me at last—of marking me, beyond any possible doubt, as his.

In an effort to reassure myself, I thought that perhaps Theo was stalling out of fear that it wouldn't work for him—that climbs were a talent reserved for my family. The delay could be a simple case of performance anxiety, which might resolve itself with time. But lurking behind this rationalization was the deep worry that his suggesting this role reversal had been only about ensuring I'd never climb inside him again, and that he simply didn't desire me in this way.

One night, after a full week had gone by without Theo mentioning his climb, I slammed the potato peeler down on the counter harder than I'd meant to. Felix, who was sitting at my feet waiting for scraps to fall, emitted a sharp bark. Theo looked up from his kitchen table, where he was reading as I cooked.

"Yes?" he said, though from his expression, he clearly knew.

"Are you going to do it?" I asked.

"Do what?"

"Come on."

Theo slowly folded his medical journal closed. "Be patient," he said.

Petulantly I said, "I've *been* patient."

"Obviously not patient enough."

"Okay, *sir*."

I'd said it ironically, but it had turned me on anyway. Theo, eyes still fastened on mine, seemed aware.

"Have you kept to our agreement?"

"Of course," I said, though it was true that there were nights I had come close to breaking it. Lying beside him, his lips parted so perfectly for me, and forgoing the chance to split him open was something akin to torture. What had stopped me each time was shame: I couldn't stand the thought of breaking his trust again, and climbing inside of him before he'd even tried to reciprocate was the definition of desperate. Until he did, I couldn't be sure he wanted me, and if he didn't want me, climbing inside him was rendered hollow.

"Are you really going to do it?" I asked. "If you're stringing me along, I don't think I can take it."

"Says the person who climbed inside me in secret. Like a million times."

"Okay!" I said. "I don't deserve it. But please, please tell me. I'm losing my mind." Felix scratched my leg with his paw. I bent down and petted the crown of his head, still staring at Theo. Maybe it was thanks to these loving ministrations toward Felix, whom Theo couldn't resist, that his expression softened.

"I'm going to do it," he said. "If you have to know, I think about it all the time."

For a while, this was enough to sustain me. When I was overcome, I imagined Theo hooking his fingers into one of my orifices and ripping me apart. I started basic, picturing him inserting both pinkies into my vagina and gingerly prying it open. From there, I got more creative: I imagined him suctioning his mouth to one of my eyeballs and sucking it out, then forcing the socket open, all the way down the length of my cheek and neck and chest. With a perverse thrill, I imagined him putting his delicate fingers to my nostrils and prising open my nose. If he used the same portal as my mom, would it feel nightmarish—or gratifying?

I still had the tapes of all my entrances, which I listened to when I felt I couldn't take it anymore. But with this new event on the horizon, and having shared every recording I had with Theo, the climbs of the past were less compelling than they had been before. They were no longer secret, they were no longer mine; they were old news. I wanted new material from fresh climbs, which meant waiting, with increased derangement, for the one thing I couldn't control.

Yet the days kept bleeding one into the next. Occasionally, I even caught myself distracted by something else going on in my life. When my attention returned to Theo I was surprised and proud that, for minutes on end, I had forgotten to crave him. I was, for example, lucky enough to interview Proust scholar Adaeze Akinyemi, a conversation for which I prepped madly, determined not only to reread *Remembrance of Things Past* but also to read as much of Akinyemi's scholarship as I could by the time we spoke. Her most compelling article, to me, was about the way Proust stretched sentences in order to still time, such that it seemed, for a spell, not to pass at all.

Theo, for his part, was even busier. He spent his usual sixty to eighty hours a week at the hospital, but on top of that passed the early fall working on an article based on his fellowship research, which he and his colleagues hoped to submit to a medical journal soon.

Somehow, he still found the bandwidth to accompany me to the food pantry for the first time since we'd met there. When we walked in together, holding hands, Binita put down the box she was carrying to give us a loud slow clap; the rest of the crew joined in, and I laughed and took a bow. I glanced at Theo; he was smiling sheepishly, his cheeks a fluorescent pink. When I observed him stocking shelves from across the room, his tendon flexing as he stood, revealing for a moment that shadowy hollow, I was filled for a moment less with crushing desire than with a shocked sense of fortune. He was mine.

And, when Theo's parents were in town, he asked me to meet them for a meal. It wasn't the weekend-long affair we'd had with my mom, but I got the sense that this had more to do with his ambivalence about his family than with me. The dinner was stilted, our table's awkward energy clashing with the coziness of the restaurant, but it was also in keeping with everything Theo had told me about his parents, who he'd often claimed he wished would get divorced. I'd wondered whether he really meant it, and asked what their marriage was like: a bickering steady state, he'd told me, unless they were in public, in which case they were stiff and awkward in their attempt to portray a healthy couple. This must have been what I was witnessing. "They put all their attention into their fighting—into each other," Theo said once we'd left dinner. "And I was an only child. So, it was lonely."

"Are you still lonely sometimes?" I asked, thinking back to our first date, when we'd talked about how strange it could be to live alone. But now he had me.

"Sometimes," Theo said, and my breath caught. Was I not enough for him? What if he was even lonelier in my company than when he was alone?

"Our nights apart are—"

"What?" I asked with dread.

"Hard," he said.

A piñata of giddiness burst inside me, spraying its confetti everywhere.

"I thought you liked our nights apart," I said, wanting him to repeat that he didn't, not anymore.

"I used to. But now I miss you. It honestly scares me a little."

"Why?" I said. "It's the fucking best!"

"It's not a version of myself I've known before."

"It's an awesome version of you."

"I know *you* think so."

I bit my tongue, willing myself not to get defensive. He was only pushing me away out of fear. He *wanted* to stop spending nights apart. Maybe, if I waited long enough, he would suggest it.

"I'm afraid to lose myself," he said after a while.

"You won't," I said.

"How do you know?"

"I just know."

But still, he didn't climb.

I turned thirty-four; Theo turned thirty-six. I went to New Orleans for Yom Kippur. It was a Dad Year, so Talia, Romi, and I spent it with our father, his wife Iris, and Iris's children—my *stepsiblings*—Jane and Ben. My stepmother was the principal of the high school where my dad taught; he'd met her about a decade before when he'd left his job as a consultant to teach math, which he'd apparently been dreaming about his whole working life. Jane and Ben were pleasant enough, if dull. I had the sense my mother was envious that Jane and Ben both still lived in New Orleans, while of the three of us, only Talia had stayed. I didn't have that sense with my father; if anything, it was the other way around. I never asked how much time he spent with Jane and Ben, pretending to myself he found them as dull as I did.

As for Talia, Romi, and me, our habit was to convene in New Orleans for whichever of the High Holidays fell closer to a weekend. Since this year it was Yom Kippur, I spent Rosh Hashanah, ten days beforehand, in Brooklyn at my local synagogue, having gotten in with a free ticket from a friend who belonged. My mom called the afternoon before the holiday and left me a voicemail—"*L'shanah tovah,* sweetheart!"—and, when I didn't call back within an hour, sent a follow-up text (a string of repeating apple and honey emojis) and an e-card. In the wake of her visit, she had begun calling me daily; before that, she'd rotated between my sisters and me, as if to project that she didn't really need any one of us. I'd immediately made a habit of setting my phone to Do Not Disturb and claiming, if she told me I'd missed her, that I hadn't received the call. But this was Rosh Hashanah. When I got home from the evening service, I called her back.

"*L'shanah tovah!*" she reiterated, her voice like a bell.

"You too!" I said, mirroring her singsong. As I did, I conjured Barney and rolled my eyes at him, trying to feel less angry and less alone.

My mom asked what I'd been up to for the holiday and I told her. "So nice!" she said, in a tone that suggested she wished I were spending it with her, though my sisters and I had maintained the same custom since I'd graduated from college. I asked what her plans had been: "Same as usual," she said. Usual meant getting together with my grandmother and my Aunt Deb and her family. Subtext: *It was sad and embarrassing that Aunt Deb had all her children with her, but I didn't.* Even Talia hadn't been there, I knew: she'd spent the holiday with her in-laws. I shook my head at Barney and just said: "Sounds like a great time!"

"It was. Very, very nice."

My mom said she'd called a few times over the past week. My stomach lurched. I cursed myself for calling her back, but immediately, guilt squashed my regret.

"You did? That's weird—I didn't get any voicemails."

"I always leave one," she said. "Honey, do you need a new phone?"

"Probably, but I don't want to spend the money right now," I said, my innards pinwheeling with anxiety.

"I'll buy it for you!" she said. "Belated birthday present."

Fuck, I mouthed to Barney.

"You already got me a birthday present," I said. She'd gifted me and Theo a couples massage at a fancy Manhattan hotel.

"Early half-birthday present, then."

"I really like my phone," I said lamely. "I'm used to it."

"But it's not—"

"Shoot, mom, I'm getting a work call, I've got to go. Have fun at services tomorrow, love you!"

"You too, sweetie, and don't forget you're the most amazing, wonderful, brilliant—"

"I've really got to go—"

"—daughter."

"Love you. Talk soon."

"I love you more and always."

Though Talia brought her wife to my dad's and Romi brought her family, I'd chickened out on inviting Theo: he wasn't Jewish and I didn't want him to feel embarrassed for not knowing any of the prayers, but even more than that I was afraid he wouldn't be able to come, or wouldn't want to. Despite our recent transition to sleeping together every night, the prolonged wait for his entry into me had left me feeling fragile, and this was a rejection I wasn't sure I'd be able to withstand.

After synagogue the morning of Yom Kippur, Talia, Romi, and I took our customary slow, long walk in Audubon Park to pass an hour of the fast. I was on high alert, afraid we'd run into our mom ("what a *coincidence!*"), but she was nowhere in sight. I took the opportunity to mimic her thrusting her painted nails toward Theo and batting her eyes. My sisters cackled with delight, exhilarating me.

A bike whizzed past. I led Talia and Romi off the main path to a bench overlooking a body of water at the edge of which an abnormal number of birds had congregated, squawking loudly. I told my sisters that our mom was still calling me every day and that, when we'd spoken over Rosh Hashanah, she'd offered to get me a new phone so I would be sure to get all her messages.

"She's going to do it," said Romi.

"And then what am I going to say?"

"Say you don't want to talk to her every day."

"Yeah right. As if you'd ever do that."

"Guilty. I wouldn't."

"Has she said anything to either of you?"

"She's asked me if you were okay," Romi said. "With that edge in her voice, you know? Is Olive *okay*?"

"What'd you say?"

"I said, of course she is. She just has a boyfriend."

"Which probably only made her more irritated."

"Not that she showed it. She went into her hyper-chipper mode, 'La la la!'"

"Talia, has she said anything to you?"

"No, but she knows I don't gossip—not with her, anyway. Unlike someone we know."

"I resent that," Romi said.

"She's probably still worried I'm angry with her," I said. "That, or punishing me for having her stay in a hotel." Minimal as this limit was—and weak as I'd been in enforcing it, given that I'd told a half-truth to avoid flat-out denying her—it was still one of the first times I'd told her no.

"One of the first times?" Talia said. "Or *the* first time?"

"Maybe *the*."

"Brutal," said Romi, and my anxiety spiked. I clutched my stomach, and not just because I was hungry.

"You think I was wrong to?" I asked.

"No! *No,*" said Talia.

"Where does she usually sleep when she stays with you, anyway?" Romi said.

"The couch," I lied.

"It's okay for her to stay in a hotel," Talia reassured me.

"She's not like this with you two," I said. "Right? She lets you have your partners!" But even as I protested, I knew it wasn't the same.

Talia echoed my thoughts, tenderly: "It's different with you."

"You two have your own . . . special thing," Romi added. Less tenderly.

"As if I chose it!" I said. But wasn't I choosing it now, by not sharing with them what I'd realized about her nighttime entrances? I wondered if Romi was jealous. For most of my life, I'd been so envious of the two of them—insulated from the divorce by being out of the house, insulated from our mother by the fact of each other—that it hadn't occurred to me that either of them would be envious of me. Before Talia was born, Romi had gotten a taste of what it was like to command the entirety of our parents' attention—something that until now I'd thought of only as a burden. Maybe, to her mind, in having our mom to myself for so long, I had received a kind of love that had been, for a precious few years, hers.

"What do you think I should do?" I asked.

"Talk to her," Talia said. "Tell her you need space right now. Better in than out."

Well, that I wasn't going to do.

Instead, as soon as I returned to New York, the leaves blooming ochre and orange, I asked Theo if we could make last-minute plans to spend a few days in the Hudson Valley, to catch autumn's climax. Though we were together whenever we weren't at work, I anticipated several days of uninterrupted Theo time with something like madness. If he was going to climb inside of me, I couldn't imagine why he wouldn't do it while we were away.

In the days leading up to the trip, I spent all my spare time researching, imagining, packing and then repacking everything from undergarments (sexy or casual?) to "stylish" hats I knew I'd never wear. In an effort to conceal my overexcited energy, I booked us a house charming only for its lack of obvious appeal, in a town I'd never heard of. Peeling light blue exterior; graying awnings. I'd insisted it was a surprise—a huge mistake, I realized as we pulled our rental car up to the ramshackle place at the end of the road, which, it turned out, mostly functioned as an auto repair shop. Car carcasses were strewn across the lawn; through the windows of the bottom floor we observed hanging machinery that resembled an elaborate medieval torture device. "Kinky," Theo said, without conviction. As we ascended the rickety wooden staircase to what was apparently "our" floor, I prayed the inside was better, but no: frayed floral-printed quilt; splintering dresser with a faded Monet print propped on top; thin blinds that hung, crooked and bent, halfway down the windows.

"I chose terribly," I said.

"It's fine!" Theo said.

"I didn't want to look like I'd tried too hard," I said. "You know, researching it for hours or something."

"Oh, is *that* it," he said, coming over and touching his hand to my waist. "But trying hard is cool."

"Cool?" I asked. "Or hot?"

In answer, he slipped his hand into my travel spandex and between my legs.

After, we went online to find a new place. On the map, Theo hovered his mouse over a huge house a short drive away, in a town called Babson. When the per-day price popped up, I sucked in air.

"Don't even click," I said. "It'll make me sad."

Theo usually paid when we went out; it was obvious—from my roommate situation if not my job—that he had a lot more money. But he hadn't, as yet, explicitly offered to cover this trip, and I wasn't about to ask, especially since it had been my idea.

Now, though, he said, "What if I pay for it?"

"No, no," I insisted, though I absolutely wanted him to. "Let's split it."

"Come on." He clicked the listing open: a floor-through, sunlight pouring in through the huge windows.

"The owner clearly knows how to take a photograph," I said.

"There's even a terrace," Theo said, scrolling through the images.

"They all have terraces. And I'm sure that vase of tulips isn't there anymore." I pictured straddling Theo on the perfect white couch.

"So you *don't* want to stay there?"

"Okay," I said, holding my palms face-out. "I want to."

The tulips were, surreally, in the apartment when we arrived, accompanied by a note: "Welcome, T & O!" We unpacked, then got naked and climbed into bed.

When we awoke it was dark out, and we were both starving, but too dazed and lazy to go out. Our hosts had left us some breakfast food, so I made two bowls of oatmeal and poured in the sweet nut mix I'd snacked on in the car, plus a little honey.

"Actually good," Theo admitted through a mouthful. We ate in bed, still undressed, now watching television on his laptop; before we'd even brushed our teeth, we'd fallen back asleep.

The trip passed in this kind of milky dream. It was almost enough to forget what I was waiting for. Who needed to be opened up when normal life could be so full? An hours-long walk, ice creams in hand even in the biting wind, my scarf wound over my head in a way that prompted Theo to call me "babushka." Huddling together in the clear brisk air on a bench in the town square, people-watching. Here was an older couple, each reading a different section of the newspaper. There was a middle-aged woman with a dog panting on her lap, her outfit immaculate: black pants, black pumps, little jacket cut exactly to her waist, black too with flashes of royal blue. And there was a young couple flirting coyly, the woman swinging her feet against the dusty floor, thick scarf coiling her neck. On our second day, the Babson Museum of Nature, which one internet commenter had described as containing "every piece of random animal-related shit you could dream up, and a bunch you couldn't." Theo and I strolled, holding hands, by the placid-looking stuffed fox in a glass case, through the room of dog paintings, by the bejeweled wild boar and the dinner table flanked by two enormous bears. We saved for last the little room whose ceiling was a mosaic of taxidermied owls. Theo stood behind me, pressing himself into me. I turned around and grabbed his hipbones like a steering wheel.

The last night of our trip, I couldn't sleep, thinking about our return. We'd get in late the next night—we were determined to have one last dinner in Babson before driving back—and go to bed barely a few hours before Theo had to head to the hospital. I would try to keep sleeping after he left, waking up only at the last possible minute before work, but I knew I wouldn't manage it; I'd be lying awake as I was now, the emptiness on his side of the bed a rebuke.

There was a warmth to this anticipatory distress. It was a detour I took to feel even more intensely Theo's presence beside me now. It attuned me to the heat of his skin, pressed against mine and radiating underneath the covers; to the soft rumble of his snoring; to the flutter of his eyelids mid-dream.

I hoped that when we got back, I would be able to preserve this feeling as a touchstone, that it would carry me through the pain of having to be separate from him once more. But I feared that, instead, it would resume: my excruciating and all-consuming obsession. The whole weekend, he hadn't climbed inside me. I didn't know how much longer I would last.

14.

The leaves fell, collecting in heaps around lampposts and leaving branches stretching disrobed and spindly toward the sky. Any thought I'd had about storing up our time in Babson as reserves for the days following our trip proved delusional. It was as though on vacation, the fullness of our connection had ballooned inside me, only now to vanish, leaving a cavity behind.

Whatever equanimity I'd found about Theo's failure to climb inside me had disappeared along with it. If before Babson I'd been in distress, now I was in agony. Vacation was where you proposed marriage, conceived children. Vacation was where, if you were going to climb inside your partner, you did it.

And he hadn't.

I wondered if Theo was afraid not of being unable to access me, nor of hurting me, but rather that, once he'd crawled inside me and sealed me back up, he'd be stuck inside. Did he fear that he wouldn't be able to figure out his exit, or even that I wouldn't let him back out? The thought sent a chill over my neck and scalp. If he never did it, how could I go on believing that he really loved me?

After six excruciating weeks, I was nearing sleep when Theo pressed himself into my side. It took me a moment to reorient myself—Felix was snoring at the foot of the bed; only the three of us were here; there was Theo's dresser; we were in his apartment—and another moment to register his erection. Heat surged through my limbs. I turned to face him. His lips were parted, his breath thick in his throat. He threaded his fingers through my hair, tugging hard. Now wide awake, I wound my leg around him and pulled him toward me; Theo put his hand to my throat, pressed his fingers hard into the muscles of my neck, then shoved me onto my back. We locked eyes, mouths open, predators.

He was going to do it.

He untied my pajama pants, ripped them down, pushed my knees into my chest and traced, with his finger, my asshole. I emitted a guttural sound.

"You like that?" said Theo.

"I like it," I said in a hard whisper. My body felt electric. Was this how he'd open me? Even though neither of us wanted to have anal, even though Theo looked at assholes all day long? In all my imaginings, I hadn't bothered to picture Theo entering me here. But if he wanted to, he could: he could open me wherever he wanted.

Felix had perked up as my breathing grew sharper and, into the space between Theo's body and mine, wedged his head. Theo nudged him away. He pried my ass cheeks apart with his fingers, then pushed one inside the tight rim. I let out a gasp of pleasure.

"So you *like* that," Theo said again.

"I like it." My voice sounded strange to me, husky and deep.

He pushed another finger inside.

"You like that?"

Mutely I assented. I liked it so much that I felt, shockingly, like I was about to come.

There were multiple fingers inside my asshole. It hurt and I liked it.

"You like that?"

"I like it."

He leaned down as if to go down on me, his hair tickling the delicate skin, but then his tongue was on my asshole, inside it.

"You like that?"

"I like it."

He probed my asshole with his tongue, moved up to my clit, inside my vagina, back to my asshole. He was probably giving me a UTI but I didn't care, my whole body was shimmering like heat in the distance. I lost track of where he was and where he wasn't, where I was and where I was not, when I came I felt like I was going to break open and I did, I squirted all over the bed in a big puddle.

I started cackling uncontrollably. "Holy shit," I said. And now he was going to do it. I kept my eyes closed, still laughing, waiting for the feel of his fingers on my asshole, prying it apart. Time passed. I stopped laughing. Theo's weight shifted as he lay next to me. I opened my eyes.

"Goodnight," Theo said.

* * *

By our six-month anniversary, veering between the high hum of anxiety about whether Theo would ever climb inside me and the low moan of despair that he hadn't had become unbearable. I tried to put the whole thing out of my mind and focus instead on the relationship we had, the fact that we'd made it a full half-year: the longest I had ever dated anyone. It helped that my hair, which had grown brittle despite my leave-in conditioner regimen when I'd been inside of Theo regularly, had returned to its normal texture; my skin had stopped flaking. I changed the file names of my recordings from "Climb 1," "Climb 2," "Climb 3," and on, to the dates on which they'd been recorded and moved them to a separate folder titled "A Dumb Story." I stopped listening to the tapes, stopped allowing myself to imagine his hands anywhere near any of my orifices, much less inside them, for anything other than sex.

I leaned hard into the role of "normal girlfriend." I surprised Theo with a halfiversary celebration—got him a pint of ice cream, sliced a neat diameter into it, and threw half into the garbage; cut chocolate truffles from the bodega in half and then rewrapped them; bought him a card with a ghost on the front that read "My boo" and, before writing on it, cut it in half, too. I bought him a shirt from my favorite store in New Orleans; as he unwrapped it I panicked that it was overkill. But he only said, "I'm so relieved you didn't cut this in half—it's perfect." I was trying to ignore my disappointment and embarrassment that he hadn't gotten me anything, hadn't considered this anniversary worth celebrating, when he said, "So—" and told me to get dressed, he'd made a dinner reservation to celebrate.

On the street, the sun was deep into setting, and threw amber light across his face. He looked like he'd stepped out of a film. The image thrust itself into my mind of his chin, neck, torso splitting open, revealing his organs—against this vision I slipped my hand into his, tried to guess where he was taking me and chose right on the first try: Inga's, a candlelit place that served simple dishes and was our favorite spot in Theo's neighborhood. We always got the focaccia, always the ricotta; each time we chided ourselves for unwaveringly following such a basic routine, but each time we did it anyway and were happy. Before we'd left, I'd slipped my recorder into my bag; it was off, and I figured I would wait until we were seated to ask, in a sexy way if I could muster it, if Theo wanted me to turn it on.

As we walked, my phone rang: it was my mom. Theo urged me to pick up, seemingly out of politeness. I didn't need to, I said, we were on a special date—but he waved me away.

"Sweetheart!" my mom said in singsong. "I haven't heard enough of your voice lately."

"I'm here now," I said. Since my conversation with Talia and Romi, our mother had continued to reach out to me at least daily. I'd tried to return her calls just enough to outmaneuver irritation or suspicion, but apparently, I hadn't met the quota.

"Is everything okay? You sound tense—" my mom said.

"Everything is fine! Theo and I are just walking to dinner, so I don't have much time."

"Oh—well, I wouldn't want to interrupt."

"It's fine," I said. "We aren't there yet."

I asked about her gardening. She listed everything she'd planted for the fall in excruciating detail. *Sorry*, I mouthed to Theo, signaling that my mother wouldn't stop talking, but he shook his head, banishing my apology. I kicked a rock and it skittered down the sidewalk. When we caught up to it, Theo kicked it again. Finally I couldn't take hearing about one more vegetable and said I had to go.

"Sweetie, are you mad at me?" my mom asked. She hadn't asked me this in a while. My insides seized up. "Have I done something?"

"Of course not," I said, my heart pounding. "What would you have done?"

"I don't know—"

"I'm just in a rush right now," I said. "Theo's right beside me and I'm being rude. It's nothing to do with you." This was a version of something I'd said in the past when it *hadn't* been about my mom but rather about my own private mood. *Are you mad at me?* she would intrude. *You can tell me.* As if I thought of, reacted to, nothing and nobody else.

"All right. Enjoy your dinner, sweetie, and tell Theo I say hello, okay?"

"I will." I wouldn't.

"But if you change your mind and want to tell me whatever it is, I'm here."

"There's nothing to tell."

"Okay," she said, her voice lonely. My stomach lurched in the familiar way.

"I love you," I said.

"I love you more and always." As I pulled the phone away from my ear to hang up, I heard her tinny voice continue, saying something I couldn't make out. I held the phone back up to my ear.

"What?"

"Can I say a quick hi to Theo?"

Too startled to say anything else, I said, "Okay." I handed him the phone: "She wants to say hi to you."

He raised his eyebrows and took it. "Hi, Mrs.—" He paused as my mom cut in, then smiled. "Cecilia. Right. Sorry, sorry." He paused again, listening, and laughed. "Formal, or polite?" Paused again. "Well, you're definitely not that." I was desperate to hear what she was saying and afraid to find out. Had she said being called Mrs. made her feel old? She'd always insisted my friends call her by her first name, too, even before she'd ceased to be a Mrs.

Theo was laughing again. What the hell was my mom saying? I felt as left out as I had when she'd visited and I'd incarnated Barney across the table. Theo was barely speaking, just "Mmm-hmm"-ing and "Really?"-ing and "Well, of course!"-ing. Of course *what*? When we arrived at Inga's, they were still talking.

"We're here," I said flatly.

"Oh, Cecilia, I have to go, we've reached the restaurant." He paused, laughed yet again. "I won't. Bye. You too."

He hung up. So my mom hadn't wanted to get back on with me for a bookend goodbye.

When we entered the restaurant, I kept my eyes trained on the hostess, unable to look at Theo. She greeted us by name—it was that kind of place, and we'd come that often—and bent to slide two menus out of the hostess stand. "Right this way," she said. We followed her to our table, passing two women talking with animated hands, a family with a bored young kid staring at his phone, a party table. Theo put his hand on my lower back as we walked, as though nothing was wrong.

We sat at our favorite table, in a dark and cozy corner. It was a busy night, which meant that Theo had requested the table specifically. I tried to soften, but I felt too abandoned. Theo always let me sit with my back to the wall, as I preferred, and though under normal circumstances we'd play-fight for it—I'd dart into the seat and poke his stomach with a percussive "ha!"—that night I sat down without fanfare and immediately opened my menu.

"What is it?" he asked.

"What did my mom have to say?" I asked, eyes still trained on my menu.

"She misses you," he said.

"Well, there's a reason for that."

"I know. But you still love her, right?"

"You think I owe her something, after all that?"

"I didn't say that."

I didn't respond.

Our server came. We ordered the focaccia and the ricotta, as we always did; separate mains; a bottle of wine. We waited without speaking. The din wasn't enough to make it not awkward. The wine came; Theo tasted; our glasses were filled, and I ran my thumbs along the raised lettering on the bottle's label, studying it so I wouldn't have to look Theo in the eye. He reached across the table and took my wrist in his hand, then lowered his head to look up at me, trying to meet my gaze.

"What did you say 'Of course' to?" I asked.

"What?"

"With my mom."

"Oh—it's a surprise."

"You're planning something together?"

"For you."

I blinked rapidly.

"Tell me what it is," I said.

"It's a nice thing. I promise." Theo looked away, indicating he wouldn't say more. Surely, I thought, he had absorbed enough about my current dynamic with my mother to appreciate that I wanted space from her. Ideally they were co-arranging some gift from afar—nothing that would invite her into our orbit. Something Theo would deliver to me when it came. But his comments about her missing me, about whether I still loved her, worried me. What if it *was* a visit? Without me involved in the planning, would she manipulate her way into staying with me? My own climbs exploded back into my mind: Theo's heart contracting and expanding in his split-open chest, the shushing sound of air flooding his lungs, his hot slick organs against my skin, the tannic scent of him. I wanted to be inside him, I wanted him inside me, I wanted to be closer than we could get sleeping side by side or even fucking, closer than it was possible for two bodies to be.

I reached down toward my bag to pull out the recorder.

"We haven't in a while," I said. "Do you want to?"

"It's not on already, is it?"

I said it wasn't.

He nodded: *do it*.

ME: So.

THEO: So.

ME: Can I ask?
THEO: Ask what?
ME: You know.
[Pause]
ME: Why haven't you—
THEO: The food—
[Clang of plates being served]
ME: Please, tell me.
THEO: Why haven't I what?
ME: Stop it.
THEO: Say it.
ME: You're being cruel.
[Long pause]
THEO: What if I'm not able to do it?
ME: That can't be it.
THEO: It's a reason.
ME: Please at least try. I need you to. *Please.*
[Pause]
ME: Are you scared of being inside me?
THEO: I've been *inside* you before—
ME: Don't deflect.
THEO: What if it hurts you?
ME: Are you actually afraid of that? Or is it that you still haven't figured out where to enter me? Because you don't—think of me that way—
THEO: You're testing me.
ME: I'm right.
[Pause]
ME: Aren't I?
THEO: I do know where.
ME: Where?

THEO: I'm not telling.
ME: Come on.
THEO: You don't get to be in charge of everything.
ME: Have you always known where?
[Long pause. The screech of a knife scraping against a plate; diners' murmurs; wineglasses chiming.]
ME: You're really going to do it.
THEO: You have to wait now. That's your only job. Wait.

That night, in Theo's bed, I nudged Felix from in between us to the foot of the bed and turned on my side to face Theo. He was in his bedtime uniform—an old, holed T-shirt and boxer briefs, this pair patterned with dancing dinosaurs—and I thought I'd never felt more tenderly toward a human being in my life. He was going to do it. I had to wait, but he was going to do it: he knew where. I lifted the hem of his shirt to his nipples, gave him an inquisitive look; he nodded, sitting up so I could lift the shirt over his head.

I undressed Theo as delicately as though I were peeling the skin from a grape. Even as I slid his boxers down over his penis, it was stirring to life. I pulled them past his knees, down his shins, then unearthed one foot and then the other, pressing my thumbs to their arches. My fingertips moved over the tops of his feet and then up his calves and thighs and toward his groin; his penis lifted in response. Before I took it into my mouth, I let a thin line of spit descend onto it like a spider. At the touch of my saliva, Theo sucked in air.

Soon he was in my mouth, and then moaning; soon his breathing was ragged in his throat; soon he had wrenched me onto my back and grabbed my wrists. I kissed him hungrily, biting him, and he bit me back, on my shoulder, my neck, my earlobe. With his tongue he moved along the crease behind my ear, flicked the shell of cartilage at the top, moved sinuously toward my earhole and licked circles around its rim. The wet sounds of his tongue echoed loudly. I tensed away.

"Relax," Theo whispered. The tip of his tongue pressed into my earhole, hard and then harder, like a sexy snail.

"It's loud," I said.

He retracted his tongue—"Shh"—then shoved it in again, so hard it hurt, so deep it felt like he was licking my brain. My earhole must have widened, because suddenly I couldn't hear out of that side anymore. I could only feel the wet meat of his tongue moving deep inside my head.

The split felt less like the ripping agony of first sex and more like an all-encompassing ache. I pictured the opening as enormous—a black hole where my tiny earhole used to be. I was still intact; from that angle, nothing appeared different at all. My ear pulsed with a hungry kind of pain.

"Lie on your side," said Theo in a forceful tone. Felix, who'd been licking my toes, flung his head up and yipped.

"Give him a rawhide," I said, my heart pounding, and gestured toward the drawer. Theo did as instructed.

"Now. Lie down," he said to me.

I obeyed, my open ear facing the ceiling.

Theo's fingers hooked into me; the ache spread; I imagined a gust of wind passing by and sweeping my brain out onto the floor. There was a tickle—Theo's hair against my cheek—and then a colossal pressure as he pushed himself inside my head. I cried out, but the pressure only deepened—were his own ears inside of me already, such that he couldn't hear me? I lifted my head in an attempt to see what was going on, a contortion that pushed Theo back out. He blinked rapidly, wiping the slime out of his eyes, his hair slicked into sticky peaks.

"Stay still," he said firmly, strands of slime stretching between his lips. My middle wrenched with nausea. I lay back down, stared at the wall, listened to Felix gnawing, the rawhide cracking between his teeth.

The ache; the pressure; my nausea transmuting into a pulsing pleasure. I shut my eyes and focused on the sounds: the packing-tape rip; the squelch of my brain shifting to accommodate him; the faint slurp that meant he was fully inside me and had made me, once again, whole.

And then it was Felix and me. My head felt only slightly heavier than usual, as though I'd had a glass of wine too many. How had Theo fit himself in? He must have shrunk more than I had; was he lying with my brain pressed to his stomach, spooning it, his back pressed to the underside of my skull? Or was he coiled underneath the brain, feet dangling into my throat? Had he shrunk so much he could fit himself into one of my brain's folds? I wondered, with a start, if he could read my mind; but when I'd inched myself up toward his head from inside him, I'd heard only those faint sputtering sparks, a code indecipherable from the outside. If only it were possible, I could think at him now: *I love you. I miss you.* But no; I knew that Theo could no more access my thoughts than a fetus could those of its mother.

Sounds floated toward me: a baby's cry; a car horn; a loud, barking laugh. Slowly, so slowly, I shifted to my back, taking care not to jostle Theo, afraid to lie on my other side because who knew if that would suffocate him? I beckoned Felix to curl up next to me, but he stared at me from the foot of the bed, still chewing, unblinking. Like this, we waited.

The sounds outside shifted further nightward: music from a tinny smartphone speaker turned up too loud; drunken yelling; low-throated teen boy laughter. I tried to fall asleep to make the time pass faster, but I couldn't. What was he doing in there? I lifted my head, sending the bulk of Theo sliding toward my neck, to let him know I had that power. I could still breathe, but I'd been right to worry when it had been me doing the crawling: my breath came short and shallow with him there.

I tried again to sleep. I could not. I tried to meditate, which was basically half-sleeping—but every few moments my eyes flew open, disobedient. I cursed my failure to specify an amount of time that he could reside in me before opening me back up again. Was he staying in there longer and longer to spite me? I tensed my neck muscles, trying to push him out. No response. I reached toward my ear and circled the hole: it felt soft as peach skin, normal as could be. I stuck my pinky inside, trying to touch Theo. Could he see my fingertip, poking through? Was this a way of communication? I curled it, beckoning him. But still: nothing.

In one world, having Theo inside me forever wouldn't be so bad. It would mean I'd get to be with him all the time: I'd carry him to work with me and on my walks with Felix; I'd lie down in bed with him every night; I'd eat meals I knew he would enjoy, even if he could no longer taste them. I'd never have to say goodbye when he went to work, never have to wait for him to come home, never feel the spike of resentment when he said he'd be late, to just give him an hour, two hours, the night. When I wanted to say hi, I'd stick my finger inside my ear, wiggle it around. If he wanted to say hi, he could poke at my skull from the inside. If he poked me hard, it would mean he wanted my attention, and I would press my hands to my forehead, soothing him.

But this could only last for a few days, maximum, before the questions would start. What would I say to the hospital when he hadn't shown up, or called? How would I explain it to his family? How, even, would I explain it to mine? They'd invite Theo over for

Thanksgiving and I'd explain that, actually, he *was* here, just not *here*-here, ha ha, if that made sense!

Felix had finished his rawhide. I called to him again, begging him to come lie next to me and keep me company, but he continued staring at me from the foot of the bed, as if he knew what I was imagining and was judging me for it. I slapped at the spot right next to me, but still he sat staring, finally laying his head down on his paws and closing his eyes.

Of course, the worst part of keeping Theo inside me was that I wouldn't be able to talk to him anymore, my favorite thing to do. How I crave it now: a simple conversation. I could bring him to the Met, but I wouldn't be able to hear any of his insights; it would be no different from going to the Met with Felix. I could read a book aloud before bed with Theo nestled inside me, and though I was confident he'd be able to hear the broad outlines of my voice, I doubted the words would come through with any definition—a theory I've since tested and know now to be true; it's more akin to music. Even if he *could* make out everything I'd said, I would never know, with him housed inside me, whether he'd been moved or perturbed, whether it was a book we should continue or one he'd rather let go. I would never hear if he thought the protagonist's longing for her father was convincingly drawn, if he thought her imagination was a stand-in for something greater or a diversion.

It was at this moment that my impatience bled into worry: why hadn't he come out yet? Was something wrong? And then I realized that I couldn't remember what Theo looked like.

"Theo!" I yelled. Felix shot up at the sound of my voice, barking, then finally came over to me and stuck his head in my face; I pulled him to me, clutching him and praying for Theo to come back out. Theo, who had maybe gotten stuck inside me, against his will and against even mine, Theo, whom I'd never again be able to press myself against, whose laugh I wouldn't hear throating its way through the room, whose hand I'd never feel cupping my skin—

And then there it was again, the aching pressure, this time with a slight accompanying burn, as though I were being singed at the edges, a feeling that spread from that little hole throughout my head, down my neck and torso, enveloping me in delicious throbbing pain, pain that meant Theo was emerging, that he would again be next to me, would talk to me again, would laugh with me, would again be able to hold me. By the time he had slithered out onto my pillow and zipped me back up, I was doubled over with insane laughter.

"What, do I look like shit?"

"More—like—brain," I said in between my gasping, hiccupping hysterics.

"You're laughing because I have your brain juice on me?"

"No—I—" But I couldn't finish my sentence. Theo grabbed a pillow to wipe his face on, and even as I recoiled at the thought of my own innards on my daisy-patterned pillowcase, watching him set off another round of laughter—which, abruptly, morphed into tears.

Theo dropped the pillow and put his arm around me.

"Did I hurt you?" he whispered.

I shook my head, said I was just completely and utterly relieved.

"I didn't think you'd come out," I said. "What took you so long?"

"I fell asleep . . . it was really relaxing in there. . . ."

"I was freaking out."

"I assumed you'd know," he said. "Seeing as you slept inside me?"

"Can you not guilt me right now?" I wiped snot from my nose with the back of my hand.

"I thought this was what you wanted," he said.

"It was," I said. "I thought it was. It was much harder than I imagined."

"What about it?"

"Missing you," I said.

"But I was with you," he said. "*In* you."

I shrugged.

He scratched the back of his head. His fingers came back with slime on them.

"This is disgusting," he said. "I'm going to take a shower."

As he got up from the bed, leaving behind a yellow smudge, his eyes snapped open as if he'd just remembered something. He asked if we'd recorded the climb.

I shook my head. We'd turned the recorder off before we'd left the restaurant, and in the chaos of being opened up and having Theo inside me, I'd forgotten, for the first time ever, to turn it on.

"Fuck," he said. "I can't believe it."

"I'll turn it on for when you get back," I said. "We can recount everything."

By the time Theo returned, towel tied around his waist and skin pinky-raw from scrubbing, I'd changed the sheets and stuffed the soiled ones into a trash bag, which I shoved into my closet. I would deal with it later. I set the recorder on the desk next to my bed.

ME: It's on.
THEO: How could we forget?
ME: We can turn it on next time.
THEO: If there is one.
ME: You don't . . . want to do it again? You didn't like it?
THEO: I *liked* it—I mean, I fell asleep—
ME: It's relaxing. Right?
THEO: Right. But . . .
ME: It grossed you out?
THEO: No, more like . . .
ME: What? Say it. It won't insult me.

THEO: . . . it was boring?

ME: *Boring.* Are you kidding?

THEO: It felt a little like a workday. But slimier. More squish, less perspective.

ME: That is the wildest thing I've ever heard.

THEO: I prefer to mess with organs from above. But come on, would you want to, like, interview people on your off time?

ME: Yes. I thought that was obvious.

THEO: Well, okay. So we're different. I have . . .

ME: What?

THEO: . . . compartmentalization.

ME: You were going to say *boundaries*.

THEO: Maybe.

[Pause]

ME: So you don't want to do it anymore? You hated being inside me that much?

THEO: I didn't say that.

ME: —found it dull? Found *me* dull?

THEO: Were you listening to me?

ME: Then what did you say?

THEO: I like it better when you do it to me. That's all.

ME: Oh. *Oh.*

THEO: Aren't you happy?

ME: I mean—yes.

THEO: You look weird.

ME: I'm in shock.

THEO: Why?

ME: The agreement, you taking so long to do it, then saying it was *boring*—well, I figured it was over. That this was the finale.

THEO: Surprise.

ME: So I can still climb inside you.

THEO: Right.

ME: Whenever I want.

THEO: That's not what I said.

ME: *[Loud sigh]* What the fuck?

THEO: No need to be so exasperated.

ME: You want me to be exasperated.

THEO: Can you let me finish?

[Pause]

THEO: All you have to do is ask my permission.

ME: Fine. That seems fair.

THEO: At least a week in advance. So I can prepare.

ME: Come *on*! You expect me to wait for an entire *week*?

THEO: Would you prefer never?

ME: No.

THEO: Okay then.

[Pause]

THEO: Oh. And one more thing.

[Pause]

THEO: I want you to record inside me. Every single time.

15.

For a month we went along like this, with such normalcy that I marveled I'd ever thought it would be a problem. Each Saturday, I would request permission to access him the following Friday night, and he would grant it. He always wanted to be awake and sometimes would ask for a particular soundtrack, or that I wear a certain outfit, which I would remove piece by piece prior to my entrance. The rhythm became as predictable as I'd heard married sex could be. I figured we could go on like this forever.

Buoyed by this routine, our bond flourished. Together we lay in bed, reading side by side or watching a show on the computer or having sex. Together we cooked and ate dinner and talked about our days. (His article was accepted; I got to interview Bonnie Ko, a poet I'd been after for a year; some patients died and others lived.) We spent Thanksgiving in New York—Theo's call schedule didn't allow him to travel—eating sweets and watching movies. We talked to my mom on speakerphone and sent her flowers to let her know we missed her at the holiday (Theo's idea, which sparked a flash of insecurity, but which mollified my mom). We made plans to spend Christmas in Poughkeepsie with his family (*this* I postponed telling my mom about). We watched Felix sleep, watched him lick himself, watched him nose into my closet and extract a sock from my laundry pile, shaking it as though it were prey. He would prance over to us, the sock dangling from his mouth; one of us would tug at it, lowering our gaze to his and play-growling back at him. When he released the sock, we tossed it to the other end of the room and Felix bunny-hopped over to it, mouthed it and shook it again—"You killed it!" we praised him—and then pranced back over to us.

Things with my mom, meanwhile, had improved. She'd returned to calling me only every few days, giving me that modicum of space. Why, I had no idea, nor did I have it in me to overtly wonder. Since the conversation on Theo's and my six-month-iversary, she hadn't asked again whether I was angry at her. She hadn't even asked about my poop. Our conversations centered on the bare facts of life: her gardening, my work, the New York restaurants I'd been to, the people she'd seen in our New Orleans neighborhood. She was interested in my relationship, but I sensed she was trying not to pry. Nor had any surprise co-planned by her and Theo materialized; I figured they'd both forgotten about it. During our calls, my mother avoided making innuendos about Theo's and my sex life and asked only what we'd done that week and whether I was still happy. On one occasion, when I told her I'd barely been at my own apartment in a month, she asked if Theo's apartment was safe enough: were there locks on the doors of the building, apartment, and rooms within? I rolled my eyes—her anxiety about safety irked me—but I felt cared-for, too. I assured her there were locks everywhere, though we didn't tend to lock Theo's bedroom at night, since we were the only ones in the apartment. This, she said, made total sense.

I felt happier, calmer, than I had since I could remember. Ever since Theo and I had met, I'd been craving this stability and terrified it would never come. And before that had been the seemingly interminable, torturous yawn of singlehood. I had made it, at last. Even asking Theo to officially move in together seemed doable. We never slept apart. What was at risk? Getting through and beyond the conflicts we'd already scaled—the recordings, the climbs—was a far bigger deal. Now that we'd arrived, and now that we were practically living together already, how could he say no?

One Thursday night, on the first snowfall of the year, as we stood at his counter chopping red peppers for shakshuka, I rehearsed the question in my mind. But each time I was about to ask, I stalled, telling myself I'd do it when I finished this pepper, or when I moved on to the garlic, or the onion. We chopped without speaking, companionably. Music floated in the background, a cooking playlist I'd made at work. Felix sat at our feet, waiting for scraps. With his toes, Theo scratched at the opposite ankle. His phone, face-up on the counter next to his cutting board, flashed with a message. He looked at it and gave that lopsided smile I'd loved since the first day we met.

I'd asked him before not to leave his phone out during "together time," and from time to time he was able to comply, but if he was on call, the discussion was a nonstarter. Though I understood this on a rational level, I still could never help the swell of irritation at being left out of whatever conversation was transpiring.

"Who is it?" I asked.

"Nobody," he said coyly.

I laid the knife on the cutting board and turned to face him.

"Seriously," I said.

He turned the screen to black, put it back on the counter.

"I can't say."

I snatched the phone and started inputting his password. Theo snatched it back.

"Okay—it was your mom," he said.

I stared at him.

"My mom?"

"Is it wrong to text your mom?"

Rationally, no, it wasn't wrong. Plenty of people had relationships with their partners' parents. Plenty of people *wanted* their partners to have relationships with their parents, even when they had complicated feelings toward those parents, weird histories with them.

But this was *my* mom. Even though we'd been doing well lately, the thought gave me a sick feeling. In all our phone calls, she'd never mentioned texting Theo. I'd figured that, despite taking his number, she'd never used it. I thought about her desire to eat off the same communal plates as Theo and me the first time I'd introduced them, her finger-waggling, how she'd kissed his neck when she'd said goodbye.

"What does she text you about?"

"Usually she asks about you."

Perhaps this was why my mom hadn't been reaching out to me as much lately, or prying for details about my relationship: unbeknownst to me, she'd had access to me all along. Imagining the texts ("What are you and Olive up to tonight?" "Dinner and a movie." "And then . . . ? ;)") made me queasy. If I were to confront her, she'd say, *What's the harm? This way I can check in on you without bothering you!* She would say, *Theo doesn't mind, because*—and she'd say this part pointedly, suggestively—*I'm not his mother.*

"It started out planning this surprise," Theo continued. My stomach somersaulted. "Which is what she was just texting about—why I didn't want to tell you."

"I thought that was just a passing thing," I said. "Like when you run into someone on the street and say you'll make brunch plans soon."

"Yeah, no. She actually wanted to plan this."

"What is it?"

"You really want to know?"

"I hate surprises. I figured you knew that about me."

Theo held up his hands.

"She was insistent," he said.

"But this is *my mom,* the person who—"

"But you still want a relationship with her, right? And you want me to have one?"

"I guess so—"

"And you said not to say anything to her about that, so what was I supposed to do?"

"Tell me what the surprise is."

He sighed. "She's coming to visit again."

My head went light. After my mom's last trip to New York, I'd made plain that the next time, I wanted ample warning. I'd tried to phrase it in a way that would flatter her: I wanted time to plan special activities for us, to secure dog walks for Felix, to make reservations at restaurants that filled up far in advance. She had said, "I'll tell you at least a month in advance," to which I'd replied, "You'll *ask* me at least a month in advance." She'd repeated the phrase back to me and added: "I promise."

And here she was, "surprising" me, as if that conversation had never taken place. Theo hadn't been there for it, so she could safely assume he wouldn't be aware that what she was proposing was a breach. He might even think it was kind. Maybe she'd said to him, "Only if that sounds good to you!" Who but my mother's daughters would know this meant, "I will get what I want, and there's nothing you can do about it"? Did she suspect that I'd figured out about her climbs and wasn't ever going to make myself vulnerable to them again if I could help it? I would stay up all night if I had to.

"But why was she texting *you* about her visit?" I asked. "What's there to plan with you?"

He looked down and resumed chopping. "She wants to cook a meal for us while we're at work," he said. "I thought it was sweet. I said she could use my place."

His eyes were trained on his cutting board.

"Is there something you aren't telling me?"

"No." He still wouldn't look at me.

"Yes, there is." I stared at him so hard I hoped he could feel it on his skin.

"I said she could sleep there," he said.

I felt the blood drain from my face.

"How did she get you to do that?"

"I mean, I offered. She said she knows there isn't room at your place."

He only thought he'd offered freely. Of this I was positive. My mom had probably asked for hotel suggestions as close to his place as possible, then exuded disappointment when he said it wasn't really a hotel area. Maybe she'd given him impossible requirements: a hotel with a spa that was under two hundred dollars a night, or one whose rooms just happened to all have working kitchens, terraces, and views of Manhattan.

"So the idea is that we'll all stay here together? Or what?"

"The couch in the office is a pullout," he said.

"I know what your apartment has in it."

"So we can stay on that and give your mom my bed. If you want."

My mind raced. What was she playing at? Images presented themselves to me: my mother looming above me, distorted to monstrous proportions; my mother prying apart my nose; my mother peeking at me from inside my body—my *pool,* as I still called it to myself— before she sealed herself inside. Was she maneuvering to stay in the same apartment as me so that she could climb inside me again, with Theo right beside us? Maybe keeping the secret from both of us at once titillated her. Or maybe she wanted him to watch. Was he helping her execute this plan—knowingly?

"You said you didn't tell her you know about what she did," I said slowly.

"I didn't."

"Do you promise? Because it seems like—"

"I swear. I would never."

But I was hardly comforted. My own boyfriend, who knew what my mother had done to me, had still invited her to stay with us, in his apartment. It felt as though he was choosing her over me. As though he was offering me up as some kind of sacrifice.

"I don't know why you thought—" I began. I couldn't bring myself to spell out for him the possibility that she would climb inside me again, with him right beside us. If he hadn't yet pictured it, I didn't want him to start now. "I don't want to sleep in the same place as her" was all I said.

"I thought about that, and, well—you don't *have* to stay if you don't want to," he said. "You could always stay in your apartment, and I'll stay here and host your mom."

"You'll stay here alone. With her."

"It'll be just for a couple of nights, and then we'll be back together. You know, to placate her. I mean, you do love her, right?"

"Could you stop asking whether I love her? It has nothing to do with that!" A diffuse panic had set in, and I didn't know where to direct it. "I don't know how you don't get it, why you thought I'd be okay with any of this—"

"I'm trying to be polite to her," Theo said. "It was selfish, okay? I don't want her to be mad at me!"

"Are you twelve?" I asked.

"You're the one who refuses to talk to her about anything real!"

"She's scary!"

"How do you think I feel?"

To this, I had no response.

"At least you're used to her," he said. "I have no idea what to do when she starts pushing. Actually, it was her idea for you to stay at your place—she said she could tell you needed some space."

I felt my panic sharpen. If it was my mother's idea for her and Theo to stay in his apartment alone, there was only one reason I could fathom. She didn't want to climb inside of me: she wanted to climb inside of Theo. Was this why she'd asked whether the rooms in his apartment had locks on them—because she wanted to know how much trouble she'd have accessing him in the night? I imagined her sneaking into Theo's office to find him on the pullout. In my mind's eye I watched her kneel next to him, as I had done so many times, reach into his mouth, and rip his body from the teeth on down. Nestle herself inside of him, as I had done. Take residence in the space that should be mine.

But why would she want Theo instead of me? Had she taken my hints about space so strongly that she'd completely given up? Would she never try to climb inside of me again? If so, shouldn't I feel relieved instead of forlorn?

Perhaps it really had nothing to do with Theo at all. Perhaps my mother had realized that if she couldn't have me, she could *be* me.

By now my head was throbbing with alarm. I could try to get her to cancel the trip—maybe contract some illness and pass it on to Theo? But that wouldn't deter her: she'd come to take care of me when I was sick before, even the time I was vomiting nonstop. (She'd vomited the whole next day.) I could get Talia or Romi to find out when she was planning to come, then surprise Theo with a trip out of town at the same time. But what if he said no, either because he didn't want to be rude to my mom, or worse—horrifyingly—because he preferred to stay and see her, because there was a part of him that envied the attention I got from her? If he felt this way, he definitely didn't understand what he was wishing for, given who we were dealing with. If he was even aware of his envy at all.

"We'll make it through," he was saying now. "It's a short trip. She'll be gone by Sunday."

My heart started to hammer.

"Sunday," I repeated. "As in *this* Sunday?"

"Fuck, I guess I spilled everything. Yeah. She gets in tomorrow afternoon."

What options were left to me? Even if I got Theo to stay at my place instead, my mom would outmaneuver me. She'd give me bad meat so I'd be stuck in the bathroom all night, or poison Felix so I had to rush him to the vet, or concoct some emergency with one of my sisters that only I could tend to. She'd find a way to get him alone.

There was only one solution that made sense, one path that ensured his protection.

I turned back to the cutting board and resumed chopping. "Let's finish making dinner," I said.

"It'll be a nice visit," he said. "I promise. I'll make sure of it."

I nodded and smiled, but I'd made up my mind.

Once we'd gotten into bed, Theo fell asleep within minutes. I waited the requisite amount of time to ensure he was deeply, truly sleeping before, with silent slowness, I peeled back the covers, slid out of bed, and crept over to my desk, where I sat and opened my laptop. In order to find a thumb drive, I needed to open the top drawer of my desk and rustle through it. Theo stirred and mumbled, "What are you doing?"

"I had an idea for a radio story, so I'm typing it up," I said.

I'm still not sure if he heard me or if he'd already fallen back asleep, but by the time I found the thumb drive and inserted it into the body of my computer, he was snoring.

I transferred all the recordings I'd ever made of us onto the drive: the dinners, the sex, the walks, the sleeps, and, of course, the climbs. At least thirty minutes must have passed while the data traveled. Once I'd ejected the drive, I hooked my recorder into the same portal. Its memory capacity was small, only enough to hold a small percentage of the recordings, so I spent a long time choosing, relying on memory. I picked our first food pantry shift together; the walk where we'd talked about peeing in the shower; a night of sex; the first time I'd touched his teeth; another walk in the park; the night his teeth first budged for me; the night we'd said *I love you;* the first time I'd climbed inside him; the tape I'd made from within; dinner the night he'd done it back to me, and our conversation after. I didn't know that I'd be able to play the recordings back to myself from inside—usually my arms were pinned down, barely mobile—or whether, should I be able to, the sound would be distorted. But it would give me comfort to have them with me.

I thought about bringing snacks, but quickly dismissed the idea: they would get disgusting inside him, and if I put them into a plastic bag would be too hard to retrieve; besides, I felt confident that at some point I'd be able to feed off whatever Theo ate. I wondered about going to the bathroom, and whether I ought to swaddle myself in a diaper; I had never before been inside of Theo long enough to need to poop or pee. It was also possible, though—and, I've discovered, true—that, once I was embedded within him, the need would leave me.

I thought, briefly, about leaving Felix behind, and even got out notepaper on which to request that Theo either care for him or get him to one of my sisters, but before I'd written even one word, I'd glanced at Felix—deep brown eyes staring at me forlornly from his perch on the bed—and changed my mind. Of course he would come with me. Instead, I wrote:

> We are inside you.
> xo,
> O.

As if, on waking, Theo wouldn't know.

I closed the computer, placed the note on my pillow, shed my pajamas as though molting and shoved them underneath the bed. Picturing Theo finding them crumpled sadly, I thought they made too rude an image for him to come upon—too college-dorm-room, too strong a stench of abandonment—and tossed them into my hamper. I arranged the thumb drive and recorder next to Theo on the bed, then gingerly arranged myself next to him, too. I leaned over and opened him up, an act that had become so second-nature that its individual components barely registered.

But his body, as always, stopped me cold. His heart going *squeeze, squeeze, squeeze* of its own accord. The glistening pink pasta of his intestines. His ever-growing-and-then-shrinking-again lungs. The ridged cartilage of his trachea, behind which I knew lay his vocal cords, though I couldn't see them. I wondered, as I had when he was inside me, what I would be able to hear once I was enclosed: never before on a climb had I heard him speak.

Finally I grabbed the thumb drive and recorder and entered him, my process the same as ever: one foot and the other, then the slow lowering until my butt dipped below the surface of his organs. Felix stared at me over the rim of Theo's body. I nestled the equipment into some pink inner folds to free my hands, scooped Felix up, and, pressing him to my chest, snuggled us both inside. It took a bit of shifting until we were laid comfortably on our sides, me curled around Felix, but once we'd settled into place, we fit just so. I was the seed inside of Theo, and Felix was the seed inside of me. Felix whimpered; I shushed and stroked him. I zipped Theo back up. This time, I fused first his skin and then, underneath, his fat and muscles and fascia, layering myself in.

That was some time ago now. Weeks, I think, but I can't be sure. Inside, it's difficult to keep track.

I hadn't intended to stay inside for this long. At first, I meant only to wait out my mother. I assumed that with me gone, Theo would forestall her visit. What he'd tell her, I had no idea; perhaps he'd simply say I'd gone missing. I do regret the bind I've placed him in, forcing him to tell her, my dad, my sisters, my friends, even Ava that I've inexplicably disappeared. Has he done it by now? I wonder, but try not to dwell on, how the mundane facts of my life—my apartment, my work—have rearranged themselves around the hole I've left behind. I try harder not to think about how Talia and Romi feel, not knowing what could have happened to me, or about how Theo is coping without me. I tell myself that he still feels my companionship from inside him; after all, when the situation was reversed, he insisted he was with me the whole time. Anyway, it seems that my gambit worked. I would recognize my mother's voice anywhere, including from in here. If ever she does visit, I will know. And if she still dares to open Theo, I will be waiting, right here.

I kept count for the first few days. I could tell when we were waking up: the body would shift dramatically, shuttling Felix and me from our sleeping position—nestled on our sides—into an upright one: me crouching, Felix balanced on my thighs. We walked (a bouncy jostling, something like a ride); we took the subway (the rush-and-halt rhythm felt the same inside as out); we went to work (of course he still went to work even with me inside him: classic Theo). But there have been too many iterations of a day now, and I no longer know when we are.

As time passes after waking, my ankles and knees ache and creak; but as more time passes, my legs grow tingly and then numb. At work, I hear the muffled sounds of others speaking, of machinery beeping, and the louder but still indistinct music of Theo's voice, the vibrations of his vocal cords reaching all the way down to the top of my skull. At night, Theo might come, his hips thrusting Felix and me to and fro—Felix craning his eyes back to me, though he can't move his head, the whites bulging around the irises—but just as easily, Theo might shift onto his side, interrupting his arousal, sending me a message. Felix hasn't whined about food for a while, so I suppose he's no longer hungry, and neither am I.

For some time I thought wistfully of the snow the night I climbed inside: the muffled hush, the soft dots filtering into the glow cast by the streetlamps, the branches outside my bedroom window outlined in white as though painted. I longed for that sight, and wondered if the snow would melt by the time I'd emerged, and then, as more time passed, if I would ever see snow again. It's one of many losses. I miss work, though with Jenny, who's covered for me anytime I've been ill, I know the show is in good hands. I've figured out how to maneuver my arms and hands so I can play the tapes from inside Theo, but the sound comes back tinny, muted by his close-pressed organs. I crave the clear sound of his clarinety voice. I miss his fingers, his face, his brain. I sometimes want my mom to hug me.

Most of all, I miss talking to Theo. I miss the surprises of his mind; I miss the way his thoughts stretched mine to places I can't get to on my own. I miss being reassured, and complimented, and loved. I miss being made to laugh.

But when I feel this way, I remind myself that I can emerge whenever I want to. I remind myself it's better this way—better I'm in here than anybody else. And once I've waited for a moment, sitting with the feeling, it doesn't take long for it to trickle away. It's enough, for now, the rush of sounds from within and the softer outside noises trickling through. It's enough, the shifts from lying down, curled around Felix, to crouching together, then back again. It's enough, the slick warmth of Theo's organs, the sharp smell of him, the way his sounds reverberate through me. The music is enough, the textures are enough, the sensations, the sustenance. It feels as though Theo's body is a home that's been built to house me, and I was built to live here. My mother can never come in here. I may never come out.

Acknowledgments

I owe this book to everyone who was kind to me over the six years I spent writing it, but especially the people below.

Thank you to my agent, Stephanie Delman, who offers reassurance and realism in equal measure, knows just when to push me and how much, is an incisive editor and a brilliant hype-woman, and also happens to be a person I like very much. And thank you to the rest of the team at Trellis, my dream agency, especially Tori Clayton, Allison Malecha, and Elizabeth Pratt.

Thank you to my editors at Abrams: Abby Muller, who fell for my bizarre book and whose vision and meticulous edits helped mold it; Ruby Pucillo, who brainstormed with me with alacrity and originality and whose edits were equally scrupulous; and Zack Knoll, who oversaw the process with wisdom and gave this book a springboard into the world. Thank you to Florence Rees at A.M. Heath for championing this book in the UK and guiding it to an ideal home. Thank you to Ellie Steel, whose every edit was sharp and perfect, and to the rest of the team at Harvill Secker.

Thank you to my film and television manager, Tara Timinsky, for evangelizing this book across Hollywood with unflagging energy, passion, and optimism. Thank you to Gabby Canton, Rachel Jacobs, Priyanka Kapoor, Lauren López de Victoria, Adrienne Love, Alana Mayo, and Steven Prinz for working to translate this book to the screen.

ACKNOWLEDGMENTS

Thank you to all those who read this manuscript in part or whole, and whose feedback not only shaped this book but also inspired and enlivened me: Nina Boutsikaris, Kate Devine, Lane Florsheim, Sabine Jansen, Kyle McCarthy, Mike Pezley, Alice Robb, Abby Ronner, Jess Smith, Rebecca Swanberg, Anna Van Lenten, and Genevieve Walker.

Thank you to Beth Ann Bauman and Leah Sophia Dworkin, in whose online courses I wrote sections of this book.

Thank you to the groups that provided vital accountability and writing company: the Texas Tech University Women Faculty Writing Program and my former colleagues at The New School, Rachel Aydt, Shahnaz Habib, Liz Latty, Kyle McCarthy, and Bureen Ruffin.

Thank you to the doctors who spoke with me about their careers and the human body: Natasha Coleman, Anne Fallon, and Elizabeth Rubin. I admittedly took some liberties with the information you so generously shared.

Thank you to everyone who answered questions about audio production, told me their partners' weird hobbies, shared descriptions of city sounds, or otherwise brainstormed with me: Catherine Cushenberry, Andrew Gross, Amy Schoenfeld, Esther Schwartz, Jillian Steinhauer, Natasja Wells, Paul Wells, and especially my husband, Matt Hunter, who talked through the ideas of this novel with me from the very start.

Thank you to my mother and to Mercedes Mendez for bonding so beautifully with my daughter and giving me vital writing time.

Thank you to my analyst, who helps me make sense of my life.

Thank you to my family: my parents, Julie and Larry, who brought me into this world and have supported me ever since; my brother, Andrew, who is also my friend; my step-parents and in-laws—Jill, Emily, David, Sarah, Abby, Evan, Gabby, and Elizabeth—who enrich my days; my husband, Matt, whose love sustains me; our dog, Benji, who has been such a tender companion; and our daughter, Orli, who is a miracle.